meeting mr. ADORKABLE

ALI RYECART

DEDICATION &
ACKNOWLEDGMENTS

Mark, thank you for your unstinting support and
encouragement.

With thanks to Angela, Barbara, and Iola.

Cover by Rhys at Etherial Designs
etherialcovers.co.uk

SYNOPSIS

Two wounded hearts. One small town. A romance with the power to heal.

Dumped by his older lover and left jobless in the family business, life isn't looking too rosy for Lucian, a sweet but awkward English florist. At rock bottom, he's determined to make a fresh start, and the Wyoming town of Collier's Creek might just be the place to do it.

After years living in New York's fast lane, Arlo's come home. No stranger to heartbreak, all he wants is a simple life after his relationship with a younger man crashed and burned. The last thing he's looking for is love. Those days are long gone, and they're never coming back.

But fate has other plans for Lucian and Arlo. A clumsy encounter in a cheesy bar, a spilled pitcher of beer, and their worlds are turned upside down. Life will never be the same again.

Will the reticent silver fox be the key to piecing together Lucian's fractured heart? And will Arlo find the courage to open himself up and let the dorky Englishman restore his belief in love and life? Find out in this always heartfelt, often quirky, cross-cultural romance that proves age is just a number when it comes to affairs of the heart.

CHAPTER ONE

"I think I'm going to make a move. It's—"

Oh god, was it really only eight o'clock? Lucian smothered a sigh. Friday night, and he was making plans to make a run for it and curl up with a cup of tea and Netflix for company; it may have been pathetic, but it was better than spending any more time trapped in the hell that was Randy's Rodeo Grill and Bar.

"No way, Luci. Loosen up and have another drink. It's Friday night, and you're staying right here." Bibi grabbed his glass and filled it from one of the pitchers of beer littering the table, a glint of mischief and a touch of alcoholic glaze in her eyes.

Luci... He'd given up trying to stop her from shortening his name.

Lucian found himself wedged in the booth, trapped between a tattooed cowgirl who seemed to be asleep, a selfie-taking muscled guy with alarmingly orange-tanned skin, and Bibi's glower. He sipped the thin, sour beer and wrinkled his nose. At least it was cold, which was the best thing he could say about it.

More people joined them, forcing those already seated to inch along. More pitchers of the beer that tasted like cat's piss were slammed down and his glass was topped off again and again. The background music went up a notch, and the warbling, syrupy tones of the woman pining for her dead dog, or horse, or whatever, competed with the ever rising volume of the Randy's Friday night crowd. Everybody was shouting to make themselves heard as pitcher after pitcher found its way to the table.

"No, I don't—" But it was too late. His glass was refilled to overflowing, the foam soaking his hand. He took a mouthful. It really wasn't bad. Or not that bad.

"Chicken wings. Tenders. BBQ ribs. Steak. Salads, fries, onion rings, corn." A waitress landed a huge tray of food in the middle of the table, the various plates of fried and breaded animal piled up high. Not a sign of a veggie burger in sight.

"Excuse me? Miss?" Lucian called out. Several heads turned his way, including the waitress's, whose pencil thin, plucked brows arched, and all but disappeared into her piled high, sunshine yellow hair.

"Been a while since anybody's called me Miss," she said, laughing. With her scarlet lipstick, bright blue eye shadow, too high heels and too tight uniform, and with her hands planted on her hips, she was intimidating, but her smile was warm and her eyes friendly.

"I ordered a veggie burger."

The waitress peered at the tray as though she might find the offending article hiding between a breaded chunk and a battered chunk of something crispy and uniden-tifiable.

"Sorry, honey, but the vegetable burger isn't available. I can get you a regular burger. One hundred percent prime local beef." The kindly eyes now dared him to demand why a veggie burger was listed as a menu item. Lucian decided he wasn't that brave.

"Okay. Sorry. I'll, erm, just have the chips — sorry, I mean fries — and the vegetables. Really, it's no trouble at all." Lucian gazed in dismay at the oily lumps. At least the salads looked as if they were less likely to induce a sudden heart attack.

More beer arrived. It really wasn't too bad. In fact, it was more than okay. What had been sour was now sharp and refreshing, cutting through the—

"Oh." The piled high platter was now only a pile of bones, the salad reduced to a few, leftover mayo covered lettuce leaves.

Lucian slumped back into the seat and drooped against the sleeping tattooed lady. Sleep, that sounded good. Sere-naded by the woman's syrupy voice, his eyes closed as she bemoaned her jail bird man…

"Errgghh!" he screeched, as an eardrum shattering, high-pitched squeal thrust him awake. His heart beat wildly. What the fuck? He blinked at the tens, hundreds, thousands of eyes all boring into him.

"Don't worry, he's English." Bibi waved her arm toward him.

The owners of all those tens, hundreds, thousands of eyes nodded.

"I'm not surprised you hollered. The feedback on that microphone's loud enough to raise the dead."

Lucian blinked at the ink adorned woman, awake for the first time all evening.

Lucian laughed. "A little embarrassing, though, so—"

A sudden thunderclap of applause drowned out the end of Lucian's words as a group of five men, resplendent in plaid shirts, leather chaps, cowboy boots and hats, trooped onto a small stage, clutching guitars and fiddles, as they smiled and waved at the crowd.

A small, round man, wearing much the same as the cowboys but who definitely was not rocking the Wild West look, waddled onto the stage. "Give a warm welcome to the Collier's Creek Cowboy Combo! On your feet, everybody. Let's make this a real Randy Friday night."

Lucian snorted. Seriously? A randy Friday night? He couldn't remember when he'd last got randy on a Friday night. Or any night. Everybody was pushing to get out of the booth, stampeding for the dance floor. This was it. His way was clear. Now he could make a run for it. Everybody was on the dance floor, connecting with their inner cowboy and cowgirl. Or everybody except the muscly guy, who was digging through the gnawed remains of the meat fest.

Tugging his wallet from the pocket of his jeans, Lucian pulled out some notes. He'd missed out on the food, thank god, but he'd had a glass or two of cat's piss. Or maybe three. Or four. Which all came to… He had no idea. Would thirty dollars cover it? He put the money in a neat pile on the food strewn table and started to edge his way out before he remembered… He dug a five-dollar bill from his wallet and added it to the pile. No way did he want to be chased along the street — again — by an angry server demanding an upgrade in the tip. The squirm wriggled in his gut. The huge, hairy man who'd come after him hadn't been over interested in his arguments that his employer should pay him a proper wage… He added another couple of dollars.

A bright green exit sign near to the bar beckoned. He'd be home soon. A cuppa and some custard creams. His lips lifted in a grin. Proper English biscuits that were definitely not cookies. Good old Mum, or maybe he should say Mom, and her care packages. His stomach grumbled, urging him on as he ducked around the line dancers, keeping his head down and hoping to god Bibi didn't catch sight of him and haul him into a Cha Cha Slide, or a Harlem Shake, or—

"Oh, fuck." His feet skidded. Spilled fries, squashed and greasy, making the smooth flooring an ice rink. His legs buckled, his arms windmilled, sending a tray with a pitcher flying in one direction as he flew in another.

CHAPTER TWO

"My god, are you okay?"

The thin, dark-haired guy sprawled on the floor blinked then blinked again, reminding Arlo of an owl. His heavy glasses had parted company with his face and lay next to him, along with his jacket and the contents of its pockets.

"Errrgg…" The guy attempted to push himself up, but all uncoordinated arms and legs, he flopped back down again.

"Here." Arlo thrust his hand out to help the guy up, whose grip was strong for somebody who resembled a gangly puppy.

"I am so, so sorry." The guy tried to straighten out his wonky glasses but though they defied all his efforts, he put them back on; they started to slip down his nose.

It was Arlo's turn to blink. The guy's clipped English accent reminded him of the BBC period dramas he binged on.

"It was the chips. I mean the fries."

"I'm sorry?"

The guy looked down at the squashed fries. "I slipped and… Oh, you're soaking." The guy's eyes, behind the ugly glasses, widened. "Honestly, I can't apologize enough. Let me get you another pitcher of the house cat's pi—whoops, sorry. It might be your favorite tipple. Which I've inadvertently bathed you in." The guy frowned, pulling his dark brows into a V, further displacing his glasses.

"What?" Arlo looked down at his sodden shirt and pants. How the hell hadn't he noticed he was soaking wet? He should be annoyed, even angry, but it had been an accident — and it gave him a great excuse to head for home.

"Let me clear this up for you." A waitress, armed with a mop and bucket, loomed.

"Just a small mishap and—" Arlo turned to the guy, and stared into the space where he'd been just seconds before. "Where did he go?" Arlo's head snapped back and forth, scanning the crowd, but the man had vanished. His wet clothes, which were now soaking through to his underwear, were the only evidence the guy had been there.

The waitress shrugged as she quickly cleared the mess before she, too, disappeared.

Arlo pushed his hair away from his brow, his fingers coming away damp with sweat. Drenched in beer, or the local cat's piss — his lips twitched with a smile, because the dorky young Englishman was right about Randy's most popular brew — and sweat from the packed bar, it really was time to take off. But not before he found Hank.

About to push his way through the crush, a dark shape on the floor caught his attention, knowing what it was. He swooped down and caught up the slim wallet. It had to be the guy's, fallen from his jacket which, like him, had gone flying. He'd leave it behind the bar... the guy would realize what had happened and would come back and collect it... he had no reason to open it up and look inside, because he had no wish, no wish at all, to be found rifling through somebody else's wallet.

He opened it up and stared down at the international driver's license.

The guy gazed up at him from the photo. He looked about fifteen, his eyes wide and startled, as though he'd been caught out raiding the cookie jar.

"Lucian Arbuthnot Blaxston. Arbuthnot? Who the hell gets to be called Arbuthnot?" Arlo muttered. Posh, dorky, young Englishmen, obviously. A couple of bank cards, and a few notes, and—

Arlo pulled the business card out.

Bibi's Blossoms, Blooms & Bouquets.

Collier's Creek's one and only florist. Did Lucian Arbuthnot Blaxston work there? Arlo snorted. The guy was thin and gangly and didn't look like he lifted anything heavier than a flower stem or two. He'd hand the wallet in at the bar, and Lucian Arbuthnot Blaxston could collect it tomorrow. He weighed it in his hand. Or, he could drop it around to the flower store in the morning... He shoved the wallet into the back pocket of his pants, just about the only part of him that was dry, the decision made almost before he was aware.

Arlo made his way over to the table, where his friend sat waiting for him. Hank raised his brows.

"So, Randy's Rodeo Grill & Bar is out of beer?"

Arlo laughed, and called over one of the roving wait-resses for a pitcher, and quickly told Hank what had happened. "Which means I'm going to take off. I'm soaked through." He plucked at his shirt, now stuck to his chest, which in the heat was drying and stiffening up.

"I thought I'd heard every excuse from you to either get out of coming to the Creek's finest nightspot, or leave early, but having beer thrown over you by a Brit is the most inventive of all. Sure you didn't upend it over yourself?" Hank grinned, as he poured them each a glass from the just arrived pitcher.

Arlo pushed his glass towards his friend. It was thin, tasteless stuff, maybe not quite the cat's piss the young English guy had claimed it to be, but not too far off. He had some good artisanal gin at home; a glass over ice with tonic, with one of his BBC dramas was beckoning … A light shove on his shoulder claimed his wandering attention.

"You still haven't said if you're coming over next Sunday. For Francine's birthday BBQ?"

"I can probably swing by."

"She'll be mortally offended if you don't, which'll make my life difficult. You're my oldest friend, so don't you want to save me from that?"

Arlo groaned silently. There was no way he could get out of the invite, and no excuse he thought up would be good enough to back out of Hank and Francine's extended family gathering, with the conversation confined to football, baseball, and the one hundred and one best sauces for ribs and steak. It was a mean thought, and he pushed it aside. Hank and Francine were good friends, and doing their best to make sure he settled back into Collier's Creek.

"Of course I'm coming." A couple of hours, max…

"She's got a cousin visiting with us from out of state."

Hank buried his face in his beer.

"What? Ah. Okay." Jesus, not again. Sweet Francine... who was a Rottweiler in her attempt to play matchmaker.

"His name's Wilbur, and he's a dentist from some hick town in Colorado."

"He sounds — interesting? At least I'd get a discount on dental work."

"Don't knock it, not with the price of insurance."

"You know, back in high school when we were all trying to work out what our futures would hold, I never imagined cut price dental work would be the route to my heart." Arlo pressed his fists to his chest and sighed.

"I'm sorry, man. But you know Francine. She wants everybody to be happy. It's just the way it is."

Arlo squeezed his friend's shoulder. "I know, and I appreciate her concern — I do," Arlo proclaimed when Hank's brows shot up into his hairline. "But I'm not looking for The One. Honestly, I'm not. I've been there, remember, and I've no intention of going back."

"But—"

"There's no 'but'. If I meet somebody who I want to get to know — and it's a big if — then great. But if I don't, then that's great too." Arlo got up. "I'll come and play nice with Wilbur and make Francine happy for an hour or two."

Grabbing his jacket from the back of his seat, Arlo slapped his friend goodbye on the back.

Outside, in the cool night air, Wilbur and Francine's matchmaking machinations were forgotten, as his thoughts turned to dark floppy hair and a pair of battered glasses that refused to stay perched on an upturned nose. Making for one of the waiting cabs, he tapped his back pocket, finding the slight bulge of a slim wallet.

CHAPTER THREE

"Can I suggest something more classic? Timeless in its simplicity and beauty?" Lucian gritted his teeth into what he hoped resembled a professional smile as the woman pouted. "Cream and pale pink roses, with lots of greenery, tumbling down into a teardrop. It would off set your wedding dress perfectly." And distract from the rhinestone encrusted bustier...

"My, but that does sound good, Tiffany. Very pretty." The older lady accompanying Tiffany glanced between the two of them. "What did you say, young man? Perhaps you could remind me?"

"Certainly, madam," Lucian said, ready to give it some posh, as his dick of an ex used to say, but The Shit Formerly Known as Miles was the very last person he wanted to think about. He wanted to think about him even less than the petulant pouter standing in front of him with her long suffering, sweet mother.

Lucian smiled and inclined his head. "The design I'm suggesting is a classic, first carried by Princess Bontempie…" If there was ever a Princess Bontempie in the annals of royal history, he'd skipped that page back in the classroom. "It soon became a standard for royal brides of yesteryear and is now very much coming back in vogue. You will, literally, look like a princess on your wedding day to Bert."

"Bart." The truck tires that were masquerading as Tiffany's lips pouted some more.

"My apologies, madam. Bart. And when might you and the lucky Bart be tying the knot? I don't believe you said." If she had, he hadn't heard, because he was too busy fighting the thumping headache that had plagued him since he'd got up. Okay, hangover. Who knew cat's piss was that strong?

A dark look passed between mother and daughter, dinging Lucian's gossip antenna.

"A date's not as yet been set. Not for certain." Tiffany jutted her chin out.

"They're just getting everything set up." The sweet, older lady wrung her hands.

"So, how far have you got in the preparations for your nuptials?"

Lucian looked from one to the other. Who the hell ordered a wedding dress, any wedding dress, let alone a baby pink, rhinestone encrusted one, just because they might get married at some point in the—

"Hey Tiffany, hey Amanda. Lucian here been looking after you? Oh, what a pretty dress," Bibi enthused, glancing at the photograph on Tiffany's phone. "Lucian, there's a consignment just come in. Would you mind sorting? I'll take over. Tiffany and me, we go way back." Bibi's smile was shark-like. *Get away before I bite you…*

"Ladies." Lucian dipped his head. "I'll leave you in the expert hands of Bibi herself. I'm sure she can help you make the right choice for your wedding day. Whenever that might be."

"Thank you, Lucian." Bibi's smile split her face in two. She was going to bite, chew, and spit him out.

In the room at the back of the store, Lucian batched up the flowers and placed them in the cooling cabinet. Most of the flowers he knew, but some he didn't, because they were native to mountainous Wyoming. He pulled out his phone and took a photo of the blooms he wasn't familiar with, so as he could find out more about them on the specialist horticultural site he subscribed to. Laughter drifted in from the front of the store, full of familiarity. Bibi was a native of the little town, and she seemed to know everybody who came in. He wasn't, and he didn't. His hands fell still.

He'd been in town, and working in the store, for almost two months, yet it felt like a lifetime. A wave of longing and regret swept over him, weakening his knees; he slumped against the table. He closed his eyes, fighting down the urge to run and jump on the first flight home. It rose in him like nausea, just as it did every day since he'd arrived, but like nausea, it would settle and fade.

Taking a deep breath, he opened his eyes. Come on, get a grip… At least he was working with flowers, even if Bibi's Blossoms, Blooms and Bouquets offered only unimaginative, uninspiring bunches of blossoms and blooms and basic bouquets. It wasn't much of a florist, but it was the only one around.

Picking up a cloth, he cleaned down the table of scattered leaves and the cut ends of stalks. He could do so much to make the store... more. He could make it spectacular. Hadn't he been the head floral designer at Danebury Manor? Breathtaking bouquets for brides, stunning table arrangements for high class, stylish weddings, eyecatching contemporary displays for corporate events... He'd done it all and covered himself with glory. Until BridezillaGate... Which had led to his dismissal... Which had led to here.

Another wave of homesickness engulfed him, this time a real and physical pain.

He was here because he needed a change... It wouldn't be forever... When he went home he'd be making a new start... It was what his family had said, what he'd said... The faces of his mother, brother and sister filled his head. They were right. He agreed they were right. He knew they were right, but sometimes — just sometimes — all that good advice to take some time out to reset just made him feel like he'd been banished.

Lucian jumped as the door crashed open before being thrown closed. Bibi collapsed against it.

"I'm sorry, Luci, but I had to jump in. Tiffany's wedding... it's complicated."

"Not as complicated as that dress of hers."

Bibi laughed. "She's never going to wear that dress, nor any other. Not this side of the next ten years. It's her little fantasy."

"What do you mean?"

"Bart."

"The fiancé?" Lucian frowned before his eyes widened. "You don't mean that he doesn't exist? He's literally her fantasy?" He'd dealt with some seriously deluded brides at Danebury Manor, but a non-existent one took the biscuit. Or should that be the cookie?

"Oh sure, Bart exists. He exists in jail, where he's been for the last three years, and he's going to be there for a few more. They jailed him for theft and a ton of other things. It's not the first time he's been incarcerated, and when he's finally freed, it won't be the last. Tiffany's a sweet girl, but she's not the brightest star in the night sky. Any dreams she has of a picket fenced house, kids, and a dog would soon turn to a nightmare with that guy."

"So, has she put in an order — or not?"

"Of course she hasn't. We talked about what might work and that's all. I kinda feel bad for feeding her Bart addiction, but that girl's nothing if not determined." Bibi shrugged as she pushed herself off the door. She narrowed her eyes at him. "Forget about Tiffany — but if she comes in again, you call me. I wanna know what happened to you last night. You disappeared. You meet somebody?"

"In Randy's? The temple of fried and breaded animal pieces? I'm a vegetarian, remember, so no, I really don't think so." Or not unless he counted the tall guy he'd drenched in beer. The tall guy with the good natured wonky smile, when he'd really had nothing to be good natured about. The tall guy with the sandy blond hair with a few silver threads running through it, and warm green-gold eyes. He coughed. "I went home. Had an early night. Thanks for the invite, but…"

"No need to apologize. You like what you like, even if it isn't a night out at Randy's." She laughed. "It's fun if you're with a crowd, but the Collier's Creek Cowboy Combo were playing, so going was a no brainer." A soft, misty expression appeared on Bibi's face, one Lucian wasn't sure he'd seen before. "The lead singer, Brad, we went to high school together. We even dated for a while and he's as good looking now as he was then."

"Well, if leather chaps and plaid shirts float your boat…" Lucian squirmed under Bibi's glare.

The jangle of the store's bell announced the arrival of a customer.

Saved by the bell. Literally.

"At least it won't be another delusional bride-to-be. The Creek can only take so many of those," Bibi said, striding into the store front.

Lucian picked up a broom from the corner and began to sweep up, his drifting thoughts stopped dead as Bibi stuck her head around the corner of the door and grinned.

"Hey, Luci, you've got a visitor."

CHAPTER FOUR

"I think you might be missing this."

The guy from Randy's, the guy he'd drenched in bad beer, the guy who was holding up his — wallet. Lucian's jaw dropped. How the hell had he missed his wallet? His credit and debit cards, his driver's license, all contained in the soft leather that was the only good thing to come out of his time with the Shit Formerly Known as Miles.

"Don't you want it back?" The guy with the sandy blond hair and the crooked smile quirked his head to the side.

"Yes! Yes, of course. Thank you." Christ, the man would think he was an imbecile, but then he wouldn't be the first, nor the last probably.

The guy held it out across the counter. Taking it, their fingers brushed, sending a tingle over Lucian's skin. He swallowed as he shoved it into the back pocket of his jeans.

"Don't you want to check everything's there?"

"What? Oh, no. I trust you. I mean, you don't look like a thief."

"I'm glad to hear it."

"Sorry. No. Sorry. That came out… Sorry."

"They say the British are forever apologizing. I guess it's true." The guy's good-natured smile broadened, matching the amusement glittering in his eyes.

"You're right. We say it all the time. But the secret is, we're not really apologizing. Or not most of the time. Sorry doesn't always mean sorry. Sorry about that."

The guy threw laughed. "Two peoples divided by a common language. Isn't that how the saying goes?" He held out his hand, the one Lucian had taken his wallet from.

"I'm Arlo McDonald."

Lucian took the proffered hand. It was warm and smooth, and big, swamping his own. The squeeze was firm but not crushing, hinting at the strength tucked out of sight.

"And I'm Lucian Blaxston — oh, and who's this?" he said, as a snort and a snuffle snagged his attention. Leaning over the counter, he looked into the chocolate brown eyes of a small, wire haired mutt, curled at Arlo's feet.

"This is Peanut." Arlo bent and petted the dog, who stuffed his snout between his bent front legs. "He's a shy little cutie who's not too good in company, but I force him to make the effort sometimes so he doesn't become too much of a recluse."

"Sounds like me. The shy bit, I mean. Not the cutie, 'cause I'm not a…" Oh shit… Could he really make himself look like any more of a dork? He stood up straight and shoved his hands into his front pockets, looking everywhere except at Arlo McDonald.

"I hope you don't mind," Arlo said, as though he'd not heard him make an idiot of himself, "but I had to check the contents to see who it belonged to. I kind of guessed it was you. You must have dropped it when you disappeared. Why did you do that?"

"Ah, yes." Lucian looked down as he shuffled from foot to foot. "The woman who came to clear up. As soon as I saw her, I thought I'd make a dash for it before she threw me out."

"Why would she?"

"Well… it's not the first time I've caused havoc there." Lucian grimaced. "Bibi dragged me along one night, soon after I arrived. Somehow, my feet got caught up in somebody's coat and I stumbled into one of the waitresses carrying a loaded tray of food. Honestly, I didn't think it was possible for breaded chicken wings to fly so high.

"Later in the evening, I was persuaded to give line dancing a try. Big mistake. I just couldn't get the hang of it, and I kept going the wrong way and bumping into everybody — including an old lady who I knocked over, and who happened to be the mayor's wife. I think Randy and his staff only tolerated my presence because of Bibi, who seems to know everybody in town, but I think it's safer if I steer clear from now on."

Arlo shook his head and chuckled before they fell into silence. The only sound in the store was the low background buzz of voices from the radio Bibi had switched on in the back room. He scratched the back of his neck, unsure what to say or do under Arlo's steady gaze. Big, tall Arlo. Very attractive Arlo.

"You're obviously a long way from home. Collier's Creek attracts way more visitors than it used to, but it's not exactly high on the world's radar."

"Yes, I am. It's a long story." And not one I want to tell.

Arlo nodded, as though he'd picked up on the unspoken message. He opened his mouth to say something, but before he could, the doorbell rang and two women arrived.

"I guess I shouldn't keep you any longer," Arlo said with a smile. "Maybe I'll see you around?" He lifted his brows in question.

"I'm an Englishman in Collier's Creek, so I'm a difficult one to miss." Lucian smiled, but it felt like it was being held up by piano wire, as the lie of his own words bit into him. He was very easy to miss.

Arlo waved his goodbye, smiling at the two women as he left. The door clanged shut on his big, warm presence. A cough caught his attention, and he turned to the two women, a practised smile settling on his lips as he wondered where and how he might see Arlo McDonald around.

CHAPTER FIVE

Seconds after the door closed on him, Arlo sneezed. Not once, not twice, not three times... They came tumbling down on each other and he slumped against a wall, watery eyed and breathless. Why the hell hadn't he thought to take an antihistamine beforehand?

The cloying perfume of the cultivated flowers had been heavy and overpowering. Flowers in parks and fields he could handle, out in the open they were no problem, but enclosed in the flower store they'd been almost suffocating. If the women hadn't arrived when they did, he'd have had to make a run for it. Next time he called into the flower store, he'd make sure he took that little pill first.

He stood up straight. "Next time? Why am I thinking about a next time?" He looked down at Peanut, who cocked his head as though considering Arlo's question. He'd found and returned the guy's wallet, that was all, so what reason was there to be a next time? "I'm being ridiculous." Peanut whined his agreement, as they set off across the square.

Mid-morning on a bright, clear Saturday, the town was crowded with visitors and locals alike, making their way around the busy farmers' market.

He still hadn't gotten used to the Creek hosting a regular farmers' market, as good as any he'd visited in New York, or in any of the upscale little towns in Massachusetts he'd spent time in. Artisan small batch cheeses, breads, preserves and a whole lot more were all for sale, and commanding a high price, rather than the motley collection of fruit and veg he remembered his mom coming home with. But was it any wonder he'd not known, or had forgotten, when he so seldom ventured into town? The affluent-looking market, and the affluent-looking people spending their dollars, had been one of the many things to surprise him, when he'd come back to the community he'd been raised in, running from New York and the smoldering remains of his old life. He shook his head; it was a warm, bright day, and he wasn't going to start looking for clouds to blot out the sun.

He'd done what he'd set out to do, but now the wallet was back with Lucian, what now? Arlo looked down at Peanut, seeking inspiration in the big, adoring brown eyes of the rescue mutt. Peanut's long pink tongue swept around his chops, and Arlo grinned.

"Come on boy, let's get you a pup cup." Peanut's tail wagged hard at the mention of the promised treat.

Arlo and Peanut settled into a corner table in one of the many coffee shops that had sprung up in the Creek. It was busy, with locals and visitors, families and groups of friends, and those on their own with headphones glued to their heads as they tapped away at laptops.

"Hey, Arlo?"

Arlo looked up and over at the counter, his order — and Peanut's — held up by a smiling barista. Instructing Peanut to behave, Arlo made his way across. The guy's smile widened as his gaze traveled down Arlo's body. Arlo bit back on his groan.

The barista, whose name was Mike or Mick, Arlo could never quite remember, had made his interest clear, but Arlo always sidestepped the light flirting. The guy was good looking, tall like he himself was, but his too solid, too gym honed frame wasn't one that pressed his buttons. Not that he was on the lookout to have any buttons pressed.

Arlo smiled, keeping it bland and polite, hoping Mike or Mick took the hint. He should have tried to get a table at CC's, which was the best coffee shop in town and where the staff didn't try to hit on him, but as he'd passed by, there had been a line of people waiting for tables.

Mike or Mick held his black coffee and Peanut's pup cup just out of reach.

"Saw you at Randy's last night. Didn't think that'd be your kind of place."

"It's not. But I was meeting a friend, and it's where he wanted to go." Arlo shrugged.

"Hank? You go way back, don't you? All the way to high school? If I'd escaped to New York, not sure I'd be buying a one-way ticket back to the Creek."

Arlo nodded, but added nothing. Even though the town had grown over the years he'd been away, at its heart it was still a small community, a place where everybody knew everybody else and all the lines connecting them. The anonymity of the city didn't exist in Collier's Creek, and he'd do well to remember that.

"Hear you got a pitcher of beer thrown over you by that British guy who works in Bibi's. He's cute, but seriously weird. He's been in here a few times. Jeez, that accent." Mike or Mick laughed and jerked his head towards his co-workers; he leaned forward as though settling down for a long chat. "They love it. One of the girls got him to read out the specials board, but I can't understand half of what he's saying. It's got to be phoney because who speaks like that?"

"Let me get my order, please."

Mike or Mick's eyes widened at the snap in Arlo's voice, and he handed over the order, which Arlo accepted with a tight smile.

Back at the table, as Peanut buried his snout in his creamy treat, Arlo's mind wandered back to Lucian. He smiled, he just couldn't help it. There was just something about the guy that brought out the sunshine — even when he'd doused him in beer, or cat's piss. Arlo chuckled under his breath.

Lucian Arbuthot Blaxston. He pulled out his cell and started to key in the name before his fingers fell still. What the fuck was he doing? He stuffed it back into the side pocket of his jeans.

The guy was cute, just as Mike or Mick had said — no argument there — his awkwardness part of his appeal. He took a quick gulp of coffee, wincing at the burn in his throat. He wasn't interested in anybody appealing to him, and certainly not a floppy-haired young Englishman with a snub nose scattered with a light dusting of freckles, wide pillowy lips, and deep blue eyes flecked with silver. Not that he'd been deliberately noticing Lucian's long-lashed eyes, of course, but they were impossible not to, even though the guy wore the ugliest — and wonkiest — glasses Arlo had ever seen.

Yes, Lucian Arbuthnot Blaxston was a cute guy who'd washed up, somehow, in a Wyoming town that was nothing more than a speck on the map. Whatever reason had brought him to the Creek, he'd soon move on, or return home.

Arlo downed the last of his coffee and, pulling away the cardboard cup that had gotten wedged on Peanut's stubby snout, he left the coffee shop, telling himself he had no reason to spend any time thinking about an awkward young Englishman who was as out of place in this town as he was.

CHAPTER SIX

Mid-Monday morning, the town was quiet as Arlo led Peanut around the town square. He'd stopped several times to look through windows at goods he had no interest in, all the time throwing glances toward the flower store. There'd been no sign of either Bibi or Lucian, or indeed customers. Maybe the place was closed on a Monday? There'd be no harm in checking. As he made his way over, the details of the window display came into full focus.

"Wow."

It was beautiful. Late summer flowers, intermingled with vibrant greenery in a colorful rainbow that reminded Arlo of a French Impressionist painting, exhibited the artist's deliberate touch in its seemingly unstructured appearance. He hadn't before seen anything so eye catching in the window, but then he'd never taken the time to look.

A movement in the store's interior caught his eye. The young English guy with the craziest name, a quirky smile, and a filter-free mouth was wrapping up a bunch of flowers for a customer. The woman left the shop, and Lucian stepped over to the window and frowned at the display, oblivious to everything else. He moved one small pot of bright flowers, swapping it with another. The frown disappeared as he nodded his approval. He looked up, his eyes growing wide as he met Arlo's. A smile broke out on his face, as bright as the sunny, summery flowers.

Arlo's hand tightened on Peanut's leash, as a wave of unfamiliar uncertainty engulfed him. He could nod and move on, a friendly gesture to somebody he knew in passing. It was what he should do, but his legs had other ideas as they kept him rooted to the spot.

Lucian ducked out of view and a second later the door opened and he came out, the smile on his face making the already warm day move up another notch on the thermometer.

"Hello again. This display's been bugging me. There was something not quite right, but then it came to me, and a tiny tweak to the composition has made all the difference. You can see that, can't you?"

Lucian was looking up at him, his face eager, his deep blue eyes pure puppy dog, waiting for Arlo to agree.

"I…" Arlo wrenched his gaze from Lucian's to the window display. The change was subtle, but it had made all the difference. "It has. There's more balance. There's a symmetry that wasn't there before."

Lucian's eyes widened further. "You noticed that? Most people wouldn't. They'd know it was better than before, but not why." He laughed. "I'm guessing you're not a floral artist, but you must be another kind. A painter, perhaps?"

Just about to confirm he was definitely not a floral

artist, his words didn't even reach his lips when Lucian exclaimed and dropped to his haunches.

"Hello, Peanut. And how are you today?"

A little flame ignited in Arlo's chest. Lucian had remembered his mutt's name... A lump formed in his throat.

"Don't be surprised if he wriggles away and..." Arlo gawped as Lucian took one of Peanut's front paws in a handshake. Or a pawshake.

"Formal introductions are so important, don't you think, Peanut? I hope you don't mind my presumption, but you really are a handsome chap." Peanut wagged his stumpy tail in response and Lucian laughed, throwing back his head and staring up at Arlo, a big grin on his face.

Arlo swallowed. In the middle of the square, with the townspeople milling around, Lucian was all but on his knees in front of him. Arlo's crotch, too close to Lucian's face for comfort, tightened. Ah, shit... But if Lucian noticed, he didn't give a sign, as his smile widened.

"I've got a pet back home called Cashew. Honestly, I didn't realize nut based names were such a thing. But Cashew's nothing like this fine pooch. In fact, he's a rather vicious bunny who takes inordinate pleasure in peeing on me, and seems to think my fingers are juicy carrots to be munched on. My mother calls him psychotic, my brother has threatened to have him stuffed and mounted on the wall, and as for what my sister has said should happen to him, well, it would make a sailor blush. But I tell them, poor Cashew had an unhappy start in life and all he needs is love and understanding, as we all do. Doesn't stop him being an evil little bastard, though."

Lucian jumped to his feet. "Have you come to buy

some flowers? We've got some gorgeous tiger lilies and blazing stars in, guaranteed to brighten even the dullest of homes. Not that I'm suggesting your home is dull, of course." Lucian bit down on his lower lip.

"Of course you're not. Like you didn't think I was a thief."

Lucian's face throbbed with a shade of red that was more than equal to the flowers in the window display.

"Ah, yes. That was, erm…" Lucian scuffed the toe of his Converse against the sidewalk, and ran his fingers through his heavy dark hair.

Arlo tamped down on the smile tugging at his lips. It was a little mean to fluster the Englishman. Mean, but fun.

"Touché. I rather asked for that."

"Yet, my home is a little dull." Where had that come from? Arlo cleared his throat. His house was bright, airy, and stylish. It was also quiet, too quiet at times. But wasn't that just what he'd wanted when he'd returned to the Creek?

"Then come in, and let me add some color and warmth." Lucian smiled at him over his shoulder, and Arlo was powerless to say no.

The heady perfume of flowers hit him as he followed Lucian into the store, the closed door blocking off the fresh breeze from outside.

"So, what's your color scheme? Would you prefer to compliment it, or go for a bold contrast? I always think contrasts work the best." Lucian gazed at him expectantly.

"It's neutral. Lots of white walls." Boring and cold. The words had been spat at him, months before, but it hadn't been his decor choices that had been under attack.

29

"Excellent. So you're a blank canvas, just waiting to be painted in warm tones."

"Something like that," Arlo said, a touch of sour flavoring his words.

"If you're happy to give me free rein, I can make up a couple of bunches that'll make the world of difference to all those white walls of yours?"

Eagerness shone from Lucian's face, and Arlo nodded. He nodded because his throat and the back of his nose were already itching. It wouldn't be long before his eyes watered. And the sneezing would come, loud and explosive enough to crack the glass vases lined up on the shelf behind the wide counter.

Lucian was talking, but Arlo had no idea what he was saying as he concentrated on breathing. The itch in his nose and throat leeched out onto his skin. He wanted to scratch his jaw, but once he started, he wouldn't be able to stop. Lucian was still talking, but if he was expecting any answers, he showed no sign, as he wrapped brown paper around the bunches.

"The colors are so vibrant, and the perfume's amazing. I've also included moonflower, because the scent is so rich and sweet. It reminds me of Turkish Delight. What do you think?"

Lucian held the bunch out, but Arlo backed away as if Lucian had thrust a blowtorch in his face.

"Wonderful." Was that thin, reedy whine really him?

"Are you okay?" Lucian's brow pulled into a tiny frown.

"Yes," wheezed Arlo. Why the hell couldn't he just tell the guy he was allergic to cut flowers?

Lucian nodded, but he didn't look convinced. He didn't look like anything other than a smeared shape, as Arlo squinted at him out of watery eyes burning to be scratched.

Lucian rang up the bill, and Arlo all but threw his card at him, the need to get out in the fresh air an imperative.

"Thank you," he rasped, as he bundled the bunches up. "I have to go." Dragging Peanut behind him, he dashed for the door, throwing it open.

"I hope you enjoy your blooms. Come back and tell me if—"

But Lucian's words were cut off as Arlo dived through the door and slammed it behind him, sucking in fresh, flower free air as he sagged against a wall around the corner from the flower store. A tiny whimper and a warm press against his leg forced him to look down. Peanut stared up at him, floppy ears flat and stubby tail pointed down, as he raised himself up onto his hind legs and pawed at Arlo.

"Hey, little fella. I'm okay, now I'm outside." Arlo stroked his anxious dog's head. "I shouldn't have gone in there, not without taking an antihistamine first. But why should I have taken one, because I wasn't planning on going in there. It just kind of happened."

Peanut whined his disbelief. Christ, even his dog didn't believe him. Arlo sucked in a breath, his allergic reaction already waning. Soon, it would be gone completely, but not if he took the tightly clutched bunch home with him. The flowers were beautiful, but other than thrusting them into the arms of some shocked passer-by, there was only one place for them.

He eyed the dumpster at the end of the narrow alleyway behind the stores. With a surge of relief that fought with more than a twinge of regret, Arlo lifted the top and slung the brown paper wrapped bunch inside, before he led Peanut away to stock up on antihistamines.

CHAPTER SEVEN

The door crashed open, and Bibi burst in. "Hey, sorry I was a little longer than I said I'd be."

A little longer? Lucian looked at his watch. Three hours to get a trim? Bibi's sleek bob didn't look any different. Maybe it was the large, bulging bag from the pricy boutique across the square that had been the real reason for him being on his own for most of the morning.

"I suppose you've got to look your best for your big date with Brad, the singing cowboy."

Bibi swatted his arm. "You're so mean, Luci. And anyway, I'm meeting Dean tonight, not Brad. I dated him in high school too…"

Lucian made coffee and filled her in on the morning. A steady stream of customers flowed in and out of the store, barely leaving them alone for more than a minute or two. Eventually, by mid-afternoon, the minute or two stretched into five, ten, then fifteen. Lucian leaned against the counter and inspected his nails, digging out the dirt that had got lodged there.

"That guy came in. The one who returned my wallet a couple of days ago." He scraped harder, focusing all his concentration.

She sniggered, forcing Lucian to look up. "Arlo, you mean. Who you decided would look good drenched in beer."

"It was an accident. It could have happened to anybody."

"Luci, I haven't known you for too long, but I think it's been kind of long enough to know if stuff like that was going to happen, it'd happen to you."

Lucian tried to look affronted. But she was probably right.

"So what about him?"

"Nothing. Just saying." He returned to examining his nails.

Bibi laughed. "If you're asking if I know him, the answer's yes, but not too well."

"Oh, so there is at least one man you didn't date in high school?" He dug at a spot of dirt that refused to budge.

Bibi sniffed. "Arlo must be ten or so years older than me. And gay. And he moved out east for a few years. So no, we didn't date."

Lucian peered up at Bibi through his lashes. "So, erm, what do you know about him?"

"Other than we never dated? Oh, okay," she said, sighing long and loud. "He's been back in Collier's Creek for a few months. He grew up here, but spent much of his adult life in New York. I think it was there. Or was it Boston? We've met a few times, through mutual friends. He likes to keep to himself and lives on the edge of town on the land that belonged to his family. The house he lives in, he designed it, because he was an architect back east. It's awesome, according to my friend Francine, who's also a friend of Arlo's.

"I like him. He's interesting, smart, and cultured and always super polite, and incredibly handsome, which I'm sure you've noticed. When he returned, he received a lot of attention and broke the hearts of several local ladies by letting them know he wasn't interested. And before you ask, no, I don't know if he has a boyfriend. I've never seen him with anybody, but like I say, I don't know him too well."

"You know a lot about him, considering you don't know him that well."

Bibi snorted. "If I didn't know you, I'd say you were being snarky. It's a small town, Luci, people like to talk. But maybe you could find out more for yourself."

"Excuse me?"

"Ask him out on a date."

"Oh, no, I couldn't do that."

"Why not? Honestly," she huffed, "don't be so British!"

How can I not be, when that's exactly what I am? But why not ask? Arlo was drop dead gorgeous. Tall, well built and with eyes like the trees back at Danebury, when fall, which was really autumn, crept in to steal away the summer. And older. He did a quick calculation. About ten years older than Bibi, which made him, what? Forty-three? Forty-four? He swallowed hard. There were too many red flags for him to take Bibi's advice. Not that Arlo would be interested in him. But even if he were, he wasn't interested in Arlo. Not one bit. Not at all. Not really.

CHAPTER EIGHT

At 4:00pm, Bibi let Lucian leave for the day. With a wave, he ducked out of the door, glad to be in the warm sunshine. It was too nice a day to go straight home, and he headed instead to CC's, hands down the best coffee shop in town.

He took a seat outside and, sipping his coffee, caught up with messages from the few friends who made the effort to keep in touch, before he scrolled through his social media. Coming to a sudden stop, his hand tightened on his cell as with the other he clunked his coffee down, forming an unnoticed puddle on the tabletop.

The Shit Formally Known as Miles stared out at him, his good looks as undeniable as his shallow, duplicitous, lying character.

As usual, Miles looked perfect. His stubble was just the right length, and his hair was just bed headed enough to not look like he'd tumbled out of an actual bed, which wasn't in reality half as attractive and always came with sour sleep breath. With his arm slung around the shoulders of a younger man, Miles grinned out at him as, behind them, a tropical sun dipped into the ocean.

"You bastard," Lucian breathed. Not at Miles, even though that was what he was, but at the man who was with him and laughing into the camera, causing his spirits to drop and spill out over the sidewalk. The man whom Lucian had always believed to be his friend, but had turned out to be anything but, now clung onto Miles like the leech he was. HashtagLoveOfMyLife, HashtagMyMan…

HashtagFuckOff.

He powered down his phone and shoved it into his pocket. They were welcome to each other; they deserved each other; one of them would soon shaft the other and not in the good way. *HashtagYouBastard, HashtagYouCheatingSlimeball…*

Lucian sucked in a deep breath and tipped back his head, the sun's rays warm and comforting.

Think positive thoughts, happy thoughts, focus on what makes you feel good as you banish the negativity… He snorted, almost hearing his mum's voice. She was always urging him and his siblings, Eddie and Bella, to get in touch with their inner, happier selves. It's because she's Californian, Eddie would grumble darkly, while Bella would simply roll her eyes. It wasn't very British, but as his skin tingled under the afternoon sun, and as the noises faded all around him, as he focused on what made him feel good, maybe, just maybe, there was something in it as his muscles relaxed and the tension drained away… Hope I don't dribble… Happy thoughts, think about what made him feel good…

Lucian gasped as hazel eyes, sandy, silver streaked hair, and a wonky smile filled his head.

Arlo McDonald was a very happy thought indeed.

Lucian jerked upright, Bibi's words ringing in his ears… Ask him out on a date… No. Yes. No. No. He'd been told in more ways than one that the best way to get over a man was to get under another, after his relationship with Miles had imploded, but he'd cringed away from taking that road. Who'd want him under them, anyway? Miles had made it very plain that he was sub par… Sub par. The word dug into his skin and crawled beneath it, like a tick. Arlo McDonald certainly wouldn't call him that. Arlo McDonald, who for a few brief minutes had been his happy place, his positive thought, the man he absolutely would not be asking out on a date.

"Do you mind if I join you?"

"What?" Lucian jumped, pulled out of his meandering thoughts by the unknown voice. Before he could answer, a large guy with huge buck teeth pulled off his jacket and threw it over the back of the spare chair and sat down at the small table for two.

"Er, yes. Be my guest, but I was, erm, just about to go."

The guy pointedly stared at Lucian's coffee, the cup half full and still steaming.

"I'm Kurt."

Yes, I rather think you are.

"You're the guy from that flower store."

It was a statement, not a question, and Lucian wasn't sure if he was required to answer, but he needed to say something in response, if only to be polite.

"Yes. I'm Bibi's senior florist." Her only florist.

Kurt shrugged. "Never saw the point in bunches of

flowers. They die, and then if you don't chuck 'em out, they stink."

"The dead have a funny habit of doing that. Or so I'm told." Lucian grabbed his coffee and took a swig, but the still-hot liquid burned his throat and brought tears to his eyes.

"You're not from around these parts." Kurt leaned in, all heavy stares and huge rabbit teeth, reminding him of Cashew just before he took another bite out of his flesh.

Lucian was sure the right to perfect teeth was enshrined in the constitution, as he'd certainly seen some impressive dentistry since he'd arrived in Collier's Creek, but Kurt clearly had a rebellious streak.

"Erm, no. I'm—"

"Australian." Kurt said it with such conviction, Lucian didn't wish to disabuse him.

"Hmm. That's right. Mate." Lucian picked up his coffee. God, it was still too hot. He'd paid $8.00 for the privilege and there was no way he was going to leave without finishing it. He'd just have to put up with Kurt, and his distracting teeth, for the next few minutes.

"I'm not from here either, just been brought in to do a job for a couple months. I'm from…" He mentioned a place Lucian had never heard of and was even less likely to visit.

Kurt droned on, and Lucian tried his best to keep up with how Bumfuck City, or wherever, was superior in all ways to Collier's Creek. Next to them, a table became free. Would it be very rude for him to move—

"You're cute. Do ya wrestle?"

"Wrestle?" What was this guy on? Why in god's name would anybody think he wrestled? "No, I don't." What had happened to Kurt's monologue about Bumfuck? He shoved his glasses up to the bridge of his nose, where they balanced at an awkward angle. It was difficult to sound affronted with wonky glasses wobbling on his nose.

Kurt leaned in closer. "We're both strangers in town. I'm from Boomfurt. You're from Austria."

"Australia." Lucian swallowed back the first tickling of a manic, rising laugh. Boomfurt? What happened to Bumfuck?

"Yeah, wherever. Means we've got a lot in common. Maybe we can find out if there's more?"

Kurt grinned.

Fuck, those teeth were enormous… "I don't think we have anything remotely in common. Now, if you'll excuse me." Lucian shoved his chair back, ready to abandon his ludicrously expensive coffee, but it hit the coffee shop wall. He was trapped. Oh, god… He really didn't want to make a scene, but the cringing embarrassment of doing so was being engulfed by his mounting indignation.

"I'm in a motel just outside town. Mountain View, you know it?"

"No, and I don't intend to. Look, if you don't mind—"

"There ain't no view of anything," Kurt said, cutting across, "other than the dumpsters behind the kitchen. But they do a fine breakfast. Lots of eggs."

"Eggs?"

Kurt nodded and a tiny burp bubbled up on his lips, bringing with it the sulfurous aroma of lots and lots of eggs from that long ago breakfast.

"Fucking hell." Lucian covered his nose to block out the stale stench. But Kurt was undeterred.

"My car's five minutes from here, so we can—"

"Hey, babe, sorry I'm late."

A shadow fell across the table and Lucian looked up. The bright sun dazzled him, but he didn't need to see who stood over them. The deep, calm voice was more than enough to quell his rising panic.

Arlo pulled a chair across from the vacated table and sat down, casually resting an arm around Lucian's shoulders. Lucian inhaled deep, the scent of rescue, and Arlo's light, citrus cologne evicting the lingering stink of hours-old egg. Arlo smiled at Kurt, his mercifully not buck teeth bared, and Lucian shivered.

"This your boyfriend? Three's the magic number, right?"

"Wrong." Arlo leaned forward. He didn't raise his voice, but its steely menace made Lucian's blood run cold.

Kurt's gaze flickered from Arlo to Lucian, back to Arlo, before he pushed himself up from the table, his short and bulky limbs clumsy and uncoordinated as he dragged on his jacket.

"See ya around." A second later, Kurt was gone.

"God, I sincerely hope not," Lucian muttered.

Arlo's arm slipped from Lucian's shoulders, taking its protective warmth with it.

"Babe?" Lucian stared up at Arlo, the word tingling down his spine.

Arlo's lips lifted in a bashful, lopsided smile. "I was passing and saw what was happening. I could have called him out, but I thought you'd rather not risk any kind of public scene... Unless I misjudged what was going on here?" Arlo leaned back as a shadow of doubt clouded his eyes, and a bubble of panic rose in Lucian's chest.

"No! God, you must be joking. He kind of barged in on

me." Lucian shuddered. "Thank you for helping me out."
Rescuing me…

Arlo shrugged, but said nothing. Lucian turned his coffee cup around, one way then the other. The silence dragged out and a mild panic pinched his nerves.

"What are you doing here?"

"Waiting to get my toenails cut."

"Your…?" Confusion creased Lucian's brow.

Arlo's deadpan expression turned into a crooked smile, and Lucian tutted.

"I was passing by on my way home after picking up a package," he nodded toward a large padded parcel, on the ground next to him, "when I saw what was happening."

"You seem to do a lot of passing by. This is the second time you've passed by where I am today. I thought it was only celebrities who attracted stalkers." Lucian laughed.

Arlo's face closed down, the wonky smile flatlining.

Oh, fuck… Everything he said seemed to come out wrong. Arlo had saved him from Eggy Kurt and his dreams of wrestling, and here he was all but accusing Arlo of stalking him.

"That sounded… I'm sorry, truly I am. I was just making light of it all, but… I didn't mean to accuse you of being…" Could this really, truly, honestly get any worse? He took a deep breath. "You got me out of a spot of bother and I'm very grateful."

"Glad to be of help." Arlo's voice was curiously flat. Or maybe not so curiously.

He got up, ready to go. Lucian wanted to pull him back down and start all over again, telling him he was sorry for being such a prat, and yes, he was more than happy for Arlo not just to pass by, but to stop, anytime he wanted.

But his tongue had turned to stone and a lump the size of a boulder blocked his throat, and the words he wanted to say refused to be said.

"Enjoy the rest of your day. Or what's left of it."

Lucian nodded as Arlo picked up his package, only finding his voice too late as Arlo strode off, his broad frame straight backed and dignified, leaving Lucian feeling more like a stranger in town than ever before.

CHAPTER NINE

Arlo dumped his package on the kitchen table, going through the mail he'd picked up on the way in. Junk, except for one, although he wasn't too sure he wouldn't dump that one in the trash as well. He'd deal with it later, or whenever; he threw it to the side, along with the rest.

Making a coffee, he nursed it between his hands. He'd been about to ask Lucian if he'd like to stay awhile in CC's, but the younger man's comment had cut him to the bone. Sure, Lucian had made a stumbling, clumsy apology as his face had heated to the color of an overripe tomato. The guy had no filter; he opened his mouth, and ill-thought out words came tumbling from his plump, red lips… Arlo's jaw tightened. He should have thrown back some snarky, smart ass comment before they laughed it off. He couldn't, not when he was made to feel… Arlo narrowed his eyes as he searched for the right word, his chest tightening as he found it.

Foolish.

With a burst of irritation, he chucked the barely touched drink into the sink.

Fuck it. He had a thick skin, he'd grown it long ago because without it he wouldn't have survived. So then why did the eccentric Englishman make that same skin feel very, very thin?

A skitter of claws on the tiled floor snagged Arlo's attention as Peanut ambled over and pressed his warm, stocky body against his leg, looking up at him with impossibly liquid chocolate eyes. Arlo scratched him behind the ear and smiled, the little dog instantly lifting his spirits.

Arlo unlocked the door to the yard so that Peanut could wander out and collapse in a heap in the late sunshine, leaving him to unwrap his package.

Paints, mostly acrylics, but watercolors and oils too, in all the colors of the rainbow and more. His gaze drifted to the yard, and the mountains bathed in light and shadow, his mind already working on the composition, using the door frame as a literal frame. But that wasn't for today, and he packed his treasure trove away again and took everything upstairs to the light flooded space that was his studio.

The late afternoon light was perfect, and the mountains were begging to be sketched. The act of running pencil over paper, the faint rasp as it flew across the roughened surface always soothed, always took him away from whatever problem snapped at him, whatever worry troubled him, unwinding and freeing whichever knot had tightened damn near enough to choke him. But not today, because all he could think about was how foolish he'd felt, and how foolish he'd been to turn and walk away.

Back downstairs, Arlo pulled a bottle of beer from the fridge. Taking it out to the porch, like Peanut, he collapsed into a patch of sunlight. Drinking alone… He snorted. If he didn't drink alone, he'd be near teetotal. He stretched out on his recliner, the warmth, along with the soft buzz from the alcohol, urging him to close his eyes.

Against the backdrop hum of insects and the whisper of a cooling breeze in the trees and shrubs, he drifted, hanging in the vague, nebulous space between sleep and wakefulness. A face came into focus. Lucian, pale and oval, eyes of the deepest blue and fringed with long, sooty lashes. Lucian's lips parted slightly, the sweeping tip of his tongue leaving a glistening sheen. His head dipped forward, and Arlo thrust his fingers into thick, silky hair.

"Jesus!" Arlo lurched forward, fully awake, as the painful bulge of his erection pushed against the confines of his jeans. Cupping himself, he rubbed at his fully hard dick, as a light sweat dampened his face. He squeezed hard… maybe he should take a shower where he could…

His cell rang, the shrill jangle shredding the air and ripping Arlo's hand from his needy dick. Fuck it, it can go to voicemail… but he was already reaching for it, checking the caller ID.

"Hey, Hank."

"You okay? You sound like you swallowed a truck load of grit." Hank laughed against the background of hammers beating against metal, the screech of machinery, and the raucous shouts of the other men who worked in Hank's car repair business.

Arlo looked around, almost expecting to see Hank emerge from behind a tree. Stupid.

"About Sunday."

What about Sunday? Arlo rummaged through his not

quite clear head to find some clue to what Hank was talking about.

"… starting a little later, we're going for 3:00pm. Francine says don't worry about bringing anything with you."

Bringing anything to what and where?

"Arlo, have you got any clue what I've just said to you? No, don't answer. The BBQ. We're starting later. Do I have to send somebody to pick you up, in case you forget?"

Of course. But now he remembered and wished he hadn't. Francine's birthday, and Cousin Wilbur, produced out of nowhere to be his gift, as though he were the birthday boy. Fuck.

"No, I've not forgotten. How could I do that?"

Hank snorted. "Just make sure you don't. Okay, I know a family BBQ isn't your thing, that it's not a fancy-pants New York restaurant—"

"Hank—"

"But if I didn't drag you out of that big ol' house of yours, you wouldn't go anywhere. Admit it, man. I'm right, ain't I?"

"I won't admit it, because that's not so. I go plenty of places." But he was stumped to think where. Hank was right, and it was an unsettling thought that his old friend had, once again, read him so well.

"You're not supposed to be a hermit, Arlo. That just ain't you. We'll see you Sunday."

CHAPTER TEN

Lucian slumped onto the couch and groaned. Why did he always stick his enormous foot into his very wide mouth? Why didn't he engage his brain before even thinking of uttering one solitary, single word? And why did he do it over and over and over again? He was twenty-four, not four, so shouldn't he have grown out of whatever it was he should have grown out of? Maybe he had a death wish? Or maybe he was just congenitally stupid.

He lay back and closed his eyes. Arlo had got him out of a fix, and all he'd done was piss him off by accusing him of being a stalker.

"Errggghh..." Lucian groaned as he shoved his fingers through his hair. He liked Arlo. The man made him smile and laugh, a big solid gold star in his favor when no man had done that for what felt like a lifetime. Arlo had all the makings of a friend — or he had until he'd opened his big, unfiltered mouth, and screwed up that chance.

A friend. It was a warm, welcoming thought. Apart from Bibi, he'd made no other connections in Collier's

Creek. It'd be good to have Arlo McDonald as a friend. A very good-looking friend. Lucian's lips twisted in a wry smile. Just a friend, and definitely not a boyfriend, because that was just ridiculous and totally the last thing he wanted. Hadn't he come halfway around the world to one hundred percent, absolutely not have a boyfriend?

"I should apologize," he said to nobody but the silent room. But how?

There was no way Arlo was going to return to the flower store, so other than finding out from Bibi where his house was, how was he going to make his apology? Lucian snorted. Yeah, right… Turning up unannounced at Arlo's door… Who was going to look like the stalker then? No, he was just going to have to hope he ran into Arlo in town. And then he'd pounce.

A loud, complaining growl from deep in his stomach was the reminder he'd not eaten since early that morning, an incinerated piece of toast.

He dug through his refrigerator, finding not much more than a dry lump of cheese, a tub of butter, and a wilted lettuce. "What's my name, Old Mother Hubbard?" The food cupboard wasn't much better — or not until his gaze fell on a jar of instant happiness. He smiled. Joy in a jar, butter, and the remains of a loaf of bread he could toast. Dinner was all but served.

Less than five minutes later, Lucian unscrewed the top on the big brown jar and breathed in deep. Heaven. Heaven on toast. Literally on toast. He dug the knife in, piling up the thick, dark brown paste, trailing a thin thread between jar and the thick slice of heavily buttered toast.

"Oh, Marmite, how I love thee," he muttered just before chomping down.

Lucian slumped back in his chair and closed his eyes as the salty, savory, unctuous goodness overwhelmed him. It was a taste of home, in the midst of the pretty little town he'd discovered by a crazy act of sheer randomness.

He took his time chewing. As much as his family, he had known he'd needed and wanted some time out, just for a few months… and Collier's Creek was as different from his life at home as it was possible to get. He'd struck lucky with the Wyoming town. There were worse places to be lonely in.

Licking away the salty smear of Marmite clinging to his lips, Lucian eyed the rest of the loaf. Another slice of toast, and then the rest of the packet of custard cream biscuits — thank you, mother dearest, for the care package — along with a cup of strong tea, and that would be dinner done and dusted. He should get some veggies and fruit, but he wrinkled his nose; he didn't much like them, which was pretty inconvenient for a vegetarian.

As he picked up the knife to hack off another slice of bread, his cell phone burst into life, buzzing and vibrating across the tiny kitchen table, the familiar ringtone instantly lifting his spirits.

"Mum!"

"Honey, how are you? Thank the lord you haven't been eaten by grizzly bears."

The distinctive tones of her Southern California accent were still strong, despite the many years she'd spent flitting between the family's London house and Danebury Manor, the ancestral home of the Blaxstons deep in the rolling hills of the Hertfordshire countryside.

"Er, no, I don't think so, especially as I'm talking to you."

Down the line, and thousands of miles away, his mother snorted.

"Did you get the care package I sent you, with all your favorites?"

"I did, but next time add in more Marmite, and tea bags, lots more tea bags. And Marmite."

"Are you being disrespectful of US tea, young man?"

Lucian smiled. "Of course I am. I learned it from you."

Across the ocean, his mother laughed. "I'm on it, honey. So how are you coping? When I said you should take advantage of your dual nationality to put everything behind you and find yourself, I meant L.A., or New York or Boston. Miami, even. Even Pennsylvania. At a stretch. Honey, I have so many contacts, I could get you—"

"Mum…" Lucian closed his eyes. He'd lost count of how many times he'd had this conversation. Yes, she had contacts. There didn't seem to be anybody she didn't know and could call on for a favor; even the job with Bibi had resulted from a contact of a contact, who knew somebody's aunt or neighbor, or pet poodle or something. "Doing this — leaving for a while, getting away from it all — I had to do it myself, for myself."

"But I only wanted to help. I wanted to make things easy for you, honey. You're my youngest, my baby," she said, her voice softening.

"I know. But I'm not a baby, Mum. Things here are going well." With his free hand, he crossed his fingers.

They were going well, if he didn't count having no friends other than his employer, or going nowhere much other than Randy's, which he was just about keeping from being barred from, and watching Netflix on his own before going to bed early. Or royally pissing off Arlo McDonald by accusing him of being a creepy stalker when all he'd done was to be really nice to him, and who'd rescued him from the unwanted attentions of Eggy Kurt. He sagged into his chair. Yeah, things were going really well for him in Collier's Creek.

"How's everything at home?" he asked, keen to have the spotlight turned away from himself.

"All good. We're fully booked until Easter, and the rest of next year is filling up fast. Who knew so many couples wanted to get married in a castle?"

"Danebury isn't a castle, it's a manor. You should know the difference by now."

"Lucian, honey, every stately pile is a castle to this California girl," she said, good humored laughter edging her words. "But a castle or a manor, people want to mark the most important day in their life somewhere special, and Danebury sure delivers, as the healthy bookings testify." She hesitated, so slight it would have been unnoticed by most. But not by Lucian. He bit down on his lower lip, waiting for her to say whatever was on her mind.

"We settled with Mr. and Mrs. Beaumont-Hughes. The lawyers wrapped it all up. It was costly…" her voice trailed off. Lucian's grip on the cell tightened; he was sure he heard her swallow. "But the main thing is, it avoided a whole heap of adverse publicity, which is so important in such a competitive market."

Lucian's mouth dried to a dust ball. Mrs. Beaumont-Hughes, the former Miss Petrelli. The Bridezilla from Hell, whose special day had been very special indeed, courtesy of an angry bee and a ruined antique dress made from paper-thin lace.

"I'm sorry, Mum. I know it was all my fault—"

"Honey, it's finished with. We've put it all behind us. Mrs. Beaumont-Hughes is fully recovered and the dress has been repaired. Or as much as it can be."

Lucian cleared his throat. "What's the new florist like?" The one they'd had to get in quickly to replace him. He'd been told their name, but he didn't remember and didn't care.

"Adequate. Not a patch on you, of course, but then nobody could ever be. Maybe, when you come home, we should buy a little flower store for you. You'd still do all the Danebury work, of course, but we could look at hiring somebody to deal with the client interface, leaving you to concentrate on the creative, artistic side of things. How does that sound?" she asked, her voice bright and upbeat.

Somebody to deal with the client interface.... In other words, creating a buffer zone to stop him from causing any damage by opening his big mouth, telling a blushing bride-to-be that the red roses she so desperately wanted for her bouquet would clash horribly with her sallow complexion, or that the corsage for the hatchet faced future mother-in-law really needed to be a statement piece, because how else could they deflect attention from the large, hairy mole on the side of her nose?

Lucian groaned. He did it every time, all the time, putting his foot in it, insulting, upsetting, or angering everybody, just by opening his mouth. Nobody was immune, he was an equal opportunities offender.

"Lucian, honey? Are you okay? You sound in pain," his mum asked, a hint of panic running through her words.

"No, just, erm, indigestion."

"Tell me you're eating properly…"

After assuring her he was, with his fingers re-crossed, they said their goodbyes.

He lay back on the couch and stared up at the ceiling. Life at home was progressing without him. Fully booked for weddings and corporates, and a new florist, too. Despite what his mum said, they'd be very good, as the business masterminds that were his older brother and sister would never allow the merely adequate for Danebury Manor's phenomenally lucrative society weddings and big ticket corporate events. He'd only been gone a few weeks, and he already felt as though he were fading from the place that had always been his home.

CHAPTER ELEVEN

Arlo was convinced his face was about to crack and his bland, polite smile would crash to the ground. His eyes had glazed over long ago as Wilbur droned on about dental implants, whitening products, the pros and cons of fluoridation, and dire warnings not to travel beyond the state line for dental care and, under no condition, to ever, if you valued your life, sanity and all things oral health, to contract such care in Arkansas, Alabama, or Alaska.

"Excuse me." Arlo's limbs twitched, and he jumped up. He couldn't take any more, but if Wilbur thought him rude, it didn't show, as he promised to tell Arlo later on about the highly acclaimed article about him, published in World of Dentistry.

Arlo had to stop himself from running across Hank and Francine's yard and crashing through the gate to hightail it back home. He sucked in a deep breath, and veered instead toward the door leading to the kitchen, hoping to find a moment's release in its air-conditioned emptiness.

He'd give it an hour, enough time to have something to

eat before coming up with an excuse to leave that both Hank and Francine would believe. Shit, he needed another beer to drown the guilt in his stomach. Pulling open the refrigerator door, he grabbed a bottle and flipped the top. He drank deep. It was a local brew, on the sweet side but good, and he snorted, spraying a flume of beer as he wondered what Wilbur would think of all that sugary booze washing over his teeth.

Wilbur. The guy had been set up as much as he had. This wasn't the first time Francine had attempted to match-make. She seemed to pull gay cousins and friends out of her purse the way a magician pulled a rabbit out of a hat. But it would be the last time. He'd have to break it to her gently — or not so — that he could handle his own love life. Which was one fat lie.

He peeked out the window. More guest had arrived as he'd sought sanctuary. Much as he wanted to, he couldn't hide in the kitchen all afternoon. He emerged into the sunny backyard. An hour, he'd give it an hour.

On the edge of the porch, Hank was brandishing a long fork, turning, prodding, and poking at what looked like a complete cow on the huge BBQ, all shiny gun metal gray and the size of a small car. BBQ, it seemed to be all every-body ate when folks got together. He'd forgotten, having been away for so long. Collier's Creek had grown, had become more affluent. The tourist dollar was riding high, and the town had welcomed a couple of good coffee shops and some stores specializing in local artisanal products. It was a good place to live, but the small, mountain town where he'd been raised wasn't feeling like the home he'd dreamed of returning to.

Maybe he could slink off now. There were plenty of

people milling around in the yard, Hank and Francine's kids, and members of their extended family. Neighbors and co-workers. A few he recognized from way back, but most were strangers to him. He could tell himself he wouldn't be missed, but he knew that wasn't true. Francine would be upset, and Hank would be pissed. And with good reason. They were solid people, and solid friends, and they deserved more from him. He sucked in a deep breath, plastered the smile back on his face, and made his way over to the BBQ.

"Hey," Hank said, a sheen of sweat covering his face, glowing red from the thermonuclear heat thrown out by the BBQ that, on closer inspection, resembled not so much a car as an alien spacecraft.

Hank lowered his voice. "Sorry about the whole Wilbur thing, but even Francie's avoiding him. She's sent him off with a bowl of chips." He nodded to a far corner of the yard where Wilbur, in between mouthfuls, was thrilling another guest about the noble profession of dentistry. Whoever they were, they looked like they were enduring cranial implants without the benefit of anesthesia. Arlo pitied them, but at least it wasn't him, and that was all that mattered.

"Hey, you made it!"

Arlo turned at Francine's enthusiastic call as Bibi entered the yard from the side of the house, holding a large display of colorful flowers. Francine's enthusiastic appreciation for the gift floated across. Both women looked back towards the house and he was about to turn away when Lucian appeared, beckoned over by Bibi.

A lump lodged in Arlo's throat and all but stopped his breath, all thoughts of feeling foolish crumbled to dust. In black jeans that were so tight they were probably illegal, and a blue shirt Arlo knew was the exact color as Lucian's eyes, the young Englishman was breathtaking.

Lucian handed over a package to Francine, and she gave him a hug in return. A second later, balancing both the enormous bouquet and the gift, Francine was chivvying Lucian in his and Hank's direction.

"Hank, Arlo, this is Bibi's co-worker, Luci-Ann—"

"Erm, it's Lucian, actually." Lucian shuffled from foot to foot.

"Sure, that's right. Luci-Ann put this wonderful bouquet together for me — and all my favorite colors, too. Thank you so, so much. And a darling little gift basket of real British chocolate." She beamed, holding up the box of candy bars nestling on a bed of pink shredded paper. "I've never had Tunnocks Tea Cakes, Double Deckers, Crunchies, and Walnut Whips, but I'm sure I'm going to love them. Hank'll look after you while I find a vase for this cute bouquet."

"Let me get you a drink, Lu—Luci…," Hank stumbled over the name; his face, already red, was turning an alarming shade of crimson.

"I'll do that," Arlo said. "You need to tend the meat."

Hank gave him a grateful smile, as Arlo jerked his head to a huge bucket sitting a few feet away in the shade, which had drinks piled up in icy water.

"Here, have one of these — I brought them. They're from a micro brewery upstate. It's good."

"No cat's piss then?"

"I wouldn't bring—" Arlo's words came to a halt as Lucian's dark blue stare and long, thick lashes captured his attention, despite the ugly glasses perched on his nose.

Lucian's lips curved upwards in a smile that seemed full of secrets and promise. Arlo's cock thickened and twitched against the confines of his jeans... oh, fuck... He coughed, and twisted the cap, upending the bottle and swallowing too much, the alcoholic sting at the back of his throat bringing tears to his eyes.

Lucian took a tentative sip and nodded. "This is good." Shifting his weight from one side to the other, he looked everywhere but at Arlo. "What I said—"

"About stalking you?" Arlo pressed his lips together to stop himself from wincing. Jesus, the guy's lack of filter was infectious.

"Yeah. That was — wrong and unforgivable, especially as you got me out of a hole with Eggy Kurt."

"Excuse me — Eggy...?"

Lucian's lips twitched and his gaze shifted to Arlo's. "In my mercifully brief encounter, he revealed a disturbing penchant for eggs. Lots of eggs. And wrestling."

"Wrestling? It's a popular hobby around here. Nothing weird about that."

Lucian laughed, his entire face brightening. "Then maybe I should have taken him up on his offer to... wrestle. Or maybe not," he said, giving a shiver. "It wasn't the first time I've been accosted in a coffee shop, but never by somebody who was so..."

"Eggy?"

"Definitely eggy, but don't forget creepy and weird. And there was me thinking Collier's Creek was a normal, straight down the line little town. But then he did say he came from somewhere called Bumfuck City—"

Arlo threw back his head and laughed. How could he stay pissed with this guy?

"But before we wandered into the murkiness that is eggs and wrestling, I was trying to apologize. You've probably noticed I have a tendency to, erm, say the wrong things, or say them in a way that's easily misconstrued. And I'm sorry, I honestly am. I offended you when all you did was come to my rescue."

Uncertainty, as though unsure whether his apology would be enough, flittered across Lucian's face, as he pushed the horrible glasses that had slipped back up his nose. Arlo's stomach knotted. He wanted to wipe that uncertainty from Lucian's face, as much as he wanted to sweep away the heavy fall of hair across his brow. His grip tightened on his beer.

"Accepted. Perhaps we should start over?"

Lucian nodded, all the anxiety that had dogged him melting away like mountain mist.

"So, Luci-Ann—"

Lucian groaned. "Luci I've kind of learned to tolerate, but I hate it when people call me Luci-Ann. It really gets to me. It's all about where to put the stress, so it was an honest mistake on Francine's part, but I had to correct her, although," he said, as a worried frown broke out on his face, "I hope I didn't offend her?"

"No, you wouldn't have. And what's the problem with correcting somebody's pronunciation? She looks like butter wouldn't melt in her mouth, but believe me, that lady's a tough cookie."

"It's what the bullies at school used to call me, when they decided it was my turn to take a beating." A heavy frown creased Lucian's brow, and he stared ahead of him, back into the past. His voice dropped. "But it was also what Miles—" Lucian stopped, as private thoughts teetered on becoming public words. "So, erm, yes, there are reasons why I really don't appreciate being called Luci-Ann."

"And it's not your name." Arlo smiled, wanting to bring back the sunshine to Lucian's face that had disappeared behind a cloud.

"So, how do you know our hosts?"

"Oh, Hank and Francine, I've known them since high school. Even though I moved away for school and then got caught up in building a life in New York, we stayed friends. They've been great at helping me settle back in. I hope you realize they'll adopt you and declare you part of the family." Arlo laughed and Lucian joined in.

He'd been only half joking. He appreciated the invites to family gatherings and the various town functions Francine seemed to be the organizer of, all part of reuniting him with the town, but he'd found himself increasingly scrabbling for excuses not to be dragged into every musical recital of this, every amateur performance of that, every Saturday evening potluck gathering.

"You grew up here?"

Arlo hesitated before he nodded, unsure how much he wanted to reveal.

"If you don't want to say anything more, that's okay."

Lucian stared up at him and straightened his glasses on his nose. They weren't the ones he'd been wearing before, but they were just as ugly.

"It's okay, there's no secret. My parents had some land — not enough to be called a ranch — just outside town. It barely provided a living, but they were determined I was going to take over."

"And you had other ideas?"

"Yeah. It caused a lot of arguments, and stuff was said on both sides we later came to regret.

"When I went east for school, we didn't talk for a couple of years. It was hard, because I loved my mom and dad and I knew they felt the same about me, but I guess pride and stubbornness got in the way for all of us. I think it was why I made sure I kept up the friendship with Hank and Francine; they were my lifeline to the Creek.

"I came back for their wedding, and I went to see my parents. We talked, and we put a lot of things right. They could see I was happy and that I'd made the right decision for me."

"So you became reconciled? That's good. My family drive me nuts, and I know I do the same to them, but I couldn't imagine being without them. Even if they think I'm incapable of running my own life." Lucian huffed out a laugh. "Which they're right about, more often than not. Do they still live here? Your parents, I mean?"

"No. They died, within three months of each other, a few years ago. I later sold off some of the land and built a new house, where I now live — the old place was rickety as hell, and freezing cold in the winter. So I came home in the end, just like they wanted."

They lapsed into silence amid the laughter and chatter. Yes, he'd come back to the town that had been his home, to carve out the life he kept telling himself he wanted, but sometimes as he sat alone in his big, beautiful, silent house, maybe what he'd really done was run away.

"How are the flowers holding up? They should be good for seven to ten days."

The sudden change of subject threw Arlo, but he was glad to leave his return to his hometown behind.

"The flowers…"

"Yes, the blazing stars, sand verbena, and mock orange?" Lucian's brows arched in question. Arlo wriggled beneath their steady, level gaze, when he never wriggled under any man's scrutiny. "I always think potted plants are fine, and if you're careful to pick the right ones, they can really make a room come alive. But there's something special about cut flowers, don't you agree?"

"There certainly is." Although he didn't think Lucian would want to know what he really thought was special about them.

"It's so unusual to meet a man who loves to fill his home with flowers. All that heady, rich perfume filling the air. It's wonderful, isn't it?"

"Sure." Arlo wrinkled his nose and cleared his throat at the itch that was forming. Just the thought of his home filled with brimming vases, infecting the air with heavy sweetness, was enough to make him want to reach for the antihistamines.

"Next time, when you come in, we'll go through all your favorite colors and scents, and I'll make you up a centerpiece for a table, or a cabinet."

Next time… The words sent a frisson dancing the length of Arlo's spine. But cut flowers… He'd better come clean.

"There's a slight problem with them."

Lucian's eyes widened. "A problem? Don't tell me they've died?"

"Not exactly. I gave them away." No way could he tell Lucian he'd thrown them in the trash.

"You…?"

"I'm allergic to cut flowers," he blurted. "They make

me sneeze, my chest gets all wheezy, and…" He trailed to a stop. Lucian was smiling, then grinning, before he burst out laughing.

"I'm sorry. I know I shouldn't laugh, but why didn't you tell me?"

"Because you were so enthusiastic about making up a bunch for me." And because I wanted to stay and talk to you some more…

"At least I know. I promise not to force any more flowers on you, but pot plants—"

"Hey, everybody, come and get the best BBQ in the Creek!" Hank's hollered out invite was met with whoops and cheers, as everybody made their way across. Arlo and Lucian joined them.

"There's enough here to feed an army," Lucian murmured as he looked at the piled up stack of meat.

Hank speared a sausage and waved it at Lucian.

"Thank you, it looks marvellous, but I'm veggie."

"You're what?"

"Vegetarian. I don't eat meat."

"You don't eat…?" Hank squinted, a pained expression creasing his face.

Arlo looked away, biting down on the grin aching to break out on his lips. In Hank's world, men ate meat. Period. He knew his friend well enough to know he was asking himself how this non meat eating English florist had ever ended up at his back yard BBQ. It was no doubt a story he'd be telling his buddies in the workshop, the entire crew of them shaking their heads in disbelief.

"I'm awfully sorry, but no, I don't. But the salads and all the side dishes look wonderful."

Hank looked from the sausage to Lucian, and back

again, his pained, constipated look turning to one of near horror. Lucian might just as well have said he only ate babies, well seasoned and slow cooked in the oven.

"Stick it on my plate, Hank, along with a burger and a couple of steaks. Come on," he said, nudging Lucian towards a table groaning under the weight of various salads, sides, and breads, "I'm sure we can find you something that hasn't been up close and personal with half a cow."

Piling their plates high, they found a shady spot and sat down.

Arlo was bursting with questions, and now was the perfect time to ask why and how the quirky young Englishman had found his way to a small town even most Wyomingites wouldn't have heard of. He also wanted to know who the guy called Miles was, the one who'd brought a frown to Lucian's brow, had made his lips turn down, and a shadow cloud his eyes. He stabbed hard at his baked potato, but the angle of the fork was wrong and it flew off his plate and rolled across the finely mowed lawn.

Lucian laughed. "Spud croquet. Oh my god, I haven't thought about that in years. We used to play it on the lawn near the ha-ha. It was the one thing I could always beat my brother and sister at. They hated losing, and especially to me." Lucian grinned, his face bright with memory.

"Spud I know is potato. Croquet's a game, because I watch far too much BBC period drama. But a — ha-ha?"

"Ah, yes." A flush colored his cheeks. "It's a type of sunken fence, commonly used in landscaped gardens and parks in the 18th century. The point was to give the Lord and Lady of the manor, or indeed anybody admiring the garden, the illusion of an unbroken, continuous rolling lawn, whilst at the same time providing boundaries for grazing livestock. I thought you'd know, being an architect."

"How do you know that's what I was?"

Lucian's flush deepened. Had he been asking about him? The thought was… intriguing.

"Bibi mentioned it. She wasn't gossiping, honestly. She just, erm, mentioned it."

Lucian squirming was great fun, and kind of cute, but Arlo put him out of his agony.

"I was, but I specialized in industrial architecture. Ha-has didn't feature much in plans for factories and ware-houses. So, a home with Lords and Ladies, landscaped gardens, and ha-has? Does that mean you're an aristocrat?"

Lucian shrugged, his face reddening further. "Only minor aristocracy. We don't get invites to take tea with the royal family. Or not in recent years, but…"

Arlo's gaze fell to Lucian's moving lips, glossy with a touch of smeared mayo. His stomach tightened, along with the crotch of his jeans. The sun shining from the hazy blue sky was too hot, the colors in the garden too bright, and Lucian's voice too far away. He blinked and tried to catch up with whatever it was Lucian was saying.

"… family took a tumble, as they backed the wrong side in some court intrigue. In the mid-nineteenth century they needed money, so a great however many times grand-father married into trade. It caused quite a scandal, but he got the cash which revived the family's fortunes, and she got a title. My brother became Lord—"

"Hey, guys." Bibi stood over them, balancing a piled

up plate in one hand as with the other she pulled a chair across and joined them.

Arlo pasted a smile on his face, bland and insincere, perfectly designed to disguise what he was thinking. He'd been a master of it, back in New York, in the life he'd put behind him.

"My god," she said, lowering her voice, "I had to get away from that Wilbur guy. He told me my teeth could do with a bleach, and he tried to sell me a half price dental package. Can you even believe that? Jeez. I'm sorry, Arlo, Francine told me the guy's your date, but—"

"What?" Arlo jumped, almost upsetting the contents of his plate into his lap. He glanced at Lucian, who stared at him openmouthed.

"You brought a date? Oh my god, and here's me, manipulating you. I'm so sorry. Wilfred—"

"Wilbur," Arlo and Bibi said at the same time.

"He's probably pissed off and with good reason—"

"There is no good reason, because he's not my date."

"But Francine said—"

"No!" Arlo cut across Bibi. He steadied his voice. "Francine's decided she needs to fix me up with somebody. Even somebody like Wilbur. But he is definitely not my date, never was, and never will be. I hadn't met the guy before today, and I have no intention of ever meeting him again." Christ, the thought that he could ever be interested in Wilbur…

Bibi leaned forward and gave his upper arm a quick squeeze. "You don't know how relieved I am to hear that." She stared hard at him, her shrewd eyes locking onto his, before she cast a quick glance at Lucian. "But just think of all that free dentistry you'd be missing out on. You'd save yourself a fortune. It really is something to consider."

Arlo pretended to think. "It's a tempting thought, but I've always been able to resist temptation."

"Have you?" Lucian asked, his eyes growing larger. "I find giving into it surprisingly easy."

"You do?" Something deep in Arlo's chest skipped.

"Or maybe think of all those flowers instead." Bibi picked up her plate, laughing as she wandered off.

CHAPTER TWELVE

Afternoon bleached into early evening, and Lucian yawned as he stretched out. It had been the best time he'd spent so far in Collier's Creek. He'd not felt... lonely. His gaze settled on Arlo who was chatting with Hank and Francine. Arlo's affection for them, and theirs for him, was clear in their easy laughter, and in Francine's light touches.

Though still early, he was tired in a relaxed, loose-limbed way, the way his old dog Wally was after spending a tiring afternoon snoozing in front of the fire, or in shafts of rare, warm sunshine. He closed his eyes and let the chatter of the remaining guests wash over him.

His thoughts drifted, as they so often did, to home. He missed it desperately, yet for the first time since he'd stepped off the plane, the persistent urge to make a run for the airport and book the first flight he could back to Heathrow wasn't tugging at him.

"Hey. Do you want to walk back with me? I'm passing your place."

Lucian opened his eyes and looked up. Arlo stood over

him, but he was in partial shadow, and he couldn't read the expression in the lovely hazel eyes that were staring down at him.

"But you don't know where my place is."

"Bibi told me. And she's gone, by the way. Says she'll see you Monday."

Lucian said nothing. Tomorrow was Sunday. No work to go to. The day stretched out in front of him.

"Don't be pissed with Bibi for telling me where you lived. I asked her, so I kind of put her on the spot. If you don't want to walk back with me, I can arrange for a cab."

"What? No." Lucian pushed himself up straight, the note of uncertainty in Arlo's voice sending a tremor of panic through him.

"I'm not in the least concerned Bibi told you where I'm living. I mean, I can't imagine you're some sort of mad axeman who'll come for me in the dead of night, or would be the slightest bit interested in breaking in when I'm hard at work floristing — which isn't a word, but I like it, so there. Honestly, I came out here with bugger all, so there's naff all to steal. Not that I think you're inclined to theft, as we've already established. You never stole my wallet, after all."

"Okay... I think somewhere in that I'm getting the message that, yes, you're happy to walk back with me?"

"Erm... would a simple yes work?"

Arlo smiled. "I think so. Come on, let's go."

They found their hosts in the kitchen.

"Thank you so much for inviting me. It really was a splendid afternoon."

Francine battered away his words. "You're more than

welcome, Luci-Ann. Any time. I hope you won't be a stranger?"

"Thank you. I—I appreciate it." Lucian coughed to clear his suddenly blocked throat.

Homely and plump, Francine was the polar opposite to his tall, elegant, poised mother, but they shared a warmth and a generosity of spirit. The tug of home pulled hard on his guts, and he didn't want that, not today, which had been perfect and the first and so far only time he felt he'd truly had a foot in Collier's Creek.

"I want you to take this home with you." She bustled over to the fridge and pulled out a huge Tupperware box. "Salads and sides, and some of the angel cake. You're too thin." Francine's expression defied all arguments, her directness leaving him speechless. She put the box into a large carrier bag and thrust it at him. "Return it to me when you can."

Minutes later, after goodbye hugs, they were out on the sidewalk. They walked for a while in near silence; it didn't feel awkward, and for once in his life, Lucian had no desire to fill it with nervous chatter. The sky was already turning pink and purple as the sun began setting behind the mountains.

"My mum asked me if I'd been eaten by grizzly bears. Which clearly hasn't happened. Are there really bears? It's hard to imagine because the most dangerous wild animals we have at home are probably disgruntled deer."

Arlo laughed. "We don't have any disgruntled deer, because the grizzlies ate them all. But yes, there are wild bears in the mountains. Wolves too. Camping in these parts isn't for the faint of heart."

"The last time I camped, I was a rather limp and

useless Boy Scout. All that outdoorsy stuff really wasn't my cup of tea. I think I only joined up for the uniform."

"So, what brought you to a mountain town like Collier's Creek? If you don't mind me saying so, it doesn't seem like the obvious place to find—"

"A dorky vegetarian English toff, you mean?"

"No, that's not what I mean. Or maybe a little."

Lucian slid his gaze towards Arlo, who was smiling. Lucian smiled back.

Arlo was so easy to talk to, but owning up to the disaster that was The Shit Formerly Known as Miles was humiliating, along with the final straw that had broken his family's back when he'd imperiled the business, was too much. He'd only end up looking stupid, because that's what he had been. The day had been wonderful, and he didn't want to ruin it by confessing to the mess that had been his life back home.

"I just… wanted a change of scenery. To experience a place somewhere very different from the one I grew up in. And I've certainly found it. I've got dual nationality. My mum's American, but I was actually born here. I spent the first couple of months of my life between the hospital and at my late grandparents' house with my mum. She went into premature labor when she was visiting." He shrugged. "Coming out here seemed to be the natural place to aim for."

"Is she from Wyoming?"

"No, California. She went to the UK to study — it was some kind of exchange scheme between universities. She met my father, and within six months they were married. As for touching down in Wyoming, I…" Oh god, was he really going to tell Arlo how random it was he'd ended up here? The man already knew he was an oddball who didn't engage his brain before speaking, but if he told him, he'd be adding screwball to the list.

"I stuck a pin in a map," he blurted out. There, he'd said it, and now it was too late to take it back.

"Okay." Arlo didn't miss a beat. "It's as good a way as any other to choose a place, so why not a pin in a map? You could have done a lot worse. I mean, you could have ended up in Bumfuck."

Lucian laughed. "The home of Eggy Kurt. I really don't think so."

Arlo smiled. "It's good to travel, to experience a different kind of life. I spent years in New York, but I've traveled a lot for work. Stints in London. Berlin, Paris. Sydney and Melbourne in Australia."

"Doesn't that make you the rarest of beasts, an American with a passport?" Lucian cringed. He'd done it again, opening his mouth without thinking. He sucked in a deep breath. This was one thing he didn't need to think about first. "I'm sorry. I really didn't mean to be judgmental or—"

Arlo shrugged. "No need to say sorry, even if by your own admittance, sorry so rarely means an apology in Britspeak."

"Ouch. But yes, I said that, didn't I? I deserved that, I suppose, even if I really am saying sorry. As in apologizing."

Arlo laughed. "Yes, you deserved it. But what you say is true. I am well traveled, both for pleasure and business, which makes me a distinct oddity around here, which I didn't appreciate fully until I came back."

"You're an oddity? Really? Makes two of us, then."

"I think so. Perhaps we're more alike than we realize."

Moments later, they came to a stop.

"This is me," Lucian said.

The street light was out, casting a pool of shadow; they both moved into it. The houses all had their drapes and blinds closed, and nobody was out and about. They were alone with no eyes looking on.

"Thank you for walking me home." Lucian slapped his hand against his forehead, groaning as he held it there. "Could I sound any more like a 1950s prom queen?"

They both loitered, neither making any attempt to move.

I should say goodnight and go... But Lucian didn't want to go, he didn't want to climb the stairs to his little, empty, silent apartment. He didn't want this evening to end. His heart thudded deep in his chest.

"We're being spied on." Arlo inclined his head slightly. "Look, but carefully, at the window by the front door. An old, bald guy's twitching his drapes."

Lucian groaned. "Mr. DuPont. I'm renting the apartment from him, which is really nothing more than a tiny bedsit. I swear the old codger can hear an ant fart. I'd invite you in, but he's strictly no visitors after 9:00pm. God alone knows what year he's living in. But the apartment's cheap. I'd like to, though. Invite you up, I mean. You know, for a cup of tea. And a Hobnob." A Hobnob...? Oh, fuck. "That wasn't some weird euphemism for... for anything that isn't a Hobnob." Please, ground, open up under my feet.

"A Hobnob. Hmm, fortunately I know that's an oat cookie, otherwise I'd think you were inviting me to take part in some weird English toff ritual."

Lucian chuckled with relief. "Tea and biscuits are a ritual, for toffs and everybody else, and a rather marvelous one. And absolutely, definitely not weird. And a Hobnob is a biscuit, not a cookie. Full stop. Period. The end."

Under the street lamp, Arlo's answering smile sent a ripple of warmth deep into Lucian's stomach. If Arlo thought he was an oddball, he wasn't enough of an oddball for him to be running for the hills.

A movement out of the corner of his eye snagged Lucian's attention, as his nosy landlord twitched the drapes too hard, partially pulling them off the rail.

"Maybe affordability isn't everything," Lucian muttered, turning back to gaze up at Arlo.

"Are you working tomorrow? Because if not, and you're free, perhaps you'd like to meet for brunch?"

"What? Erm, yes. Please. Thank you, I mean. That would be. Erm, yes…" Lucian stumbled to a stop.

"I'll meet you outside CC's at 11:00am — if that works for you?"

"It does. Sounds good. So, well, goodnight then." Lucian shuffled from one foot to the other. He really should go, but his feet hadn't got the message.

"Bye."

"Yes, er, bye then."

Arlo nodded, hesitating for a moment before he swung around and strode off. He didn't look back, but if he had, he'd have found Lucian staring after him, not smiling but beaming.

CHAPTER THIRTEEN

Lucian glared at the heap of clothes on the bed, hands on hips, as he stood in nothing but his boxers. He'd tried them all on, in all combinations, once, twice, a hundred times. Brunch. What did one wear for brunch with Arlo McDonald?

He picked up his one pair of good, expensive pants. Fine, dark gray wool, they were the bottom half of a suit, the jacket long since ruined. No, too formal. It would have to be jeans as there was nothing else left to choose from other than sweat pants and a pair of chinos that bore the ghost of a stain over the crotch, from a spilled cup of coffee. Very, very hot coffee. Black jeans. Nice and tight. And his dark blue shirt.

Exactly the same as he'd worn yesterday. Shit, Arlo would think he'd slept in his clothes. He threw the shirt in the general direction of his laundry basket, catching the faint odor of BBQ.

Twenty minutes later, jeans matched with a white T-shirt, he was ready to go. Or almost. Peering into the mirror, he groaned. "I've really, really got to get a haircut." He ran the palms of his hands over his hair, trying to push down the lightly curling ends. Wild and untamed was a generous description, but maybe a mess was the more honest. Fumbling for a tube of hair serum, he pumped once, twice, three, and four times for luck, into the center of his palm, and rubbed it through his hair.

He stared into the mirror. Oh, fuck. He looked like he'd stuck his head into a deep-fat fryer.

Rushing to the tiny bathroom, he grabbed the shower attachment from the wall in the shower and attempted to wash it out, getting more shampoo in his eyes than in his hair. Scrubbing hard with a towel, he peered through stinging eyes into the cabinet mirror. Bloodshot eyes, wet hair — and a spreading damp patch on the front of his T-shirt from the shower spray. Oh great. Terrific. Wonderful. A wet T-shirt Arlo would think was sweat soaked. Back in the bedroom, he ransacked his way through his closet again.

"Ooh, forgotten all about this." He held up a soft lilac T-shirt. It was a bit creased, but once it was on… He gave it a tentative sniff. Clean. Stripping one off, and tugging on the other, he snatched up his keys and wallet, slamming his door closed and locking up before thundering down the stairs, waving at Mr. DuPont, peering out from a crack in his doorway.

Running his fingers through his wet hair, he all but sprinted to meet the man who was definitely, absolutely not his date.

Out of breath and skidding to a halt outside the coffee shop, Lucian's apology burst from his lips.

"I'm so sorry I'm late. I had a run-in with some hair

product which resulted in a drenching. It's not…" Lucian's rushed apology fell silent. The ever popular CC's should have been buzzing with life, but instead was very quiet, and very closed.

"I was going to call and tell you, but we didn't swap numbers last night." Arlo pushed himself away from the door as he turned to the taped up sign on the door. "'Closed today due to unforeseen circumstance. Business as usual tomorrow,'" he read.

"Oh." A crushing disappointment pressed against Lucian's chest, making it hard to breathe. No coffee shop. No brunch. No certainly, absolutely not date. But there were plenty of other places, there was even Randy's, but Arlo wasn't suggesting any of them. The bright Sunday morning seemed to turn as gray and cloudy as an English summer's day as it stretched endlessly in front of him. "Perhaps we can rearrange, for when it re-opens?"

Arlo said nothing as his brows creased and his shoulders hunched as he thrust his hands into the pockets of his jeans.

No, let's not rearrange… but a small bubble of annoyance burst in Lucian's chest. Arlo had suggested brunch, not him, and if he was now squirming for a way out of his hastily offered invite—

"If the thought of having brunch, lunch or dinner no longer appeals, just say it," he snapped. "A few beers can make the best ideas regrettable in the morning light." Yeah, and didn't he just know it.

Arlo's jaw dropped, and he tugged his hands from his pockets, holding them palms out as he stepped back. It was an exaggerated response, and would have been vaguely comical if Lucian's sharp snap of annoyance hadn't already crumbled to dust, leaving him fed up and dejected. His stomach hollowed. He'd thought the man who now really, truly wasn't his date was better than that.

"The idea appeals very much. Believe me, if it didn't, I wouldn't have suggested it. But how do you feel about turning brunch into lunch? Not in town, but out at my place?"

Lucian blinked. Arlo was gazing at him through calm green-gold eyes, his face serious, his shocked surprise of seconds ago tucked away. Lucian groaned and flopped against the coffee shop window. His outburst had been too much; he felt like a tit because he'd reacted like a tit, ergo he was a tit.

"I seem to have developed a well-honed habit of having to apologize to you. I thought… Well, I think you realize. But yes, please, if the offer still stands?"

"Sure it does. And just for your info, I don't have any regrets at all. Come on. My car's in the parking lot." Arlo set off with his long-legged stride and Lucian, a wide grin breaking out on his face, followed in his wake.

CHAPTER FOURTEEN

"What a lovely house. Modern yet traditional, if that makes sense."

Arlo smiled. It made perfect sense, and he felt a tickle of pride in his chest. He locked his car, though just beyond the far reaches of town and with no other houses in sight, he had no genuine need to. The years of living in large, teeming cities would take more than a few months to undo.

"The house I grew up in needed a lot of work if it was going to be anything like how I wanted."

A lot of work was an understatement. The place had been a wreck by the time he'd inherited. Uncomfortable memories nibbled at him. Parents who'd not had the funds to get the much needed repairs done, pride steadfastly preventing them from accepting his offers to take care of the bills. The gloomy memories faded as soon as he opened the door to the cathedral ceiling and wood beamed room that formed the house's central space, flooded with warm, buttery light.

"Oh, my god. That view. It's, it's… stunning. It's the only word I can think of, but that doesn't do it justice."

Lucian was rooted to the spot, staring wide eyed and slack jawed at the mountains framed like a picture in the floor to ceiling glass wall.

"If I woke up to that every day, I honestly don't think leaving could ever have been an option."

Arlo shrugged. "This view didn't exist when I was growing up, or not from inside the house, and even if it had, I was so intent on moving away I don't think I'd have noticed. Anyway, let's get some lunch. Any preferences?"

"Oh, I'm very easy."

Arlo opened the well-stocked refrigerator and peered inside. "Whatever you want, I think I can satisfy your needs." He stifled the groan straining to escape him.

Had he really just said that? His own needs, when Lucian had rushed up to him, flushed and breathless, had made themselves known. Thank god for the blast of icy air cooling his pulsing face. Seconds later, all his mortification was swept aside as a distant plaintive whine from the other side of the glass wall nabbed his attention.

"Peanut!" Lucian strode across to the glass and grinned down at the dog. "He's got one of those faces that always looks like he's smiling. I love dogs. In fact, I love all animals. I have quite the menagerie at home, and I think I miss them more than my family, which is dreadful when you think about it. I asked Mr. DuPont if I could have a cat, but the answer was a flat no, so I asked about a house rabbit or even, at a push, a guinea pig. The old boy was horrified. He took a puff on his inhaler and wheezed his refusal. I think that's why he spies on me, to catch me out smuggling in a pet."

Arlo opened the door, and Peanut slunk in, cautiously sniffing at Lucian's outstretched hand before retreating behind Arlo's legs. He bent down and rubbed behind the dog's ears.

"You're honored. He's not too good with anybody but me, and will avoid contact with most other people, but with you…"

Lucian looked up, a shaft of sunlight picking out the deeper, darker tones of his hair, almost blue black, and begging to be touched.

"… knows I'm a friend."

"What? Sure, I expect so." Arlo scrambled to fill in the blanks he'd missed as he'd stared at those glossy strands he knew on every level would be warm and soft and would slip through his fingers like spun silk.

Arlo sucked in a deep, quiet breath, unnoticed by Lucian who'd managed, for a second time, to entice his normally reticent, nervous dog back to him and who'd now flopped down on the tiled floor, happy to be patted and scratched behind his large, floppy ears.

"I've got salads and cheeses, dips and various items from the deli," Arlo said, returning to the refrigerator, glad of the second icy blast against his burning face. Lucian made a vaguely appreciative sound in answer, all his focus on Peanut.

Lucian declined the offer of beer or wine, and so Arlo filled two tall glasses with sparkling mineral water, adding lemon, and mint leaves. Refusing Lucian's offer of help and leaving him to return his attention back to Peanut, Arlo let his mind settle as he chopped and sliced and grated, and whisked up a couple of salad dressings.

Piling up trays, they took everything out to the porch.

Peanut trotted behind and slumped down — at Lucian's side, pushing hard up against his leg. Arlo shook his head. His battered and bruised rescue dog, who kept his distance so as not to get hurt again, was learning how to trust once more. The sentiment hit him in the chest, smashing the air from his lungs. Keeping his distance... wasn't that what he should be doing?

"Wow, this is delicious. Thank you so much. I'm rather glad the coffee shop was closed, because they could produce nothing as good as this. You're an excellent cook."

"Thanks. But this is assembly, not cooking," Arlo said, his voice raspy. He grabbed his water and gulped some down, its icy tingle bringing instant calm.

"Whatever you want to call it, it's miles better than anything I can do. I can fry eggs and not ruin too many pans in the process. Frozen pizza is touch and go as I either incinerate or under cook them, so they're soggy and cold in the middle. I can, however, make a cheese sandwich — just so long as I don't grate the ends of my fingers off in the excitement of my accomplishment. But," he said, leaning forward in a conspiratorial manner, "what I'm really a dab hand at is... Marmite on toast." Lucian grinned and, looking very pleased with himself, sat back in his seat.

Arlo could feel the horror crawl across his face.

"Marmite. That's the scrapings from old beer barrels. You know that, right?"

"Yeast extract is the correct term, and most delicious it is too."

"No, it's..." Arlo wasn't sure a word existed to aptly describe the thick salty paste Brits readily slathered over their morning toast and which he'd tried once — which was one time too many — on a long ago business trip to London.

"You're nothing but a savage, Arlo McDonald. Nothing but a savage." Lucian dug his fork into his plate, the loud huff belied by the good humored twitch of his lips.

They fell silent as they concentrated on eating. Arlo threw him surreptitious glances. What was it Francine had said when she'd thrust the Tupperware into Lucian's hands? Too thin. Maybe not too thin, but Lucian couldn't afford to miss many meals. And he certainly couldn't afford to live off toast and rank leftovers from the beer making process.

With their plates cleared, without a word, Arlo retreated to the kitchen and returned with a tub of caramel ice cream and a couple of bowls. Piling up the ice cream, he raised his brow in challenge. Lucian huffed, pulled a bowl closer, and dove in.

"What were the chances that you had exactly my favorite flavor? Honestly, I could eat every kind of ice cream they sell, and probably some they don't, but this…" Lucian said with a groan, "is. The. Best. Ice. Cream. Ever." He closed his eyes and licked his lips, the pink tip leaving a damp smear as he slumped back into the seat. Arlo couldn't drag his gaze away. Lucian looked full, sated… Arlo's breath caught. He looked—

Lucian's eyes fluttered open, their blue startling even behind the horrible, heavy glasses. Arlo's fingers itched to lift them from Lucian's face and throw them aside.

"You've missed a bit," Arlo croaked. A tiny speck of

ice cream clung to the outer edges of Lucian's lips, begging to be wiped away, licked away. Kissed away.

"I have?"

Lucian leaned forward, just as Arlo did, bringing their faces closer, closer still, a ripple tumbling down Arlo's spine, his breath catching as Lucian's eyes grew darker and his glossy lips parted.

"Yeah, just here," Arlo murmured as, tilting his head, he moved closer still, breathing in the heady sweet sugar rush of ice cream on Lucian's quickening, warm breath.

"Better wipe it away, then," Lucian, just a kiss away, whispered. Lifting his head, leaning forward a little more.

"Guess I better."

"Guess you should."

And Arlo did want to kiss Lucian, he'd wanted to kiss him from the moment he'd stared down at him, splayed out on the floor in Randy's. It was a truth he couldn't deny. His breath hitched. Lucian was just a warm, sweet breath away, and an invisible rope Arlo had neither the will nor the strength to resist pulled him forward. He tilted his head one way, Lucian the other, both of them ready for — a hard, bone crushing clash of noses.

"Ouch!"

"Shit!" Arlo reared back. His hand flew to his face and cupped his throbbing nose, which was deflating the much more pleasurable throbbing that had been taking place in another part of his anatomy.

"It's not broken, just a bit bashed in." Lucian winced as he prodded his nose. "Like my glasses," he added, showing the ugly frames that the impact had knocked off his face.

"Jeez, I'm really sorry." Arlo's voice was thick and nasal. "I didn't mean—"

"To kiss me, batter my nose, or bash my specs? I rather like the first choice best because the others are a bit crap." Lucian bent them back into shape, or almost, and jammed them on his face.

"Your nose got in the way. It's big, and as for your glasses, they're still wearable, so no way am I going to cough up compensation. You want that, mister, talk to my lawyer."

"What? I'm not looking for compo, and my nose isn't—"

Arlo's lips twitched, making Lucian tut and roll his eyes before his face lit up in a smile.

Yet, the nearly kiss… Arlo's stomach clenched. What the hell had he been thinking? Involvement, beyond friendship, was the last thing he wanted, with anybody, but getting involved with Lucian Arbuthnot Blaxston felt like it'd be too damn easy.

"Maybe it's for the best," Lucian said, his smile fading as he pushed his fingers through his hair. "Not kissing, that is. Could make things a little awkward. With us becoming friends, I mean. Especially as neither of us is looking for, well, anything more. Are we?" Lucian's unsure words cut through Arlo's troubling thoughts.

Are we…? No. No, they weren't. "We're not. Looking for anything, I mean." Lucian was right, about not kissing, about not looking for more. But why did right not feel… right?

Lucian was looking at him through worried, anxious eyes. Arlo plastered a bright smile on his face to cover the cracks. The kiss that couldn't and wouldn't happen. Lucian returned his smile, but it was unsure and tentative.

Way up in the mountains, a distant roll of thunder broke the charged silence that had settled upon them. Arlo looked up into gray sky. When had the sun gone in?

"Come on, let me get you back before the storm comes."

CHAPTER FIFTEEN

"Hey, how was your weekend?" Bibi asked as she breezed into the flower store.

Lucian glared at her. She'd left a message for him to open up on his own again. And, she'd be leaving early, leaving him to close up. Again. Perhaps he should ask for a raise.

"You should know, as I spent a big chunk of it with you," he snapped.

Bibi stopped in her tracks and frowned. "Excuse me?"

Lucian's anger deflated. He was too tired to keep his temper stoked, and he rubbed his brow to ease away the niggling headache that'd been with him from the moment he woke up.

"Sorry," he mumbled. "Just a little out of sorts."

"I'll say you are. And please remember, I'm your employer." She exhaled, long and deep, and leaned on the counter. "And your friend," she said, her voice softening. "Or at least I hope I am. Come on, what's wrong?"

Lucian pushed his glasses, still slightly bent, on top of

his head and closed his eyes. Bibi rested a hand on his arm, the flame to the touch paper, and Lucian couldn't help it, he just couldn't, as it all tumbled out. Meeting up with Arlo, the almost kiss, the squirming embarrassment even though they'd both done their best to laugh it off. Bibi, her face thoughtful, said nothing, and for that he was grateful.

"You're probably wondering what kind of sad loser you've got working for you." He attempted a smile, but his lips weren't playing.

"I'm doing nothing of the sort. But Arlo wanted to kiss you?" The surprise in her voice was unmistakable, and Lucian's spirits sank further.

"Yes, unlikely though it sounds."

Her gentle touch turned to a sharp slap.

"Ow! What was that for?" He rubbed a palm over the sting.

"For being an ass. Why wouldn't he? Luci, you're super cute. If a little dorkish, but that's kind of like a part of your appeal. And that exotic accent you have."

Lucian gawped at her. A dork, with a funny accent...

"Thanks for the vote of confidence. I'm not a dork. And my accent is hardly exotic."

"Is for these parts." Bibi snorted. "'Read out the specials board... Can you repeat that, nice and slowly, and then do it again'. Oh, Lucian." She laughed, but it was affectionate and kind.

"You just used my proper name. You do realize that, don't you?"

"Don't get used to it." Her levity dropped away. "I'm not making fun of you, honestly — don't look at me like that," she said, when Lucian rolled his eyes. "If I sounded surprised at Arlo making a pass, that's honestly because I am. The guy's had a lot of interest thrown his way since he came back to the Creek, from both men and women. For months now, he's batted every single one away. I've lost count of the number of times Francine has tried to match make, although some of her choices have left a lot to be desired—"

"Like Wilbur the Demon Dentist?"

They shuddered before they both smiled.

"The point I'm making is that Arlo's rejected every-body who's thrown themselves in his way, or has been thrown, with a big fat no way. All very polite, all very charming, but a no way is a no way. And then you come along. He's interested, Luci, interested in a way he's not been interested in anybody. A fuck up of a kiss or not."

"I'm not so sure." He bit down on his lip, dialing up his courage for what he had to say next. "I don't think I want him to be interested." The words were acid burning his tongue. "I've had enough complications in my life recently. I'm not looking for any more. Plus, afterwards, we kind of agreed it'd be best if we didn't muddy the waters, and stayed as friends instead." And maybe that's for the best, because hadn't he come to Collier's Creek to keep away from all entanglements, no matter how short-lived they could only ever be?

Bibi crossed her arms over her chest and studied him, her quiet, assessing gaze unnerving. Always upbeat and irreverent, this was a side to her he'd not encountered before.

"I don't know what made you leave your home and come out here to a place where you had no contacts or connections. I've never asked, because I figured you'd tell me if you wanted to. But whatever made you move, you've got to put it behind you, just like you need to have more faith in yourself. Perhaps it's time to stop licking whatever wounds you brought with you and look out from under the stone you've buried yourself under."

"I've not buried myself under a stone. Or not a very big one."

Bibi shrugged. "Just think about what I've said. And when Arlo comes knocking, make sure you open the door and greet him with that big, beautiful, bright smile of yours."

CHAPTER SIXTEEN

The park was busy with parents pushing strollers and helping toddlers take their first steps. Over on the grass, a game was taking place. Baseball, Lucian knew, though to him it looked just the same as rounders, a game he'd played as a kid.

He bit into the sandwich he hadn't had time to eat. He couldn't taste a thing and when he swallowed, it hit his stomach with a thud. Late Friday afternoon, five days since the almost kiss, and four since Bibi had told him to open the door wide when Arlo came knocking. The door had remained firmly closed because Arlo hadn't, and with almost a week gone past, he never would.

He took another bite of his sandwich before dropping it into the trash, whatever appetite he had gone. Bibi had closed up earlier than normal, to get ready for her date. He'd been happy to escape into the late afternoon warmth, yet he had no idea what to do with himself. Making his way through the park, he headed back toward the town square, which was always buzzing with life with its busy coffee shops and restaurants. He turned a corner, and stopped.

Just yards ahead of him, Arlo leaned against a battered, mud spattered pickup as he talked into his cell phone. Indecision grabbed Lucian and held him tight. It'd be best if he just backed away, before Arlo looked up and saw him gawping, but his feet, rooted to the ground, had other ideas.

This was Arlo, but a different Arlo. The Arlo he knew had neatly brushed hair, and wore chinos or smart jeans, and button-down shirts. This Arlo didn't.

Jeans, sure, but these molded themselves to Arlo's long legs, hugging his slim hips. They were old and faded, with a few rips that didn't look like they had much to do with fashion. A loose, checked flannel shirt, unbuttoned to reveal a crisp, white T-shirt clinging to his strong, honed torso. And... Lucian swallowed... heavy, scuffed workman's boots. And that hair... oh my god. It was roughed up and messy, as if he'd just rolled out of bed, or somebody had shoved their fingers through... Oh, shit.

With his attention still glued to his cell, with his free hand, Arlo thrust away a hank of hair that had fallen over his forehead. A tight little noise that was part groan, part moan, and all want pushed its way past Lucian's lips as heat coiled in the pit of his belly. Arlo looked like something out of Hot Wyoming Man, because that magazine just had to exist, and Arlo McDonald absolutely needed to be on its front cover, rugged, masculine, and so fucking sexy.

He was staring, and he needed to stop, wipe the drool from his chin, stop fucking hyperventilating, and retreat.

Arlo frowned hard, his face thunderous, as he muttered

something and stuffed the cell into the hip pocket of his jeans. Lucian stepped back — and crashed into a parcel delivery guy, balancing a couple of large boxes in his arms.

"Hey, watch what ya doing!" the guy yelled.

"Sorry, I didn't—"

But the delivery guy didn't wait for the apology as he barged past Lucian, banging into his shoulder as he disappeared through a door Lucian hadn't noticed.

Any chance of making a quiet, unobserved escape had vanished as Arlo strode toward him.

"Hey, are you okay? I just saw what happened." Arlo frowned as he jerked his head toward the door.

"I'm fine. I suppose I did almost cause him to drop his boxes."

"He still had no right to talk to you like that — or smash into you." Arlo propped his hand against the wall, the stance barring Lucian's way.

"Honest, I'm cool about it." He didn't feel very cool, not with Arlo standing just a breath away, and looking like a wet dream as he stared down at him. "Nice pickup."

"What d'ya mean?" Arlo stood up straight, face flushing red.

"Your pickup truck." What did Arlo think he meant? Oh… This time, it was Lucian's turn to flush.

"Oh, sure. Yeah. It's better for… picking stuff up from town, and a lot better in bad weather than the car. You know, in the snow."

Lucian looked up at the sky, a perfect cobalt blue. "Well, best be getting on, I suppose. Things to do." What they were, Lucian hadn't a clue.

"Like what?" Arlo leaned back into the wall.

"Erm… I've got the afternoon off, and I thought I'd just… wander around…" Fuck, he couldn't have made himself sound more pathetic if he tried.

Arlo laughed, but it was good natured, so perhaps he hadn't sounded quite like the saddest, most pathetic fucker in the universe after all.

"What about wandering toward the coffee shop?"

"Oh, yes please." Lucian swallowed his cringe, along with the neediness in his voice. He coughed. "What I mean is, that would be good, but only if you can spare the time? If you're not busy. Doing pickup truck type things." And looking like sex on legs.

"Pickup truck type things? You mean like picking things up and putting them in the truck?"

"Hmm, I suppose so." He'd just made himself sound like a fully certified jerk, but he didn't care, not when Arlo was smiling down at him. "But a coffee would be good. And it's my treat, for lunch the other day." The day of the almost kiss, which they'd agreed would have been a big, fat mistake.

"I've got time. I might even let you throw it all over me."

Lucian groaned. "You really aren't going to let me forget that, are you?"

"Not in this lifetime."

Unease dissipated in Lucian, like a soft mist in the breeze, as they set off. Minutes later they were in CC's, open once more after its emergency closure. Although busy, the lunchtime crowds were thinning out. Arlo made to go to the counter, but Lucian stopped him with a hand on his arm. A warm tingle made him pull back.

"My treat, remember? You grab a table." Lucian dashed off and joined the short line.

"Hey," the barista — or Cameron, as Lucian remembered from previous visits — gave him a lazy smile before leaning across the counter; he tilted his head to the board behind him. "Wanna read out the specials? Nice and slowly, just take your time."

Lucian groaned. Why did this always happen? He might not have sounded like a born and raised Collier's Creek local, but his accent couldn't be that much of a novelty…

Cameron laughed. "Just kidding. What can I get you?"

Lucian gave his order for his own drink — and stopped. He hadn't the faintest idea what Arlo would want.

"Sorry, I'm going to have to ask my friend—"

"You mean Arlo." Cameron smiled. "Thought you'd know how he takes his coffee, what with you being his friend." His smile turned to a grin, sprinkled with more mischief than a CC's cappuccino was with chocolate powder.

"Erm…"

Lucian's face throbbed. Had he and Arlo become a juicy morsel of gossip for the locals to chew over? No. No way. There was absolutely, totally, one hundred percent nothing about him and Arlo to gossip about.

Cameron laughed and shook his head. "Don't worry, I've got his order. Arlo's our easiest customer: black coffee, nothing added, nothing taken away." His gaze flittered across to Arlo before settling once more on Lucian. "I'll bring them across," he said, all but shooing Lucian off before he get to work.

Arlo had found a table on the other side of the coffee

shop. Lounging on what should have been Lucian's chair was a cop, his muscles stretching his shirt tight. The cop leaned forward and said something to Arlo, who laughed, the rich, gravelly sound sending a shot of heat through Lucian at the same time it speared him with jealousy. Whatever the cop had said had been for Arlo's ears alone, and Arlo was still chuckling to himself when he reached the table. The cop looked up at Lucian, his gaze sliding to Arlo and then back again, before he got up.

Jesus… The guy was huge, his tight uniform barely containing him. Even his muscles had muscles… Closely cropped hair and a face so chiseled it was almost a caricature completed the look. He put his cap on and pulled the peak down before donning sunglasses. *Oh my god, he looks like something out of Tom of Finland.* A giggle rippled up through Lucian's body. He pressed his lips together and prayed he wouldn't get arrested for disrespecting an officer of the law.

The cop stepped away from the chair, leaving it pulled out from the table, inviting Lucian to take his place.

"Lucian, this is Ted. Or perhaps I should say Deputy Sheriff Warren."

"Ah, Ted's fine. Good to meet you, Luci-Ann." Ted held out his hand, a huge paw, and Lucian had no option but to take it as he braced himself for his fingers to be crushed to a pulp.

"It's… errr… You too." Maybe correcting Ted of Collier's Creek finest wasn't the wisest of options.

"Whoa, cute accent. Are you from Boston?" Ted raised an inquiring, exquisitely groomed brow.

Why didn't British policeman look like this?

"No. I'm from… Australia."

Arlo coughed, a strange strangled noise.

"That's great." Ted's bright white smile didn't dim by a single, solitary watt. "Got to go and catch some bad guys." Ted laughed.

"Happy hunting," Lucian said, but Ted's attention had already shifted back to Arlo.

"So I'll see you at Gilligan's tomorrow night?" Ted's bright smile became a shade darker.

Lucian slurped his coffee, but neither was looking at him. He could have been stark naked, with a bouquet of roses stuffed up his ass for all the notice they took of him.

"Maybe."

Lucian looked up through his lashes, something in Arlo's one-word answer catching his attention. Non-committal, and maybe a little guarded, just like his friendly smile was, but if Ted noticed, it didn't show on his rugged, handsome face as he pointed a finger straight at Arlo.

"I'll be waiting for ya, buddy. We're long overdue getting together." A broad wink at Arlo, and a nod to Lucian, and he was gone.

Arlo groaned as he slumped in his seat, running his hands through his sandy hair, before he picked up his coffee. Narrowing his eyes, he gazed at Lucian over the brim.

"Hope it's okay? The server said it's what you drink."

"It's perfect, and thank you." He put the cup down, and leaned forward, his forearms on the table. "Australian?"

"Why not? I could have told him anything. Your friend wasn't remotely interested in anything I had to say." Because your friend was eating you up with his eyes.

Lucian's spirits dampened when Arlo didn't respond. He was jealous, yet he had no right to be because he and

Arlo were friends, and that was all. So there was nothing, absolutely nothing, to be jealous about. He picked up the coffee he no longer wanted and put it straight back down.

"Ted's okay, if a little persistent."

Persistent. And why not? Because Arlo was worth being persistent about. Not that it was his business, but... Bibi's words came back to him. All those offers thrown Arlo's way, all the offers he was determined not to pick up.

"I knew him before I left. Like Hank and Francine, we were friends in high school, the difference being we didn't keep in touch. But he's keen to get reacquainted. A little too keen."

"That's nice. He was very, erm... Lovely smile, don't you think? Dazzling, in fact." What the...

Arlo shrugged, his expression deadpan. "Maybe he dated Wilbur."

Lucian met Arlo's eye, the twinkle in their green-gold depths unmistakable, and he laughed. As Arlo joined in, the tension drained out of him.

"So you won't be going to, Gilligan's, was it?"

"No, I don't think so. You've not heard of it?"

Lucian shook his head.

"It's a gay bar, a few miles out of town. I've been a couple times since I've been back, and a couple times is a couple too many. It's... think Randy's, with added leather."

"Oh god, I'd rather not." Lucian shuddered, but a tendril of relief threaded through him, knowing Arlo wouldn't be going anytime soon to meet Collier's Creek's very own homegrown Tom. Ouch, bitchy...

"I haven't seen you around town for the past few

days." Lucian gave himself a mental kicking when Arlo's expression stiffened.

Arlo took a sip of his coffee, his brows pinched as though he was wondering what to say, or whether to say anything at all. He let out a long and tired sigh.

Tired… God, how could he have not noticed? Arlo didn't just look tired, he looked downright exhausted. Shadows darkened the skin under his eyes, shadows Lucian was sure hadn't been there before.

"I had to go to New York. It was all very last minute, and I didn't get back until late last night."

What, or who, is in New York? But Lucian couldn't, wouldn't ask, and he bit down on his tongue.

Neither of them said anything for a minute or two. Lucian fiddled with his spoon, failing to find the words to fill in the deep hole which had opened up between them.

"Hey." Arlo leaned in across the table. "I know you're wondering, and it's no big secret—"

"You don't have to say a word. Your private life is—"

"My business? This is Collier's Creek, remember? A small community, and small communities are the same wherever you go in the world. Even Australia." Arlo sighed, his cheeks golf balling as he stared out through the window.

"I was with somebody." Arlo turned his attention back to Lucian. "In New York. We were together for a few years. When it ended, I took the chance to make some changes in my life, one of which was to sell my half of the architectural practice to my business partner, and come back here. That was a few months ago, but wrapping everything up back east, it's taken longer than I thought. It's been harder, too, and fraught with difficulties."

"Honestly, Arlo. You don't have to tell me this, not if you don't want to."

Who was the man Arlo had left back in New York? What was he? Why did it all come tumbling down? Questions he wanted to ask, questions he couldn't, because those same questions would be turned back on him.

"I know, but I'd rather you heard it from me, not through rumor and half truths."

Lucian said nothing and Arlo gazed at him, as though waiting for Lucian's permission to tell him what he wanted him to know, from his lips and nobody else's.

"Okay," Lucian said, his voice little more than a dry whisper.

"His name's Tony, and he was my partner. We were in it for the long haul. Or so I thought. I even designed a house for us, close to the beach in Massachusetts. It was supposed to be our getaway for when things got too much in the city. I paid for the construction, the fittings and furnishings, and the running costs." Arlo shrugged. "It didn't bother me, because I was the higher earner. But I registered the place in both our names. Legally he owns half, which wouldn't have been a problem if everything between us had gone to plan. It didn't, which is why he's still in New York, and I'm here."

"I'm sorry. I really am." A relationship Arlo had thought was forever, before it all went to shit. Lucian's gut tightened. He knew all about those.

Arlo stirred the remains of his coffee. "We were both trying to keep afloat something that should have sunk long before it finally did. He was — is — younger than me. It didn't matter most of the time, but when it did..." He sighed and shrugged. "But we were very different. Maybe too different, and we ended up wanting different things out of life.

"We should have been honest with ourselves, and each other, a lot sooner, but we just clung on tight, thinking it would come out ok. But of course it didn't." The rhythmic clink, clink, clink of the spoon on the side of the cup was as regular as a metronome.

"I'd been dissatisfied with the direction of my life for a while. Professionally, I was reaching my peak. We had the pick of projects, and we could afford to be fussy about who we worked with. But it was stressful and draining and I just didn't love it anymore. I kept thinking of coming back home, but when I told Tony you'd have thought I said I wanted to run off and live in a mosquito infested swamp or something. He's New York born and raised — I'm not sure he even knows where Wyoming is."

Arlo threw the spoon down and he looked up, his gaze falling not on Lucian but out of the window, all the way back to New York. The harsh ring of a cell and a peal of laughter burst the bubble that had surrounded Arlo, making him jump as his gaze darted back to Lucian.

"So I sold my half of the business, like I said, and Tony and I ended just before Christmas. I'd reached the point of wanting out of the career I'd spent so long establishing, and out of the city I'd made my home. And we both wanted out of the relationship. Not that there was any relationship left.

"It was a relief for both of us, and it put an end to the nasty arguments. Or mostly. But, we were together a long time, so there's a lot of practical stuff to unpick and settle — which includes the fight over the beach house. He wants to buy me out, at way below what it's worth. I want to sell. That's why I went back to New York, to try and sort things out once and for all. It didn't work."

Arlo smiled, but it was sad and tired, and didn't reach his eyes. Lucian ached to give him the hug he looked like he could do with, but instead, he clamped his hands together.

"So that's why I came back. To reset and re-evaluate. To live a different, simpler, less complicated life. Even if Francine doesn't believe that's a way for a man to live."

"Ah, Wilbur."

"Exactly. He's not the first, but I'm going to make sure he's the last. The one before him was a podiatrist, and the one before him was a hair stylist. She seems determined to make me over," he said with a shrug.

Arlo's words had shaken him, the parallels in their reasons for coming to Collier's Creek pulsing like a strobe light. They were both seeking refuge from pain, to reset and start again, to steer clear of heartache and heartbreak. They were both on the same page, yet something contracted in Lucian's chest, and grew smaller by the second. It made him want to cry, but he smiled, the biggest, brightest one he could dredge up.

They talked, light and inconsequential, until their fresh coffees were long gone and the staff were tidying up and sweeping the floor, the cue for them to go.

Outside, the sun had turned a hazy, soft gold against the deep cloudless purple-blue of the sky. In the distance, the mountains loomed large, the town's guardians and protectors.

"You don't get skies like this at home, or at least not anywhere near London." Lucian gazed into the wide sky. "The colors are different, deeper and more intense. More defined. Harder edged, and kind of heavier, a gritty crime drama rather than a cozy mystery. Less watered down than home. Listen to me, getting all arty-farty." He turned his head to look at Arlo, expecting to see a smile on his lips; instead, he was staring at him, his concentration as hard and sharp as a blade.

"No, you're right," Arlo said slowly, his eyes still focused on Lucian, looking at him as if he were truly seeing him for the first time.

Lucian fidgeted, the urge to dip his head under Arlo's heavy scrutiny growing stronger, but he held his gaze. People bustled by them, traffic filed past, but as Arlo continued to gaze at him, they could have been the only people left standing on the planet.

"You're a florist."

"*Ye—s*. Although the in vogue term is floral artist."

"What I mean is, you deal in color, texture, and place-ment. You create compositions. You paint with flowers."

"I suppose so. I've never really thought of it like that before." But even as the words left his lips, he knew that wasn't so.

Imaginative displays and intricate bouquets had brought tears of joy to so many brides, helping to make their big day even more special.

Each December, on the first of the month, he'd decked the walls of Danebury Manor with deep winter greenery, trailing holly and ivy, his creations traditional yet innova-tive. Fresh floral arrangements for spring, for every room, bright with the promise of the warmth to come. The church on the edge of the estate, old long before the ground he now stood on would be called the United States, a riot of red and green for Christmas, the warmth of golden blooms for Easter, and the deepest red for the poppies of Armistice Day.

The ropes of home tightened in his chest, pulling hard, all but severing his breath as his vision misted. His family hadn't exiled him, he'd exiled himself. It didn't matter that it was temporary, that it was for a few months only, the force of what he'd left behind for a place where he was alone, a stranger, as incongruous as a fish out of water, hit him with a force that took his breath away.

"Lucian?" Arlo's voice came to him as though through a fog, but the hand on his arm was warm and sure. "Are you okay? You look a little shaken."

His voice was low and deep, but soft too, concern in every word. Arlo's hand still held his arm, and Lucian craved that warmth and strength, yet he cleared his throat and forced a shaky smile to his lips.

"I'm fine. Really. I just got a vision of home, that's all, and its intensity shook me. It's silly, I came out here for — well, a much needed break from everything. Just for a few months. I should be having the time of my life—"

"But you're not?"

Lucian shook his head as a lump filled his throat. It wouldn't have mattered where he was, Collier's Creek or the moon, the feeling of being alone and being lonely, away from everything that had been his anchor even if that anchor had been pulled up and wound in, it would have been the same anywhere.

"Sorry," he said, his voice rough, as he pulled a tissue from his pocket and blew his nose.

"Don't be. You've uprooted yourself. You're feeling… disconnected. I get it." Arlo gazed down at him with sympathy in his clear eyes, but the tiniest pull of his brows, as though there was more than sympathy, urged Lucian to speak.

"Is that what you felt when you first went to New York? When you left everything you'd known behind?"

"No, not then, but I've felt it since. Believing — or trying to — that everything's great, that it's all going as it should be when it's not. Knowing that something's missing." He pulled his hand away, and Lucian felt it as though a warm coat had been ripped from him on the coldest, bitterest winter's day. Stuffing his hands into the side pockets of his jeans, Arlo looked out at the mountains, dark and brooding against the setting sun.

Tony, the ex... The man Arlo had once loved, the one he'd spent years with, the man he'd believed would be his forever. Whatever had become of them, Arlo must miss what they'd both once had.

A teenage girl walked by and bumped into Arlo, yanking her attention from her cell as she blushed an apology. The presence of others, of traffic, of life buzzing all around them, broke through the bubble they'd been in since they'd left the coffee shop.

Lucian looked around him. Somehow, they'd found their way back to Bibi's, but he had no recollection of how they'd got there.

"Well, I'd best let you get on with the rest of the day. Or what's left of it."

Arlo frowned at him as if he'd spoken in a foreign language.

"Goodbye, then. I'll let you go. You know, to get on with things. Bye." Lucian had got no further than a couple of steps.

"Lucian!" Arlo barked. "Wait."

Lucian turned. Arlo was still frowning, but it was different. A little awkward, a little... bashful? But there was more that Lucian couldn't decipher, as though Arlo had reached a decision.

"Are you doing anything this evening?"

"Other than trying to dodge Mr. DuPont on the way up to what's laughingly called my apartment, then no." No hot date, either, if he didn't count Netflix. God, it was pathetic.

"Would you like to come back to the house?"

"Again?"

Arlo's face fell. Lucian didn't even attempt to tamp down his groan. How could such a rugged, masculine man look like a kicked puppy? And how could he have been so fucking stupid?

"Just an idea, that's all—"

"I'd love to. It's just that you look exhausted — and haven't you had enough of my company for one day?"

Arlo smiled, warm and bright, chasing away the clouds that had scudded across his eyes.

"It's either you or I spend the evening trying to teach Peanut new tricks he refuses to learn. It's not really much of a choice."

Lucian pulled himself up to his full, not very tall height. "I accept your invitation, Mr. McDonald, if only to spare poor Peanut from your attentions," his voice clipped and clear, putting on the posh in every word, syllable, letter. "I'm doing this for your dog. You do understand that?"

"I've still got ice cream."

Lucian grinned. "You're on."

CHAPTER SEVENTEEN

It was a replay of just days ago, but as Arlo gathered together an ice cold bottle of lemonade and some chips and dips to take out to the porch, he knew something had shifted. It'd been Tony.

The only people in Collier's Creek who knew, for sure, that Tony even existed were Hank and Francine and that was how he wanted to keep it — although, he knew some speculated and came to their own wild and outlandish conclusions about why he'd left the bright lights of the city behind him. Yet, he'd told Lucian, spilling out not only the bare bones, but some of the flesh too. He didn't understand why, didn't want to analyze, but he was glad he had.

Placing everything on a tray, he took it outside. Lucian wasn't where he'd left him, petting Peanut, who now lounged on the flagstones.

"Luc…" The rest of the name faded on his lips as he turned and looked into the interior of the house, a kaleidoscope of soft shadow and fading light.

At the far end of the long room, Lucian stared up at a painting hung on the wall. He was immobile, his head hanging back, his dark, heavy hair falling behind him. As though feeling Arlo's scrutiny, Lucian turned, a shaft of early evening sunlight illuminating his face.

"The painting, it's stunning. It's like it's alive. How did I not see this when I last came here?"

"Because it wasn't there. I only hung it this morning." Arlo came and stood next to Lucian, stuffing his hands into the side pockets of his jeans. His artwork had always been a private passion, reflecting his inner self, far too revealing to let others' gaze fall on it for too long.

Lucian tilted his head. "You're the artist, aren't you?"

Arlo nodded, not meeting Lucian's gaze as unaccustomed shyness stole over him.

"You must have trained, because this isn't the work of an amateur."

"That's exactly what it is. It's a hobby and has been for years, but that's all it's ever been." His shoulders tensed as memories surfaced. Disinterest, worse than any criticism could ever have been, forcing him without a word to take down the canvases and stash them away, as though they'd never been.

"This is accomplished work. Have you ever considered showing them to a gallery?"

Arlo snorted so loud he coughed. "No. Like I said, it's just a hobby." Who'd be interested in his dabblings? Although, he had stopped by the gallery that had opened in town, a few months back, ostensibly to view the ever-changing display as he'd tried to work up his courage to walk through the door. Instead, all he'd done was talk himself out of it, convincing himself he'd be met with nothing more than disinterest… Candid criticism he could take, or probably, but disinterest was emotional and creative acid.

Lucian stared at him, his face solemn, his large eyes unwavering, and the words Arlo hadn't meant to say tumbled from him.

"Once, I showed my work to somebody who was in the art world. Their reaction was lukewarm, and that's being generous. But like I say, I'm just an amateur." A friend of Tony's, but no friend of his. Arlo's shoulders hunched up another notch, and he pushed his hands further into his pockets. Even so long after, the burn of humiliation was still there. Derivative… flat… one dimensional… The punches hadn't been pulled.

"Well, that's a load of old bollocks. Whoever this person was, they'd have been better suited to flipping burgers or delivering pizza. This," Lucian stabbed a finger at the painting, "is exceptional work." Lucian glared at him, his whole body seeming to shake with indignation.

Arlo jolted at the passion in Lucian's words, but it was enough for his shoulders to relax, and he pulled his hands from his pockets, glad to have somebody in his corner, even if Lucian was only being polite.

"At best, I'm a talented amateur." But didn't Lucian know about color and composition? Wasn't he an artist in his own right? "So how come you know about painting? Did they teach you that at flower school?"

Lucian raised a brow as he tilted his chin upwards. "Flower school? I hold advanced diplomas in Floristry and Event Styling, if you don't mind. But no, I didn't take art classes." His face dissolved into a smile. "I learned an awful lot from our art historian. At home."

"Who the hell employs an art historian?"

Lucian's lips quirked. "We do, but only on a part time basis because full time would be showing off." His words were bright and breezy, as though employing an art historian in any capacity was as commonplace as a person announcing they employed somebody to take care of the yard, or the housework.

Arlo laughed and shook his head.

"If you've any more, I'd love to see them."

Arlo's laughter stuttered in his throat.

"I do, but you don't—" Have to be polite.

"I'm not enquiring to be polite," Lucian said, all but stealing Arlo's thought away, "but I'd love to see if Collier's Creek has an undiscovered genius lurking in its midst."

Lucian was so bright and wide eyed, Arlo would have said yes to anything even when he should have been saying no, even when he should never have blurted out his second invite in just days.

"I've got a studio."

Lucian's smile stretched wider. "Then lead the way."

Upstairs, Arlo stood aside to let Lucian in. The sun had slipped behind the mountains, and he reached out to switch on the light, but Lucian's startled intake of breath tugged at something deep in Arlo's chest and he let his arm drop.

Lucian's reaction to the room was the same as his, months before, when he'd walked in for the first time after it had been finished. A glass wall, like downstairs, but the ceiling too was glass, as were the two side walls. The only part of the room that wasn't glass was the wall behind them.

"This is incredible. In the daytime, this'll be flooded with light. It's different from downstairs. Up higher, I feel like I'm actually in the mountains." Lucian's words were quiet, almost for himself. Arlo said nothing, hesitant to break the spell the room had cast over Lucian the way it had cast it over him.

Lucian turned, his face little more than a shadow between the very last of the dying sun's rays and the first glow of moonlight. His lips were curved up in a soft smile. Arlo's heart clenched hard, and a weight pressed against his chest.

"It's amazing. You don't know how lucky you are."

Lucian bit down on his lower lip, its full plumpness held captive. Arlo's breath hitched, wanting nothing more than to rescue that beautiful mouth, to capture it and make it his. He took a step closer, his heart jolting as Lucian didn't drop his gaze, didn't step back, but let his eyelids flutter to a close. Arlo cupped Lucian's face between his palms, holding him steady as their lips touched, releasing a bolt of heat deep into his belly.

From some dim and distant place, a faint voice whispered that this wasn't supposed to happen, that it wasn't part of the plan, but as he plunged into the wet heat of Lucian's mouth, as tongue met tongue, as body pressed into body, that insistent voice faded until it ceased to be.

The need for air forced them apart, their rapid breaths the only sound.

"I'm sorry," Arlo breathed. "I didn't mean... I shouldn't have..." But as the taste of Lucian's lips tingled on his own, everything he hadn't meant to do, and everything he shouldn't have done, faded to nothing.

"At least this time you didn't break my nose, or bend my specs out of shape." Lucian blinked up at him, his eyes huge and owlish behind his geeky glasses.

"I told you that was your fault, because your nose is too big. And anyhow, when did the sexy, nerdy librarian look become a thing?"

"Excuse me! Sexy, nerdy floral artist, if you don't mind."

Arlo smiled, reveling in the playful banter they so easily fell into almost as much as he had in the kiss. Almost, but not quite.

"You know, I'd like to kiss you again." Even though I shouldn't… Dangerous ground, ground he'd been determined not to tread again…

"And I think I might like you to." Lucian tilted his face.

"Perhaps you could take something off for me," Arlo whispered against Lucian's lips.

Lucian squeaked, and it was so damn adorable that Arlo couldn't help but throw his head back and laugh.

"Your glasses. Although, if you want to take anything else off…"

"I… But I wouldn't be able to see," Lucian mumbled.

Arlo's laughter died. Lucian was suddenly awkward, and panic speared through Arlo.

"Just didn't want to break them," he said, forcing a lightness into his voice.

"You won't."

Lucian wound his arms around him. Arlo luxuriated in

the forbidden kiss. He wouldn't let himself think about what he'd told himself he wouldn't and couldn't do, not when Lucian arched into his body, and not when he made all those moans and gasps, and not when his mouth tasted so, so good.

"Wow, those stars are incredible," Lucian gasped when they broke the kiss.

Arlo blinked, Lucian's words blindsiding him for a moment. "Oh, yeah. The night sky around here's—"

Lucian laughed, a low chuckle. "I'm not talking about the stars in the sky."

"You're…?" And then he understood. Lucian had seen stars, but there'd been nothing cosmic about them. Maybe he could make Lucian see some more, but as he leaned in for another kiss, as Lucian let his head fall back, the first bar of the Stars and Stripes ripped through the air, making them both jump as though they'd plunged soaking fingers into a plug socket.

"Mum!" Lucian barked into his cell, rolling his eyes at Arlo. "Everything's good… Yes, I am eating properly…"

Arlo mimed eating and pointed downstairs, leaving Lucian to his call. Disappointment settled in the pit of his stomach.

The ill timed call had ripped them out of the moment. But, as he put together a selection of salads and cheeses, pretty much a repeat of what they'd eaten before, maybe, perhaps, probably, the intervention hadn't been such a bad thing, slicing through the moment's madness. Because he hadn't come back to the Creek to get involved. He pressed his lips together and chopped down hard on a pepper. Yet the tug of something in his stomach and the tightening in his chest felt like so much mocking laughter.

He took everything out to the porch table, where he'd

set down the lemonade in what felt like hours before. The sky was now fully dark. The inky, velvety blackness was ablaze with stars, and a few light clouds scudded across the moon. Flicking a switch, a soft exterior light flooded the porch at the same time strings of tiny, pinpoint, colored lights pulsed softly in the trees and bushes. It was beautiful, even romantic — or it would be, if he let himself think such a thing.

A patter of claws claimed his attention, and he looked down into Peanut's reproachful gaze.

"Hey, boy. Am I late with your dinner?"

Arlo crouched on his haunches and fussed over his dog, who nuzzled into his hand and then tried to climb into his lap, seeking the cuddles he'd been starved of as a puppy. Chuckling, he stood up before scooping Peanut into his arms and nuzzling into his neck.

"Who's daddy's baby boy, eh?" Arlo turned for the house, coming to a halt as Lucian stood on the threshold of the kitchen, a soft smile dancing on his lips. "I forgot this one," he said, a warm tingle of embarrassment in his cheeks at being caught talking to his mutt of a dog in such sappy terms.

"Dogs and horses first, then the rest of the menagerie, with the two-legged animals limping along as they make up the rear. Those were the rules I grew up with, and with which I fully concur. Go on, feed Peanut."

"So, your mom's checking up on you?" Arlo said, when they sat down to eat.

Lucian groaned. "She fusses terribly. I keep telling her I'm a big boy now, but she won't believe me. I'm sorry I was so long, but she wanted me to tell her where I was and what I was doing, which I had no intention of doing."

Lucian looked down and speared a tomato, but Arlo didn't miss the faint flush that colored his cheeks.

"She has the most terrible timing, though. Normally, she phones just as I've fallen asleep, or when I'm in the shower, or when I'm, erm… Well, you know, just terrible timing," Lucian muttered. "She also asked me when I'm going to see sense, up sticks, and hightail it to L.A. or somewhere else where she has innumerable contacts." Lucian put his knife and fork down, his brow creasing into a heavy frown. "Mum was the loudest voice in persuading me to come out to the States, but she's determined to micromanage me while I'm here."

"Perhaps she's trying to do the right thing, or the right thing as she sees it. Maybe she worries?"

"She does. Too much. I'm her baby, as she keeps telling me. Like Peanut's yours."

Arlo spluttered and grabbed a glass of water. When the tears had cleared from his vision, Lucian was grinning at him from across the table.

"Peanut's a dog. He is absolutely not my baby."

"Hmm, not from what I heard."

They carried on with dinner, agreeing they'd go back to the studio afterwards so Lucian could look at some of his work. It surprised Arlo that he wanted to show Lucian when, for so long, he'd hidden his art away from the eyes of others.

The evening was easy, companionable, the silences neither strained nor awkward as it so easily could have been after the kiss that definitely, absolutely, shouldn't have happened. It was good to share dinner with some-body, to hear a voice in his home that wasn't his. He cast a gaze at Lucian, and smiled as the younger man petted a besotted Peanut, who'd come over to beg for scraps.

Besotted. The word hit him hard in the chest, a sucker punch that knocked the air from his lungs. A word that pulsed with danger and that led only to broken promises and heartbreak.

No involvement, no ties, no emotional ropes to bind him to another before they were inevitably severed, leaving him unbalanced and floundering. A kiss that was all shades of dangerous, no matter how sweet it had been. It would be so, so easy to become besotted with a guy who was ludicrously adorable and who made him throw back his head and laugh out loud, loosening the tension that always seemed to hum just beneath his skin. So, so easy for his heart, once more, to break into a million pieces.

He couldn't let it happen, not again.

Arlo swallowed down the forkful of food that threatened to stick in his gullet. Lucian was passing through, here for a handful of months at most, and then he'd be gone for good as he headed for some place else, or back to the home he missed so much and a life that was a million miles from Collier's Creek, leaving him where he'd vowed he'd never be again, shivering in the cold and so damn alone.

He pushed his plate away, all his hunger gone.

"Are you okay?"

Across the table, Lucian tilted his head to the side, concern etched across his face. Arlo dragged up a smile from somewhere and plastered it on his lips.

"I'm fine," he lied, but Lucian's stiff smile and the crease in his forehead were all he needed to know that Lucian wasn't convinced. A light wind whistled through the yard, rustling through the trees and the bushes. Arlo shivered. Somebody was walking over his grave, as his long departed mom had always said.

"It's getting a little cool. And perhaps I should be going. Thank you for feeding me — again." Lucian laughed, but it was forced and awkward; he pushed himself to standing and stood behind his chair, shuffling from foot to foot.

No, don't go… but Arlo bit back the words, killing them before he could say them aloud. It was for the best, but it didn't feel like that. The air around them had shifted, yet it had nothing to do with the quickening breeze coming down from the mountains.

Lucian pushed his glasses up his nose as he kept his eyes downcast, and Arlo hated that he'd wiped the smile from his face.

"Luc—"

"Perhaps you could call me a cab? It's a rather long walk back to town."

Arlo jolted, Lucian's words cutting him short. "No. No, I'll give you a ride back. And you don't have to leave yet. We can go inside. I'll put on some coffee…"

Lucian shook his head. "That's very kind, but I think it's time to leave. Work tomorrow. Bibi needs me to open up the store."

"Oh, okay." Disappointment gnawed at Arlo. But what the hell did he expect? He'd become quiet and sullen over dinner as he'd retreated into himself, pulling all his doubts and fears around him like a cloak. No wonder Lucian couldn't wait to get away. "I'll take you back. No argument," he said, when Lucian opened his mouth to protest.

Moments later, they were in the pickup. The night sky

was a dense black, all the stars blotted out by the clouds that had rolled in, their brightness snuffed out. Arlo glanced at Lucian, who was blank faced, his smile tucked away and nowhere in sight.

Arlo started up the engine, and in silence, they drove away.

They hadn't had the ice cream after all.

CHAPTER EIGHTEEN

"What's all this?" Lucian picked up the sashes and peered at them.

Every one in the pile Bibi had dumped on the counter was red, white, or blue, and many of them all three, and printed with either Happy Jake's Day! Or, I Love Collier's Creek.

"Jake's Day." They were the only words she said as she picked up a poster from a bag on the floor, unrolled one, and gave it a critical stare.

Was he supposed to be a mind reader? Was he supposed to have a crystal ball to find the answer to whatever the hell she was talking about?

"Luci-Ann, will you stop peering at me like that?" Bibi didn't raise her eyes from checking one poster after the other, nodding her approval to each one. "These are still good," she muttered.

"I'll stop peering at you like that if you stop talking in riddles."

Bibi huffed, nodding to the poster she held up. A

young cowboy, all leather chaps and rugged jaw, stared into the middle distance. Lucian had seen nothing as butch since his last PRIDE parade, the year before, in London.

"Jake's Day. Haven't you seen the billboards around town? The displays in the stores? The front page of the Collier's Creek Citizens' Chronicle?" She dropped the poster on the counter, planted her hands on her hips and glared at him. "Two weeks from tomorrow, the town celebrates its founder, and that founder's Jake."

"Oh. No, I haven't noticed." But he'd not noticed anything, having walked around with his eyes glued to the ground, shoulders hunched, feeling a spark of life when the store door opened only for it to go out when it wasn't Arlo who walked through.

"You have been a little quiet and distracted, I guess."

A little? He shrugged. "You want these draped in the window?"

"Sure — and you can put together some of your cute little displays."

Lucian slid his gaze from the sash to Bibi. God alone knew how she'd ended up owning a floristry business. Her knowledge and skills were barely above rudimentary.

Yes, he could do some of those, anything to take his mind off the way everything had suddenly gone cold with Arlo just as they'd been heating up.

What had he done wrong? What had he said? It might have been madness to have let Arlo kiss him, because he was definitely staying away from men, especially older men who had more than a hint of silver fox about them, while he found himself and reset... Thank you, Mother, and your half-baked New Age philosophies. But Arlo's lips on his had sparked the first genuine signs of life he'd felt since he'd arrived in town. God alone knew why Arlo had backtracked so fast. Perhaps it'd been for the best, before Arlo discovered that being involved with him was a bad idea, and that he really was sub par after all.

But sub par wasn't how he'd felt as they'd kissed, and when Arlo smiled into his eyes.

A light hand on his shoulder saved him from sinking further into the gloomy morass of his thoughts.

"Luci, are you okay? You seem so sad suddenly — way more than a little quiet."

"Really, I'm perfectly..." He swallowed. Bibi's eyes, brimming with concern, locked onto his. "Not okay," he whispered.

Bibi strode over to the door and threw the bolt, locking them in, and turned the Open sign to Closed.

"But... customers?"

"I don't think 9:00am on Monday is peak business hours. Come on, I'll fix us some coffee and we'll have some of those awesome Tunnock's Tea Cakes — do you think your mom could send some for me in your next care package? Then you can tell me what's wrong. Or would you rather have a cup of your disgusting tea?"

Lucian laughed. It was hard not to when she looked as though she'd found a skunk making a home for itself in her underwear drawer.

"Coffee's fine. But you really don't have to listen to my drivel." But even as he said it, the need to talk and offload tugged hard at him.

"Yes I do, because I can't afford your sour face making all the flowers wilt. This isn't an act of friendship, it's purely a business decision." Throwing him a wink, she strode into the little kitchen area at the back of the store, and Lucian trailed behind.

Settled at the tiny, dented metal table a few minutes later, Bibi didn't waste time.

"So, what's Arlo done, or said — or hasn't done or said?"

Lucian's jaws dropped, his shock at her words causing his cup of steaming hot coffee to slip between his hands. He clattered it onto the table before he dropped it.

"Arlo? Why…? How did you…?"

Bibi preened. "Am I right, or am I right?"

Lucian opened his mouth before clamping it shut again. How had she guessed?

Bibi sighed. "I've had enough man trouble to spot the signs in others," she said, answering Lucian's unvoiced question.

Lucian let his head flop into his hands. "I haven't got man trouble because I haven't got a man. Arlo or otherwise."

"But something's happened?"

What could he tell her without looking like a teenager brushed off by their first crush? It had been a kiss, that was all, and ill advised. It'd been stopped in its tracks before it developed. And that was a good thing, right? Wrong, because that kiss had tasted so good and had been like nothing he'd known before.

"You'll think I'm a pathetic wuss…" He looked up at her through his lashes.

"Hey, don't let me hear you say those things, because you're neither. Okay?" Bibi squeezed his shoulder. Lucian wasn't sure he agreed, but her words made him feel a little better. Taking a deep breath, it all came tumbling out.

Bibi's beautifully groomed brows scrunched downwards, and she pursed her lips. She looked like she was sucking on a foul cough sweet, and Lucian smiled despite himself.

"He got scared," she declared. "It ended badly with his last boyfriend—"

"I never told you that." Lucian sat up, ramrod straight. If Arlo ever thought he'd been gossiping about him and Tony… What would he think of him? How would he look at him? A shudder raced down his spine and made him feel sick.

"You didn't. This is a small town, and lots of folks have nothing better to do than talk about others' business." She coughed and shifted in her seat. "Francine isn't as discreet as she should be, or not after a couple of cocktails. She's dropped some pretty big hints about Arlo's last relationship hitting the rocks in a big way. And I don't think it was the first."

Lucian blinked. "He never mentioned any other—"

"Why would he?"

Why indeed?

"According to Francine which, of course, is according to Hank, and which comes from Arlo himself, he's steering clear of involvement — even if Francine and her endless matchmaking think otherwise."

"It was only a kiss." Then why did it feel like so much more…?

"Maybe it wasn't, not to him. Maybe not to you, either. And, just maybe, he knew that and it's spooked him. I don't know all the details of what happened when he was in New York, but I've been around enough to read between the lines. Francine wasn't that indiscreet. My guess is that he got hurt pretty bad. Hurt enough to pull back and retreat to safer ground. This is the first time I've heard anything about him taking any interest in another guy. The problem, and no doubt he realized it, is that you're not a good bet for him."

"Wh—what do you mean by that?"

"You're passing through. Collier's Creek, and everybody in it, is a footnote in the story of your life. In a few months, you'll be going back home," Bibi said gently. "You're here for reasons I think are probably not too different from Arlo's. Am I right?"

Lucian nodded. Why deny it? Bibi was too smart to be taken in by any story he might try to fob her off with.

"You'll be here when the snow comes, but you won't be here to see it melt. Arlo will be. He's come back home, but you'll soon be leaving for yours. I know it hurts, honey, but maybe he's done you a favor."

CHAPTER NINETEEN

The morning wore on. Lunchtime came and went. Lucian worked through it, like he mostly did. He checked in a delivery of flowers, arranging them into sprays of contrasting colors, before festooning the window with the Jake's Day sashes, and displays of flowers in patriotic reds, whites, and blues, doing it all on autopilot. No more had been said about Arlo, and Bibi left him alone, but he was aware of the concerned looks she threw his way. At four o'clock she told him to go, but he shook his head. No, he'd see the day out — after all, what else did he have to do? At 6:00pm, Bibi locked the door and waved him good-bye, after she'd given his arm a squeeze of sympathy.

With the working day no longer distracting, his gloomy thoughts found their way back to Arlo, the parallels with his own pathetic history biting at him. Arlo had loved and lost: check. Arlo had left his old life behind him to find something new, something different, maybe even some-body different: check, check, and check again. So Arlo wasn't looking for love — he wasn't even looking for a quick fling — but then neither was he. Was he? No. Check and bloody check. They could be friends and agree anything else, even casual, was off limits, a line not to be crossed. That would work. Lucian huffed a bitter laugh. They'd already kissed, so that line was already looking very fuzzy.

He didn't go straight home, an evening stretching out in front of him with nothing and nobody to fill it was depressing. If he was going to stick it out in Collier's Creek, he had to get a grip. Join some community groups, maybe, and push himself forward to make some much needed friends. A shudder ripped through him. He wasn't overly social, preferring to blend into the background, often choosing plants over people... but he could do it, he had to do it, if he was going to stick around to reset. If he didn't, what was the point of leaving home if he was only going to end up as—

"A fucking hermit."

An elderly woman, leading a beribboned bundle of puffed up fur, jumped and stared at him in alarm.

"Barkassaurus Rex! Stop it, stop it," she shrieked, as the dog started yapping and strained on its leash. "You've scared my poor Barky with your potty mouth. Bichons, young man, are highly sensitive. You've probably scarred him for life." The woman glared, and Lucian glowered back.

Let it go... But he was fed up, upset, and he'd had enough.

"Madam, if that straggly mop you're dragging around is a Bichon, I'm a boiled egg and you're a dried up rasher of bacon."

The woman gasped. Clutching a string of pearls to her

chest, she blinked hard as her mouth flapped open and closed like a landed fish.

Oh god… "I'm sorry, I shouldn't have—" But it was too late for apologies as she scooped up her still yapping mutt, and hurried away as fast as she could.

He pushed his fingers through his hair. Why couldn't he have kept his mouth shut? No filter… He had a gift for insulting or upsetting people, whether they were old ladies and their raggedy dogs, or throwing yet another misadvised comment at a bride-to-be back home. He opened his mouth, and it all came spewing out. Too honest, or maybe too fucking stupid, as Miles had always said.

Approaching the block where Randy's was, he slowed his pace. He couldn't hear the Collier's Creek Cowboy Combo, so perhaps he could call in and have a drink and get something to eat. Lucian shuddered. God, he wasn't that desperate. He hunched his shoulders and lowered his head, as if he was afraid someone would drag him inside, and scuttled past. There were other places in town he could go, but the idea trickled away like water down the sink. The sad truth was, he didn't want to sit alone, nursing a drink and getting more and more miserable. He could do that back at the apartment, and for a lot cheaper.

With nowhere he wanted to be, he set off for his apartment that was really a shoe box, ready to give Mr. DuPont, who'd be peering out from behind his drapes as he did every day, a wave and a facsimile of a cheery smile.

Mr. DuPont wasn't twitching his drapes, which must have been a first, but Lucian didn't give it any more thought as he let himself in.

As usual, a rumble of voices came from behind the closed door of his landlord's first-floor apartment. Lucian was used to hearing the TV turned up high, but the voices didn't sound like they came from the soaps the old guy seemed to like so much. Maybe he had visitors, but Lucian neither knew nor cared. As he planted his foot on the first step, Mr. Dupont's front door swung open and Lucian twisted around.

"Here he is, and he's late." Mr. Dupont had made an art form out of sounding peeved.

Did the guy log his comings and goings? Did he keep a tab on what time he went to work, came home, showered, or took a piss?

"I'm sorry you've had to wait for such a long time, but he's never late and—"

"Thank you so much for your time, and good company, Mr. DuPont. I apologize for inconveniencing you."

Lucian froze. That familiar voice, rich and low, measured and steady…

Arlo stepped out from Mr. DuPont's apartment, every inch of him relaxed and at ease as he shook Mr. DuPont's hand and thanked him for showing him his fascinating collection of knitted sailor boy dolls. Arlo looked up, his eyes locking with Lucian's, his smile wonky and warm.

"Lucian. I need to have a quick word with you. May I?" Arlo nodded to the staircase, his easy smile unwavering.

"Errhh… Yes. Alright." Lucian blinked but didn't move, his feet nailed to the spot.

"Then perhaps…?"

"Oh, yes. Right. Fine." Lucian darted up the stairs, followed by Arlo, and Mr. DuPont calling out for Arlo to visit again.

Why was Arlo here? What could he have to say to

him? Was the apartment tidy? Were his clothes slung into corners? Had he left half eaten slices of toast abandoned on the sideboard? All the questions and more jostled for space in his head, anything to distract him from Arlo just inches behind him, anything to stop him breathing in Arlo's lemon laced cologne.

He opened the door with unsteady hands, ushering Arlo inside, and glimpsing Mr. DuPont on the stairs staring after them, before he closed the door and fell back against it.

"Man, this really is a shoebox."

"Whatever you do, don't stretch your arms out because you'll touch the sides."

Arlo huffed out a small laugh, but said nothing more as he looked around the tiny space, taking it all in.

He's probably thinking how shit it all looks. At least there was no abandoned toast, nor boxer briefs draped all over the place to dry.

"I'm sorry," Arlo said. "About the other night."

"What, exactly, are you sorry for, Arlo?" Lucian pushed himself away from the door as anger mixed and melded with confusion. "Are you apologizing for inviting me back in the first place? It was you who asked me, remember, not the other way around." Arlo had pulled him in, then pushed him away, and now he was here and he didn't know why. Anger and confusion fizzed in his veins. "Just like it was you who made the first move to kiss me. Oh, not once, but twice. Okay, so that first time—"

"I'm still not paying to replace 'em, mister."

"What? I don't want—oh, bloody hell." Lucian sagged down onto the sofa, his anger and indignation spent. He wanted to be angry, he wanted to be indignant, and he had every right to be, but he couldn't, not when Arlo lowered himself down beside him, the warmth of his body so tantalizingly close, and definitely not with those steady gold-green eyes gazing into his.

"Why are you here, Arlo? I don't know what happened the other night, what I did to make you go cold—"

"You did nothing. You're right about me making the first move to kiss you. I'm glad I did because it was everything I hoped it would be — or it was on the second attempt. But…"

Lucian's heart raced, thundering in his chest. *But*. One tiny word that said so much.

"But. Why but?" Lucian held his breath, waiting for Arlo to tell him all about the *but*.

"Because I'm damaged goods," Arlo said softly. "When it finished with Tony, it broke me into pieces. I came home to put them all back together again, or as best I could, though I'm not sure I'm doing such a great job of it. Being more than friends, it's probably not wise for either of us."

"Not wise. Yeah, well, maybe you're right. Probably are. You saved us both from a fate worse than death. So what is this, some kind of Dear John speech?"

"I didn't like the way the evening ended up. It was my fault, and I needed to explain."

"So now you have."

Arlo rubbed his brow. "Perhaps it's best if I go." He made no attempt to stand.

"I could escort you to the door, but you've only got to put your arm out and you'll be able to touch it."

Arlo nodded. "I just wanted to… say what I had to.

Better go, I guess. I promised Hank I'd stop in at Randy's." He grimaced.

"So, you thought you'd call in here then go to the bar? Kill two birds with one stone."

"I didn't mean it like—who the hell…" Arlo's cell rang and he fumbled it from the hip pocket of his jeans. "I'll cancel the—"

"Answer it. It might be Hank telling you to get down there quick as there's a two for one on deep fried skunk."

"Hank," Arlo barked. "We said… Oh, right. Sure…"

Lucian got up and crossed the few steps to his kitchenette. Tea and toast, tonight's dinner. Despite his hunger, he wasn't sure he could stomach much more.

He threw a tea bag into a mug, keeping his back to Arlo, the hiss of the kettle drowning out the sound of the one sided conversation. By the time he'd made the tea, Arlo would be on his feet, ready to leave. Being more than friends… He shoved a couple slices of bread into the toaster and smashed down the lever before slopping boiling water into the mug, jabbing at the bobbing tea bag. Arlo was right. The guy was damaged goods. He had Arlo's own words and Bibi's telling him that loud and clear. Join the fucking club. The tea bag, unable to withstand his onslaught, burst, sending a cloud of leaves to the surface, just as the acrid stench of burning rose from the toaster.

"Shit." He jabbed the eject button and incinerated toast flew out and landed on the floor. He swooped them up and slung them in the trash, then chucked the ruined mug of tea down the sink.

"That was Hank. He's had to cancel."

"Really?" Lucian turned around and leaned back against the counter.

"I'm glad, if I'm honest. Not sure I'm in the mood to talk about car engines or baseball."

Lucian shrugged.

Arlo's shoulders slumped. "Okay, guess I really should be going."

"Yes, I guess you really should." Lucian crossed his apartment in a few steps, opened the door, and peered out. No sign of Mr. DuPont, thank god.

"Maybe we could get a coffee sometime?"

From a kiss that had made his heart sing to a tepid, vague invitation for coffee. His stomach plummeted. So this was how it was to be; best to just suck it up, and maybe look for flights home and swallow whatever was left of his pride.

"Bye, Arlo."

"Bye." Arlo opened his mouth, but whatever he was going to say he thought better of it. "I'll see you around?" A question, not a statement.

Lucian nodded, not trusting himself to answer as he quietly closed the door behind Arlo, slumping against it for the second time in less than half an hour.

The silence in the apartment pressed in on him, along with his crushing loneliness. But at least he had his pride and his dignity, and that had to mean something. Perhaps they could meet for coffee, just as Arlo had suggested, and talk about everything that didn't matter and nothing that did as they sat and smiled politely at one another.

Lucian gasped as a hand reached into his chest and squeezed tight, crushing the breath from him. It was sad and grim and everything he didn't want. Fuck pride, fuck dignity…

He slung open his door, just in time to hear the door to the street slam shut, the finality of its thud a punch to his stomach. He hurtled down the stairs, just catching himself from going head first, and ran out onto the street.

"Arlo, wait."

Arlo turned, his eyes wide as his mouth dropped open in surprise.

"Forget coffee. I make a mean cup of tea, so if you want…"

"If you're sure?" A slow smile lifted Arlo's lips, a slow smile that burrowed deep inside Lucian. He didn't know if he'd done the right thing in calling Arlo back, and didn't care. Maybe it was just another random act, as random as sticking a pin in a map which had led him to a small Wyoming town.

"Who knows? But the offer's there if you want it."

Arlo's widening smile was the only answer he needed.

CHAPTER TWENTY

Lucian eschewed the tea bags in a mug approach, and instead brought out the pot bearing a print of Danebury Manor on one side, and the family crest on the other. The mugs, however, were the second best Target had to offer.

He kept his mind focused on what he was doing, because what he was really doing wasn't up for scrutiny. Placing everything on a tray, and adding a packet of Hobnobs from the care package, he turned. And stopped. Arlo was studying the montage of photos that took pride of place on the wall next to the window overlooking the quiet side street.

His family and friends. The manor. The gardens. His animals.

Arlo turned and waved a hand at the photos. "Is this…?"

"Yes. Home and my family." He put the tray down and joined Arlo. "That's Mum, on the sofa, and the grizzled ball of wool on her lap wearing a Santa hat is my dog Wally. The goon grinning into the camera, because he's had too many eggnogs, is my brother Eddie, and that's my sister Bella, next to him." Lucian smiled. He'd snapped the happy, carefree photo last Christmas Eve.

"This is my favorite, though." He pointed to a smaller photo, dog-eared with age, of a boy and a man, both dark-haired, both with wide smiles, petting a puppy. "Me with my dad. It was my tenth birthday. The bundle of fluff's a baby Wally. He was Dad's special present to me."

Arlo leaned in and narrowed his eyes. "You look more like your dad than you do your mom. So your dad's Lord Blaxston?"

"Was. My brother now holds the title. Dad died the year after the photo was taken."

"I'm sorry." Arlo's eyes brimmed with compassion.

"He was lovely, and I still miss him. Got lots of great memories, though, which I'll always treasure. Anyway," he said, moving away from the wall of photos and sinking into the couch, "shall we have tea?"

Arlo joined him. "Are you sure you're not a member of the royal family? I mean, I never expected some kind of palace…"

"Palace?" Lucian laughed. "Thought you might have googled it, though."

"I did." Arlo gave a sheepish smile. "But nothing came up for Danboro."

Lucian picked the teapot up and pointed to the print with the name emblazoned underneath.

"Ah."

"Quite."

Lucian poured the tea and emptied the biscuits on to a plate. "No milk, I'm afraid, because it's turned to yogurt."

"No problem."

They drank in silence for a couple of minutes, perched on either end of the couch, nestling their tea on their knees.

Lucian dunked a biscuit, missing the vital moment to take it out before the soggy end slopped back into the mug. *Fuck. Perhaps he's not noticed.* Lucian glanced up through his lashes; Arlo was staring into his tea. The silence stretched out, growing more painful by the second. Maybe he shouldn't have rushed for the door, maybe he shouldn't have called out for Arlo, maybe he—

"Nice teapot."

"What?" Lucian jumped, dragged out from his thoughts of all the things he maybe, absolutely, shouldn't be doing. "Teapot? Nice? No, it's hideous. I can only think my sister, whose many little Danebury empires include merchandizing, was being ironic when she commissioned them. But the visitors love them, and are quite happy to shell out the dosh, so who am I to pour scorn when I can pour tea? Care for another?"

Arlo put his mug down. "Thank you, but no. It's gross. The Creek water tastes better. I don't think even letting your cookie — excuse me, your biscuit — melt into it would improve the taste."

Lucian opened his mouth before clamping it closed again. Arlo's face was deadpan, but he couldn't hide the mischief in the depths of his bright hazel eyes. Lucian laughed, the off color comment and the shine in those gorgeous eyes fracturing the tension that had bound them both.

"I've got beer."

"Then why didn't you say?"

Lucian dumped the tea in the kitchenette and popped the caps on a couple of bottles, ice cold from the refrigerator, and slumped on the couch. His gaze slid to Arlo, who was slouching, his long legs stretched out in front of him and crossed at the ankles. A friend... regret rippled through Lucian before he pushed it down. Yet perhaps it was a friend he needed more than...

"So tell me about Danebury Manor. I've never met a guy who grew up in a castle."

"It's a manor, if you don't mind, not a castle," he said with a huff before he grinned. "It's been in the family for hundreds of years. I know it's not ordinary, but to me it's always been home first, and Danebury Manor second. This time of year is when it's at its best, when all the trees are turning from green to gold." Like your eyes. He swallowed the words as he swallowed his beer.

"Everything will be in full swing, getting ready for Autumn at Danebury. It's a wonderful event, and I'm in charge of dressing the house in seasonal flowers, just as I am for Springtime at Danebury and Christmas at Danebury. Or at least I was." His shoulders slumped.

"Lucian, why are you here? I mean, really? With all this..." Arlo waved towards the wall of photos, "why would you want to leave?"

Arlo's words were gentle, caressing, and reached into his heart. Lucian looked away. Arlo had no right to ask him, not like that, not when they were just friends. Yet why not tell him? Hadn't Arlo confided in him about Tony, so why not do the same? It was what friends did, and he had nothing to be ashamed of, even if so often it didn't feel like that.

Lucian pushed his glasses further up his nose, holding them in place for a few silent seconds, before releasing them to begin their slow slip down.

"It was a perfect storm," he said, staring at the half drunk bottled beer as though he didn't know how it had gotten into his hand. "Or that's how my brother described it. That, or the unholy trinity.

"I had a boyfriend. The Shit Formally Known as Miles. Or that's how I think of him now. We were together — supposedly — for almost two years, and he was horrible to me for most of that time. Not that I could ever see it. My family warned me about him, so did my friends — the few who hung around after he drove the others off."

Falling silent, he stared at his bottle. Somehow, most of the label lay shredded on his knees. He glanced up at Arlo's gentle scrutiny. No judgement, no criticism, just a kind of quiet understanding. But of course, hadn't Arlo been there, hadn't he gotten the T-shirt?

Sucking in a breath, he readied himself to tell his story.

"I've never been the most confident person, and Miles was older than me by quite a few years. I think the thing that attracted me most to him was his supreme self confidence. It was like he knew all the answers to life. It was only later I realized his confidence was arrogance and narcissism, but by then he'd chipped away at my limited self-belief. I questioned everything about myself, and every answer I came up with left me feeling like I wasn't good enough. Sub par is how he referred to me, and that was when he was being kind — not that he was ever that. Mostly, though, he called me a moron."

"Jesus. What a piece of work."

Lucian shrugged. "We finished a few weeks before I came out here. I hadn't seen or heard from him for a while, which wasn't unusual, but then I got sent a photo—"

"Oh. Right—"

"Wrong. No, it wasn't him with another guy, which is what you're thinking. In a strange way, I'd have preferred that. No, it was a photo of a picture perfect tropical beach, along with a message telling me not to book a flight."

Lucian's lips twisted into a humorless smile at Arlo's frown of incomprehension.

"He was a banker, and he'd taken a job in the Bahamas. He relocated and hadn't bothered to tell me. I think that's what really hurt, that he didn't think I was worth him mentioning it to. Anyway, it put paid to whatever it was we were. I'm just sorry, looking back, that I didn't have the guts to end it myself, and a whole lot sooner."

"Don't beat yourself up about it. If somebody constantly erodes who you are, it undermines you."

"Was it like that with you and—" Lucian winced. "Sorry, it's not my business."

"Tony? No." Arlo shook his head. "We had our problems, and toward the end, the arguments grew vicious on both sides, but that kind of picking away wasn't part of it. So you came to the Creek to get over a guy. Sounds kind of familiar." Arlo held out his bottle, and Lucian clinked his own against it.

"I needed a change. I can see it now — somewhere different, even if I used the not very scientific method of sticking a pin in a map. But The Shit isn't the only reason everybody thought it best I take a break."

Arlo quirked his head.

"We're a prestigious venue for corporate events and society weddings. Danebury Manor is very expensive to book. There was an incident involving a bride on her wedding day. It cost the business a lot of money. I don't think it was my fault, but that's not how everybody else saw it. It was the bee," he blurted.

"The bee?"

Lucian nodded his head hard. "We were hosting the wedding for the Bridezilla from hell. Nothing, and I mean nothing, we did was right from the very moment they made the booking. And she seemed to take an instant dislike to me, but then, I suppose, I shouldn't have told her that her ideas for the design of her bouquet looked like a giant and very erect cock."

Arlo spluttered. "You said—"

"I know, I know. I opened my mouth too wide and stuffed my foot straight in. Didn't I tell you I have a problem with filter? After she had her fit, and my sister calmed her down, she deigned to take advice about the bouquet design. Or some. But at least she wouldn't have clutched a floral phallus as she walked down the aisle on her big day.

"When the wedding day came around, everything was going to plan, and the service was beautiful. She was even bearable, or just about. The weather was perfect, a rare, warm, summer's day. The photographer asked her to bring the bouquet to her face, as though she was sniffing it. And that's when it happened. The bee, which had been snoozing amongst the blooms, didn't like her nose invading its privacy, so it decided to fly off — straight up her left nostril.

"Everything went crazy. She was rolling around on the ground screaming, everybody was screaming, and a very pregnant lady went into labor. Ambulances were called, and they carted the pregnant lady off to hospital. But it was too late for the poor bee, because by the time the paramedics arrived, it was dead."

"The poor bee?"

"If you'd encountered the woman, you'd be thinking poor bee, too. Once they sting, they die. The paramedics got it out, but it wasn't easy because the bride's face had swollen up so badly. She didn't actually go into anaphylactic shock, but her reaction was severe enough to warrant adrenaline being injected into her thigh, and to be taken to hospital to be put on an IV drip and pumped full of antihistamine.

"The wedding reception had to be abandoned. We knew there'd be an insurance claim, but she also went the legal route. The compensation she was going for was eye watering. Among a whole checklist of stuff they were claiming for, all of which was utter bullshit, they were citing health and safety breaches. There was no bee in the bouquet when I checked it. What happened was down to a fluke that a bee had decided he was going to get cozy among the flowers. It was sheer bad luck. It wasn't our fault her day was ruined, because it was nobody's fault."

Lucian put down his bottle on the tiny coffee table and squeezed his hands together.

"The insurance covered some, but not all of what was being claimed for. After negotiations between our respective legal teams, we reached an out of court settlement. It was expensive, and the whole affair was very stressful for my mum, brother, and sister, who'd built the company. It was that or risk terrible publicity, which in such a competitive business…"

"Wow, that's quite a story. Did you come out to the States soon after?"

Lucian nodded. "There was a family conference, and they persuaded me to step away from the business for a while. Things had got too much for me, they said, and I needed a change and to take time out. I could hardly disagree because I was a mess, and we all knew it. Everything seemed to happen on top of each other. The thing with Miles, the ruined wedding, the fire—"

"The…?"

Lucian cringed, knowing Arlo would think he was deranged, but it was too late to backtrack, so he took a deep breath. He'd told parts one and two, so he might as well go for the hat trick.

"We have a large outbuilding where I put together all the floral displays, bouquets, etc. I'd been experimenting with some new designs for large static displays, as we were hosting an event for a major City bank a few days after the wedding disaster. They included candles. I failed to extinguish one. I went for a cup of tea in a little side room, and—and when I got back…" Lucian stuttered to a halt, and licked his dry lips. "The flames were taking hold, but I grabbed the hosepipe and I put it out.

"Although the outbuilding sustained only minor damage, the fire destroyed a lot of expensive stock. The insurers — who weren't the ones dealing with the wedding fiasco — considered it negligence and refused to pay out. The fire was completely my fault, but the bee thing… Whatever, they all thought I needed time out and in all honesty, I couldn't disagree."

"Wow. That's quite a story. Or stories."

"I'm afraid I'm a bit of an all-round disaster, and I'm surprised you want to be friends with me." *Let alone anything else.* "If you decide I'm too dangerous to be within ten feet of, I'll understand."

"They say things come in threes, don't they? Seems to me you've had yours."

Lucian retrieved a couple more beers from the refrigerator. Arlo hadn't decided it was best he left, so perhaps he didn't think he was too much of a liability to be around after all.

"What's Jake's Day like?" Lucian asked as he handed over a bottle to Arlo, glad to no longer be talking about the list of sorry events that had brought him to Collier's Creek. "Bibi had me making displays for the window and putting up banners. I must walk around in a daze, because I hadn't noticed anything around town about it."

"Jake's Day. I haven't been to one in years. If it hasn't changed, and I don't see why it would have, it's a bit like a cross between a 4th July parade and a farmers' market. Lots of stuff for kids and families, cook offs, a fireworks display in the evening. I loved going as a kid, missed a couple of years when I was a teenager, because my friends and I thought it was uncool. Local bands play, most of them terrible—"

"Oh my god, not the Cowboy Combo?" Lucian clutched at his chest, and laughed.

Arlo grinned. "They're probably the headline act, so don't get your hopes up you'll be listening to… chamber music."

Lucian widened his eyes. "Chamber music?"

"Sure. Isn't that what the aristocracy listens to?"

"Not this very minor, way down the scale aristocrat."

Arlo snorted in derision. "But still an aristocrat. A coat of arms on the teapot? Oh, I think I rest my case."

Lucian chuckled. "Bibi told me I'm going with her. Apparently, she's organizing a group of her friends. Trouble is, I've met some of them…"

"And you'd rather not repeat the experience."

"Hmm. I appreciate the gesture, though. She's a bit of a mother hen on the quiet."

"Francine's more mama bear. She's been making noises about dragging me along, and I need a good excuse to say no. I think she might have another gay cousin." He shuddered, and Lucian laughed. "Perhaps we can both escape others' plans for us?" Arlo's gaze locked onto Lucian's.

"Sorry, I don't… Oh, you mean perhaps we should go together? It'd get us both out of a fix. Although I'm not sure I like the idea that I'm a convenient excuse." Lucian grinned, in the hope it took the sting out of his words, yet the thought that Arlo might think the two of them going together was merely expedient sat like a block of ice in the pit of his stomach.

"Hey, you're not an excuse for anything, and never for me. You hear that?" Arlo's words were as steady as his gaze, and Lucian nodded as the ice in his gut melted.

"Yes, I'd like that." Just as friends, nothing more, because this was the kind of thing friends would do together.

Arlo pushed himself up to standing. "That's great. I'd better go, I guess. I need to speak to Tony. I've been avoiding his calls since I got back from New York, but I'd better get it over and done with even though I think I'd rather have my eyeballs skewered onto red hot spikes."

"Oh, right. Sure."

Lucian got to his feet, and they faced each other, just

inches apart. Arlo's smile looked easy and relaxed, but it was a facade as his shoulders hunched as he shoved his hands deep into his pockets. Lucian returned the smile, but it felt stiff and strained. Now the moment had come to say goodbye. He pushed his glasses up his nose; his finger slipped, and he dug himself in the eye.

"Ow!"

"Oh, Lucian," Arlo said softly, shaking his head. "I've never met anybody like you before."

"Then count yourself lucky." He'd been told that before, but not the way Arlo had said it. From Arlo, it sounded more like a gentle revelation, and Lucian didn't mind that at all.

"Next Saturday then. Call me to let me know what time and I'll meet you here."

Lucian nodded. "Of course. So it's a date then. But not a date date, but an arrangement. That's what I mean..." Lucian squirmed.

Arlo's answering laugh was warm and good natured. "Don't tie yourself up in knots. I know what you mean."

Once Arlo had gone, Lucian collapsed on the couch. A date that wasn't a date. He understood. He could get behind that. Just two friends meeting up for the day. They'd discussed it, like the sensible adults they were, going over the good solid reasons for their mutually agreed decision. His brain got it, but his heart, whooping in his chest, absolutely, totally, did not.

CHAPTER TWENTY-ONE

"But Arlo, all the family's getting together — and you're as much family to me and Hank as our own flesh and blood. And there's my cousin Marty, who's come to visit with us for the weekend, and he's just dying to meet you and—"

"Francine." Arlo had to shout down the phone and the answering silence was absolute and straining at the seams with hurt. Arlo sucked in a breath. He didn't want to upset her, but this had to stop. "I really appreciate what you're doing—"

"Then that's great, Arlo, real great. So you'll come meet Marty."

Arlo couldn't stop the groan, but he doubted she noticed as she'd grabbed his insincere appreciation and turned it into an offensive weapon.

"He's a suitable man, Arlo, a veterinarian surgeon specializing in farm animals. He's got a deep and special interest in goats."

Goats? What the fuck…?

"… at the bandstand for the picnic…"

Bandstand? Picnic? He was still stuck on goats. And… suitable. He scrambled to catch up, fighting against the strong current of Francine's enthusiasm. If he were to escape with his life, he needed to swim hard and fast for shore.

"What do you mean by suitable? A veterinarian who's into goats? Come on."

Francine's hesitation was tiny. It wouldn't be noticeable to anybody who didn't know her well, but Arlo did.

"He's nearer your own age. To our age. I just figure you'd have more in common with somebody like that."

"Somebody who wasn't younger. Like Tony, you mean." Arlo's shoulders tensed.

"What I mean is, what a person wants from life depends a lot on how old they are. Dreams and aspirations, they'll differ."

Her words sucked the breath from Arlo's lungs. He and Tony, what they'd wanted, what they'd needed from life, had differed and in the end they'd ripped them apart, leaving them both beaten and bloody.

"Francine," he rasped, "I'm not meeting up with you. Or with cousin Marty, no matter how suitable you think he is. I'm going to stop by Jake's Day, but I'm going with a friend." Who you won't think is remotely suitable…

"Arlo, are Hank and I not your friends?" Francine asked quietly.

Arlo squeezed his eyes closed and counted to three in his head before he spoke.

"More than that, and you know it. But please, you have got to stop trying to fix me up with random guys I have nothing in common with. I mean it. I don't want you doing this anymore. When I'm ready to meet somebody, it'll be for me to decide who is and who isn't suitable."

"Okay," she said, her voice quiet. "Perhaps I've been a little too pushy. It's just that I — we — worry about you. Hank and I. We…" she hesitated, as though unsure how to continue when she was never unsure about anything. Arlo's eyes narrowed, and he sucked in his lower lip as he waited.

"We both know splitting up with Tony hit you hard. Of course it did. But you came home to make a new start. And a new start means new attachments. Attachments of the heart. Romantic attachments. You may think I'm a meddler, always trying to hook you up. And yes, I'm guilty as charged. But somebody's got to give you a nudge in the right direction, because you won't do it yourself."

"Francie," he said quietly, "I am making a new start but I don't think I'm ready—"

"For what? Ready to live life again to the full? Ready to take a chance on somebody? Ready to put your heart on the line? Sure, you risk it being hurt, but the bigger risk is missing that special person who makes waking up in the morning worth it. You tell us you're happy, but neither Hank nor I believe it. We know you too well, and we can see you're, I don't know, unsettled, I guess. You seem kind of adrift, and you need somebody to anchor you. Arlo, you have the kindest of hearts and you have a lot of love to give. Don't waste it, because you're not meant to be alone."

A weight pushed down on his chest, crushing the air in his lungs.

"Arlo? You still there?"

"Sure," he croaked, forcing the word past the hard

lump filling his throat. "What is this, tough love?" He forced out a laugh.

"Maybe it's what you need to hear. Okay, so it's a no to Marty—"

"And his goats."

"Yeah, maybe he's not the best of matches." Arlo heard the amusement in her words, and he smiled. The tightness binding him like rope loosened. "So, who're you going to Jake's Day with?"

Who's your date, in other words. Even though it wasn't a *date* date, as Lucian had said, stumbling over his words. Arlo grinned, because it was impossible not to, when he thought of the awkward young Englishman. There was no reason not to tell her who the friend was he was going with, because she was sure to spot them together.

"Lucian. Do you remember him? He came to the BBQ with Bibi."

"Luci-Ann! My, that boy was so cute. And that accent. Not that I was always sure what he was saying. Hank told me he threw beer all over you, at Randy's. Sounds to me like he's dangerous to be around."

"It was an accident. Could have happened to anybody." His skin tingled. There was nothing dangerous about Lucian, nothing at all.

"So, you're going to be meeting up with Mr. Adorkable!"

Arlo pulled his cell away from his ear and stared at it, not sure he'd heard right. He pressed it back. "Mr... What?"

"Adorkable," she said, laughing. "An adorable dork. Just about sums him up, from what I could see. Especially with those glasses he was wearing."

"That's crazy. He's not a dork." Lucian was quirky, eccentric, and kind of accident prone, judging by the bee… and the fire… and tripping over and drenching him in beer…

"Oh, I think he is, but he's super cute, too. And very young."

Arlo's shoulders stiffened. Had he imagined a change in her tone?

"It must be hard being away from home at that age—"

"He's twenty-four." Arlo's lips tightened into a thin line.

"Is he? Well, that is young isn't it? Only a little older than the twins, so it's very good of you to befriend him while he's a guest in our town. I noticed you were talking to him for a long time at the BBQ."

"And why not?" He winced. Defensive, way too defensive. "I've spent a lot of time in London," he said, more steadily, "so we had plenty to talk about." Not that they spent any time talking about that…

"Sure you had."

"What—"

"I'm sorry, Arlo, I gotta go. Hank'll be home soon, and dinner won't cook itself. No doubt we'll see you in town on Saturday. Bye."

He stared down at his cell. The call had left him unsettled. Stupid. He shook his shoulders out to release the tension. It'd been Francine being Francine. He and Lucian were friends, that was all. They'd agreed it. Yet, as he pushed his cell into his pocket, he was starting to feel as if he were veering away from the path and making his way into the unknown.

CHAPTER TWENTY-TWO

Nerves butterflied in Arlo's stomach as he leaned against the streetlamp and waited for Lucian, who as soon as he'd rung the bell had stuck his head out of the window and called that he was on his way.

It'd been a couple of days since his conversation with Francine, but her words hadn't stopped going around and around in his head like a washing machine on a never-ending cycle. *Unsettled... drifting... young... dangerous to know...* He'd examined every one, before rejecting them. Yet, he'd picked up his cell, on the verge of calling Lucian to cancel their plans before throwing it aside. Why had Francine gotten to him the way she had? His relationship with Lucian — not that it was that — was none of her business, and he was going to make sure it stayed that way.

The front door flung open, scattering Arlo's troubled thoughts.

Lucian stood on its threshold, his smile sunshine bright. His thick, dark hair, wild as ever, framed his face;

Arlo's fingers itched to push away the heavy hank that fell across his brow. They stared at each other, neither moving, as though each were afraid to make the first move.

Crazy… This wasn't a first date, it wasn't a date of any kind.

"Quick, let's escape before Mr. DuPont sees us." Lucian bounded down the short flight of steps and chivvied Arlo along. "He keeps stopping me to ask about you. I think he's got a crush!"

Arlo shuddered. "You mean I'm an object of Mr. DuPont's affections? Along with his knitted dolls? I'm gonna need therapy."

Main Street was thronged with people lining the sidewalk on either side. Arlo pushed his way through the crowd, ensuring Lucian stayed close. The annual celebration of the town's founding, Jake's Day was the town at its best, with its party dress on and a bow in its hair, and he was determined Lucian was going to enjoy every moment.

"Collier's Creek really has gone to town." Lucian looked up at Arlo and smiled. Like everybody around them, they were crushed together, but the press of Lucian's lithe, slim body was warming up Arlo in all the right, and wrong, places.

A few cops wandered along, ready to deal with any non-existent trouble, stopping and talking to friends and family in the crowd. Ted was one of the cops on duty and, as Arlo noticed him, he chose that moment to turn around. His gaze caught Arlo's; he smiled and walked forward.

Arlo slipped his arm around Lucian's shoulders, bending so his mouth came close to Lucian's ear. Ted stopped, as Arlo hoped he would, raising a brow and a crooked smile before he waved and turned away.

"You okay?" Arlo asked when Lucian looked up at him, a question in his eyes. He had to say something, anything, to explain why he'd thrown his arm around him. "Should have asked you if you were, er, claustrophobic."

"No, I'm fine." Lucian looked as calm as a summer's morning. "Oooh, what's happening out there?" Lucian pointed to a small raised platform in front of a statue of Jake himself. Local dignitaries jostled for position as a uniformed police officer bounded up on stage to join them.

"That's Sheriff Morgan." Arlo's lips brushed Lucian's ear, a few errant strands of soft, dark hair tickling his lips. "He's a direct descendant of the man himself."

Lucian turned to face him. He was so close Arlo could feel his warm breath caress his skin, and see every silver fleck in Lucian's deep blue eyes, their beauty undimmed by the ugly glasses. His heart thumped hard, and a bead of sweat crawled down his spine. If Lucian asked him what his name was, Arlo wouldn't have been able to answer.

Lucian laughed, sending a delicious ripple across Arlo's skin. "Really? Then he must be like local royalty, having the sacred blood of Jake running through his veins."

Next to them, a pink-haired elderly lady, holding a flag emblazoned with the noble features of the main man himself, and wearing a large bag across her front, out of which a small, scruffy mutt poked its beribboned head, glared at them before turning away. Arlo straightened up and attempted to put some space between him and Lucian, but the crowd had other ideas.

"My, but he's handsome." Lucian laughed as he pushed his slipping glasses up to the bridge of his nose. "He can come and arrest me any time. Handcuff me now, Sheriff, and I promise not to come quietly!"

Arlo ground his teeth, and his shoulders tensed. It was only a joke, but…

Next to them, the old lady gasped, covered her dog's ears, and did her best to edge away.

Sheriff Morgan kept his speech short and sweet, as against a cacophony of cheers and whoops, he declared the official start to Jake's Day.

With a drum roll, a marching band led the way, woefully out of tune and out of step. The crowd reformed, the outraged old lady nowhere to be seen.

Lucian had edged in front of Arlo, leaning back into him, waving and cheering, all his focus on the parade. Arlo's breath was heavy in his lungs. It was the crush of bodies, that was all, the only reason Lucian pressed against him, his ass way too close to his awakening dick, before a sliver of space pushed its way between them, gone a second later as Lucian's back plastered once more against Arlo's front.

Ah, Jesus… Arlo's erection pressed painfully against the zipper of his jeans, but somehow, some way, he found a little space and held on tight to a hair's breadth of air between him and Lucian.

At some point, high school cheerleaders replaced the marching band, every movement crisp and sharp, the crowd greeting them with applause as they high kicked their way along. Local veterans, marching in perfectly synchronized, tight formation, provoked an explosion of cheers and frantic flag waving. A small fleet of classic cars followed, bodywork polished to blinding brilliance, chrome dazzling in the sunshine.

"Oh, my god. We have one of those at home. We hire it out for weddings." Lucian grinned up at Arlo as he pointed to a classic Bentley, sleek and cherry red, every undulating line an understatement of class and sophistication.

"What the…?" Lucian's mouth dropped open as the last of the cars rolled by.

"I'd forgotten about this," Arlo muttered. A few young children began to cry. "This gave me nightmares when I was a kid."

"I can see why. They're super creepy, but weirdly fascinating."

On a convoy of flatbed trucks, plaster statues of Jake Collier stood proudly.

Jake, or several Jakes. Ten, twelve, fifteen feet or more. Jake with a lasso. Jake taking aim with a rifle. Jake flexing his muscles. Jake looking noble, shielding his sightless eyes with his hand as he stared into the distance.

"Okay, I know this is weird—"

"You bet it is. God, I have to take some photos for posterity. Nobody at home will believe me otherwise…"

"The models are old, mostly made just after the First World War, by the returning soldiers."

"Then I can only imagine they were shellshocked."

Attempts had been made to restore the models over the years, but even at a distance, the cracks were visible, the repainted faces bright and clown-like.

A snort of laughter replaced Lucian's shock. "Eyeliner, lipstick, blusher. I expect the West was very wild in good ol' Jake's heyday."

"Young man." They both jumped. The pink-haired lady had reappeared; an even older woman whose hair was a startling shade of orange hovered just behind her. She glared at Lucian, five feet nothing of softly permed pink indignation.

"I've seen you before, your potty mouth upset my Barky—"

"What—"

"I never forget anybody who upsets my baby. I don't know where you're from, but it sure ain't from around these parts, not with that funny accent you've got. In this town we revere our heroes. If it wasn't for Jake, none of us would be here — and that includes you, with your snooty east coast — Barkasaurus Rex, stop it! Down boy, down," she shrieked as her mutt, still in the bag, began wriggling, drool dripping from its chops. "You and your disrespectful ways, you've upset my Barky. Bichons are very sensitive—"

"I'm very sorry. Honestly, I didn't mean to offend you. But I have to say, I'm not from the east coast and whatever your dog is, it's not a Bichon—"

Both old ladies gasped in unison.

"Our apologies, ma'am." Arlo stepped in. "My friend's been in the sun a little too long. He needs a cool drink to recover."

"I kinda reckon he's already been drinking, and I don't mean a root beer."

"Geraldine, come on," the orange-haired woman said, easing her friend away. "We don't want any trouble, not on Jake's Day. Let's find a shady spot and fix poor Barky's ribbons." She made to pat the dog but whipped her hand away when it growled and snapped at her fingers.

"I haven't been drinking, and I don't need—" But Lucian didn't have the chance to finish, as Arlo steered him out of the crowd.

"Where—"

"Just keep going."

"But—"

"There're no buts. Do you want me to have to bail you out of jail? Calling out somebody's mutt, and mocking the sacred image of the big man, will either get you thrown in the slammer or run out of town."

With the plaster Jakes marking the highlight of the parade, and its finale, the crowds were shifting and thinning out as people headed toward the park to picnic with family and friends, or visit the food trucks that always set up for Jake's Day.

"The Jake Collier Memorial Park," Lucian said as the park gates came into view. "This is where the Jake Collier Museum is, isn't it? I visited, soon after I got here. They have a pair of his boots on display. Did you know that? Honestly, I'm surprised they don't have the man himself stuffed and mounted on the wall."

Arlo looked down into eyes shining with mischief. He dipped his head, so his lips were just a kiss away from Lucian's ear.

"Don't let anybody hear you say that, not if you want to get out of here alive."

Lucian chuckled. "Will I be sacrificed on a stone altar, or hit by a righteous thunderbolt?"

"Man, you're going to get yourself in trouble one of these days."

"Oh, I think I already am," Lucian said, smiling, as he eased his way through the crowds.

CHAPTER TWENTY-THREE

"Hey, you two, come join us — Francie and her mom have cooked enough to feed the entire state."

Arlo swung around as a heavy hand landed on his shoulder. Hank held up a chicken drumstick with the other. "But we've got some cheese," he added, looking at Lucian.

Arlo waved at the Mason family gathering, a few yards away. But he didn't move.

"Hey, Hank, that's good of you, but I told Francine we wouldn't be joining you. This is Lucian's first Jake's Day, so I'm introducing him to the town's best tradition."

Hank smiled but said nothing as his eyes narrowed, and his chin lifted. It was so slight, few would notice, but Arlo did; his stomach tightened. Hank might as well have shouted out bullshit. It was the same look he always got every time he said something Hank didn't believe. His friend had done it since they were kids, and he was still doing it.

"Sure you are," Hank said with a smile, before he

switched his attention to Lucian, who hovered at Arlo's side. "You're in good hands with Arlo. Safe hands."

"Safe?" Lucian's head twisted from side to side as he scanned the laughing, good natured scene spread out around them. "It doesn't look dangerous — although some of the picnic foods I can see look scary— Oh, I'm sorry, it's my mum," he said as his cell rang. "I have to answer otherwise she'll send a search party out from the UK. Nice to meet you again, Hank." Lucian stepped away.

"What's going on?" Hank kept his voice low. "Francine told me you'd turned down the invite to spend the day with us." He glanced toward Lucian, a few steps away and concentrating on his call.

"Nothing's going on." Hank narrowed his eyes again, and Arlo let go of an exasperated sign. "Look, we're just friends, Okay?"

Hank answered with a quiet laugh.

"Whatever you say, Arlo, whatever you say."

"It is what I say, so don't—"

"Sorry about that," Lucian said, rejoining them, smiling as he looked from Arlo to Hank, and back again.

"I'll be in touch, Arlo." Hank waved his goodbye as he left.

"Oh, look, they're beckoning us over. Including that, um, man with the pudding bowl haircut and wearing… a poncho? I think Francine's arm will come off if she waves any harder. Maybe we should—"

"No. let's go."

"But—"

Away from the main group of picnickers, the crowds were less dense. Lucian trailed silently behind him.

"I'm sorry about that." Arlo golf balled his cheeks. "I

probably seemed like a jerk, but we'd have been trapped with them for the rest of the day."

"But they're your friends."

"Yes, they are. But today's your day. Do you really want to spend the day with them? If you do, we can go back."

A wry smile curved Lucian's lips.

"If you put it like that… Friends can be wearing, especially when they think they know what's good for you and can't resist telling you. It's why I think flowers are often so much better company."

"Better company than me?" The words flew from Arlo's lips before he could catch them. It was Lucian who was supposed to have a lack of filter.

"Oh no, not you. You're the only one I make an exception for, even if roses are more witty, and orchids more—"

"Okay, mister, you can quit with being a smart ass." Arlo tried to sound stern and intimidating, but nailed down by Lucian's wide-eyed gaze, he didn't stand a hope in hell.

"I'd rather not quit, because it's my only chance of ever being considered smart. Come on, let's see what we can get to eat because I'm famished. Honestly, I could eat a scabby donkey."

Arlo's jaw dropped, the conjured image grossly fascinating. "Never saw that on any menu," he muttered as he followed Lucian toward the food trucks.

All the local restaurants and coffee shops were showcasing their menus. There were the usual burgers, pizza, and tacos, but there were also Middle Eastern and Far Eastern foods.

"This isn't the Jake's Day offering I remember growing up." Arlo stopped beside Lucian, who was inspecting the chalked menu next to a truck selling wraps of char-grilled skewered meat, but also hummus and falafels. "The most exotic thing you could get was a cheeseburger."

"The good old days, eh?" Lucian insisted on paying for their food, Arlo being left to grumble when Lucian refused to take no for an answer.

Finding a shady patch of ground beneath a large tree, they ate in easy, companionable silence — or at least for a few moments.

"Oh, bollocks." Lucian's voice, loud, crystal clear, and as clipped as the haughtiest Lord in a BBC costume drama, drew undisguised interest from those nearest to them.

"It's okay folks, he's British." Arlo smiled at the curious faces. Heads nodded and lips curved into smiles, and some rolled their eyes, as though the explanation said it all.

Arlo turned back to Lucian, who was picking pieces of falafel and pickled vegetables off the front of his formerly pristine white T-shirt. A blob of tahini sauce oozed its way down.

"Aren't you a little old not to have learned to eat in public?"

Arlo kept his face straight as Lucian glowered up at him over the top of his glasses.

"Nanny was sacked because we caught her pilfering bottles of my father's best Lafitte from the wine cellar before she could teach me. I really am awfully feral." Lucian scooped the dripping tahini from his T-shirt, transferring more to the tip of his nose and the corners of his lips than into his mouth.

"How do you cope with dressing and washing? Do you

need a caregiver? There must be somebody crazy enough to take the job." Arlo bit into his own, more manageable, sandwich.

"Are you offering? I promise I'll be a very compliant client."

Arlo's food lodged in his throat and he took a swig from the soda they'd bought to go with their food.

Taking care of Lucian... was he offering? Yes. No. No. You've got a lot of love to give... Francine's words echoed in his head.

"This T-shirt is well and truly ruined. Honestly, I should have chosen something less messy." Lucian bit into the wrap, managing at the same time to squirt yogurt sauce onto his chin. "Oh, god..." He put the wrap down and wiped his face, but only succeeded in smearing the mess all over his lips.

"Jeez, it's like having lunch with a clumsy toddler."

"Get used to it, because I'm convinced it's hereditary. Dad was the same. If he could knock something over, or drop it, or spill food down his front, he did. He was a total klutz, as Mum always says, even worse than me if you can believe it. She says she thought it was adorable, and it was what made her fall in love with him."

"Hereditary, eh? Come here." Arlo put down his sandwich and picked up a spare napkin. Without thought, he leaned forward and wiped the mess from Lucian's nose, cheek, chin. And lips.

His fingers slowed, then stopped, nothing separating his tingling fingertips from Lucian's warm, pillowy lips, nothing except a scrap of thin tissue paper. The laughter and chatter in the park grew quieter, until it faded to nothing, leaving only the hard, racing beat of his heart and his ragged breath. What am I doing? But whatever it was, he was powerless to stop, as his fingers twitched into life, gently sweeping the napkin over Lucian's lips.

Lucian's hand came to rest on his. It was shaking, Arlo registered through the fog filling his head. Shaking, almost as much as his own hand. Taking the napkin from him, Lucian looked down at the thick white sauce, as if he didn't know what it was or how it'd gotten there.

"Thank you." His words were so quiet they were barely even a whisper; he looked up, and Arlo caught his breath.

The thud in Arlo's chest was hard and heavy, pounding his ribcage as Lucian's gaze met his own. Lucian's eyes were black, their pupils blown and distended, stealing away the deep blue of their irises.

"I'm sorry I'm such a mess, Arlo. But you've probably realized that already?" Lucian crumpled up the tissue and gave him a small, unsteady smile.

No. No, you're not... Arlo's heart protested, but before he could tell him, before he could counter the resignation threading through Lucian's words, the world crashed in on them as noise flooded where there had only been the galloping beat of his heart, as a scratchy guitar ripped through the bubble that had enclosed them.

Arlo jerked away as Lucian veered back. Clapping erupted all around them as a troupe of teenagers murdered a classic Springsteen number, strutting on a rigged up stage.

"They're marginally better than the Collier's Creek Cowboy Combo. Perhaps the Cowboys will perform later and we can line dance." Lucian smiled, but there was a self-consciousness about it. His eyes, though, were now more blue than black. Whatever had happened, it was gone. They were back on track, and Arlo didn't know whether to be grateful or despair.

The teenagers moved on to screech their way through a Nirvana number, destroying their parents' treasured memories.

"I think this is where we leave." Arlo stood and extended his hand for Lucian to take. Lucian grinned and clasped him tight, allowing Arlo to pull him up. Lucian's grip was warm in his, and regret burst inside of him when he slipped his hand free.

"Look at that sign. Over there." Lucian pointed to a big painted arrow, with the words Fair This Way.

"My god, it reminds me of home." Lucian beamed, as bright and warm as the afternoon sun, as they followed the arrow and emerged into the fair.

"At Danebury, for the annual seasonal events, we always stage a traditional fair with all the old-fashioned games. There's nothing even remotely electronic. We also have a Victorian merry-go-round, like that, but older look-ing." He pointed towards the carousel, the plaster horses pretty in pinks, golds, and myriad other colors, sedately rising and falling as they went around and around in never ending circles.

Lucian leaned into Arlo and lowered his voice to a stage whisper. "The last time I went on it was after I'd been helping to judge the cutest pet show, because having a menagerie of cute pets I was, of course, suitably quali-fied. I was mortified when they barred me from entering Percival, my guinea pig. Honestly, he'd have stolen the show. The winner was a very snappy terrier, and when I tried to attach the winner's rosette, the bloody thing went for me. I was traumatized, so naturally I had a sample of the homemade fruit wine at the Women's Institute stall. Or several. Having a ride on the merry-go-round then seemed like an excellent idea."

"And was it?" Arlo smiled, already knowing the answer.

"No. I soon got very dizzy, then queasy, and when I staggered off, I was… somewhat unwell. Over a small child."

"You barfed over a young kid?" Arlo shook his head as he laughed. Poor kid, but it couldn't have been more Lucian if he'd tried.

"It's not funny." Lucian huffed. "It was awfully embarrassing. Mum, fortunately or not, depending on how you look at it, was swanning around, in full on Lady of the Manor mode, and she saw the whole thing. To my eternal shame, I'd attempted to run away, but being unsteady on my feet due to the pet trauma, I tripped over and went flat on my face. She suggested I retire to my room for the rest of the day."

"What happened with the kid?" If anybody else had told him the story, Arlo would have given them the side eye, but this was Lucian…

"Cleaned up and given an ice cream, I suspect. After that, at all the other public events, my involvement remained strictly floral related. No more pet judging for me."

"So, a turn on the carousel—"

"Is off limits."

What else is off-limits? But Arlo buried the traitorous thought.

"Come on, let's have a look around." Lucian grabbed his hand and hauled him forward.

"Baggo!" he exclaimed, pointing to a booth with a large, brightly painted board. "I love this, and I'm pretty good at it."

"Baggo? You mean corn hole." Arlo couldn't see the point in throwing bean bags into a hole, but Lucian was almost jumping with excitement. He handed over the cash, refusing to listen to Lucian's protests. The booth holder placed a pile of colorful beanbags in front of Lucian, who picked one up, feeling its weight, his expression so serious, determined, and resolute, Arlo fought to keep a straight face.

"Right. This is a warm up shot." He rolled his shoulders, then stretched his neck from side to side. Steadying himself to take aim, his arm came around in a perfect arc, releasing the beanbag at its apex. It glided through the air — and missed, not just the hole but the entire board.

"Oh." Neither the next bag, nor the one after, fared any better.

"Here, let me." Arlo took the last bag, sending it flying through a hole without touching the sides. But it was too late, any chance of winning a prize gone.

"Perhaps I'll have better luck with the whack-a-mole."

He didn't.

"So, you were good at sports when you were in high school, huh? Because your hand-eye co-ordination is something special." Arlo dug his nails into his palms, concentrating on the pain to stop the laughter threatening to bubble up as Lucian glowered at him.

"I attended an exclusive public school, which thought very highly of itself even if I didn't, as a day pupil. It might be hard to believe, but I wasn't exactly the first choice for being picked for team games."

Arlo widened his eyes in mock surprise. "Gee, Lucian, I would never have guessed that in a million years. Not with your natural, athletic ability." Arlo's palms had long since gone numb, and finally he began to laugh.

Lucian's lips twisted into a wry smile. "I didn't fool you, then? I just wanted to win a prize for once, because I never win. Not at life or love. Not even a tenner on the lottery. My ticket's never been called in a raffle." His shoulders slumped. "Perhaps it's time to stop wasting my time and money. And yours."

Arlo's heart twisted. Losing at life and love? Lucian was sweet and good natured, too damn…. adorkable… to always have his legs kicked from under him.

"Hey, look." Arlo spun him around and pointed over Lucian's shoulder. "Ring toss. You want a prize so bad, I'll win one for you."

"You don't have to do that. Honestly." A light flush colored Lucian's cheeks.

Arlo swallowed. He did, he really did. "Come on."

Guiding Lucian toward the booth, he looked up at the star prize for getting every ring over the necks of the lined up bottles without knocking them over. A large black and white stuffed toy, a gruesome hybrid of a racoon and — piglet? It was horrible and would likely give a kid nightmares for weeks, but he didn't care what it looked like, not when Lucian was smiling at him with pure, unadulterated joy.

"My hero," Lucian said, and Arlo's heart danced. He didn't give a damn about the booth holder's gaze shifting between him and Lucian. He could think what he liked. All

Arlo knew or cared about was doing this for Lucian, for the prize he never won.

He weighed the rubber rings in his hands, calculating how much force to put behind his throws, judging the angle, the distance, the trajectory. They were, he suspected, weighted to ensure they veered off course. All of it took just a split second to calculate before, taking aim, he threw.

One, then two, then three hoops landed. The fourth balanced on the top of the bottle before it, too, clattered down. Just one more and he'd win the top prize for Lucian. Sucking in a deep breath, letting it go slow and steady, he aimed, he threw — and it landed cleanly.

A loud round of applause broke out, and he swung around. A small group had gathered, and he accepted the congratulatory pats on the back and the shoulder squeezes.

"Cometh the hour, cometh the man." Lucian flung his arm around him, burying his head into his chest before springing back, a smile so bright on his face it put the sun to shame. "My hero indeed — and I'm guessing you did do sports in school, and got picked for all the teams."

"Maybe," Arlo croaked. He'd do it all again, win Lucian all the prizes, just for that smile.

Collecting the prize from the tight faced booth holder, with a flourish Arlo presented it to Lucian.

"Your prize, my Lord." He bowed.

"Thank you, my good Sir. I will remember your bravery to my dying day. You are, indeed, my hero. I'll treasure it forever because it'll remind me of spending this perfect day with you." Lucian accepted the furry hybrid with a grave nod, before he laughed, light and filled with joy, as he hugged the toy tight to his chest.

CHAPTER TWENTY-FOUR

After the fair, they made their way back to the park. The teenage musical assassins had gone, replaced by those who could play their instruments and sing in tune.

Lying back on the grass, sharing snacks and sodas, conversation light and meandering, it was the most relaxed Arlo could remember feeling since... he wasn't sure when.

"Oooh, look. Over there." Lucian pointed. "I really hope we didn't offend them because we didn't join them earlier."

In the distance, Hank, Francine, and the rest of their group had packed up and were heading out. They wouldn't be offended, but they sure as hell would be speculating all kinds of... speculations.

His friends weren't the only ones leaving. The crowds in the park had thinned out as day turned into evening, the sky now a deep purple bruise. Soon, it would be fully dark.

"You ever been into the mountains at night?"

"God, no. I've hardly ventured into them during the day. All those bears and wolves. I joined a hiking group when I first got here, because I love walking through the fields and woodland at home, but I soon found out mountains are a tougher proposition. The average age must have been about seventy, but my god, they were like mountain goats on steroids. They kept having to stop and wait for me. It was awfully embarrassing, and I expect they were relieved when I didn't turn up again."

Arlo hesitated. It had been the best day he'd had since he'd come back to the Creek. The clumsy, sweet natured young Englishman had made him smile and laugh more than he'd done in a long time, sweeping away the niggling feeling of disconnection that had scratched at him since he'd returned to the town that hadn't felt like home anymore.

"The mountains take on a distinct character at night. We could drive up to Jake's Lookout, and... look at the stars," Arlo finished lamely.

Silence wedged its way between them. Maybe Lucian would say no, maybe he'd thank him for a lovely day, maybe he'd pretend Arlo hadn't suggested whatever it was he had suggested, and tell him it was time he went home. Maybe Lucian would—

"I'd love to."

"You would?"

Lucian nodded, a smile dancing on his lips.

It took a while to push through the crowds. Many were making their way home, but just as many were moving off toward the bars. They'd all be crowded as the townsfolk stretched out what was left of Jake's Day. Finally, they reached the parking lot, and minutes later, they were leaving the town behind them. As they climbed, taking one twisting road, then the next, Collier's

Creek finally disappeared, eaten up by the encroaching darkness.

"Thanks for today. I had a wonderful time."

Arlo cast a glance over at Lucian. The dashboard's muted lights lit up his face. He was smiling, relaxed and at ease — and still clutching the stuffed soft racoon toy that looked more like a piglet. *I'll treasure it forever... Every time I see it, it'll remind me of spending this perfect day with you...*

Lucian's words, when he'd presented the toy to him with a flourish, now dug and gouged at his heart. He'd be a memory, something warm for a little while, before it cooled and faded away for good. Lucian's brief stopover in Collier's Creek would be nothing more than a line or two in the story of his life.

Arlo pulled up on a rough, leveled out patch of grass and cut the engine. Silence hung heavy and absolute, a thick, physical weight. Arlo cleared his throat. He needed to say something, anything, to pierce the silence.

"Not too many folks bother to come this far. There are lots of easier places to see the stars, and with better parking, but Jake's actual lookout, according to local legend, is just a few minutes' walk."

"Where he stood, no doubt looking all heroic and butch."

Arlo chuckled. "Come on, we can't see anything from in here."

The only sound to be heard was the rustle of a light breeze tumbling down the mountains. Up above them, the clear sky glittered with stars, every one of them pulsing and twinkling as though they were breathing.

Arlo glanced at Lucian, who stood so close he could

feel the warmth of his body and the light brush of his arm against his own. Lucian was perfectly still, his neck craned back. His heavy hair tumbled behind him like a dark waterfall as he gazed into the heavens.

"I don't have the words…" Lucian whispered.

It would have been so easy to make a quip, a little joke, a snarky remark, and Arlo might have, at any other time, but now any words he had melted away like the last of the winter's snow.

"I thought the view was spectacular from your house, but… this." He waved an arm toward the vastness. "The only time I've seen anything even remotely like this was when I was a kid. We stayed with some relatives in the far north of Scotland, miles even from a hamlet, let alone a town. They were dreadful people, even colder than their horrid old castle.

"Late one night, I snuck out and went down to the loch with a blanket and just stared and stared up into the sky. Never, ever, did I think I'd see anything as beautiful ever again. Or not until now." Lucian turned to Arlo, his smile soft, his breath warm, his lips parted, damp and glistening.

"It is beautiful, but it's not as beautiful as this."

Arlo cupped his hands to Lucian's face, feeling the first faint signs of scruff against his palms. Lucian sighed as Arlo's lips brushed his, his mouth softening and opening, little moans escaping him. As their lips pressed together, so did their bodies. Arlo threaded his fingers through Lucian's hair, shifting his head a little, repositioning him, so as he could kiss longer, deeper, harder. He should stop, he should pull back, because this was everything he'd told himself he wouldn't do, taking risks rather than running from them, but whatever voice whispered to him, the thunder of his heart and the rising rush of blood through his veins drowned out every word.

Breaking the kiss, breathing in deep the clear mountain air, Arlo rested his brow against Lucian's. The younger man was breathing just as fast, each breath as ragged as his own.

"I wasn't supposed to do that."

"No, and I wasn't supposed to let you. But if this is what friends do out here in the mountains, I'd have made more of an attempt to make some when I first arrived."

"Oh, Lucian." Arlo laughed softly as he ran his fingers through Lucian's hair.

"So what happens now?" Lucian asked, all levity gone. "Because in all honesty, I've got no idea. You kissed me before, then pulled back. Friends, you said. But friends don't kiss under the stars. I—I'm not very good with mixed messages."

"And I'm not very good at giving them. Or that's what I always thought." No wonder Lucian was confused, because he sure as hell was.

"Then why have you?"

Arlo hesitated, the answer he didn't want to give burning on his tongue. But he'd made the move he'd vowed not to make, he'd been the one to blur the line. He owed Lucian an honest answer.

"Because I was scared. I guess I didn't want to put myself in a situation where I might get hurt again. But Francine said something to me…" She'd said a lot, some of it he'd not been keen on hearing. He swallowed. "It—it kind of dug its way in and I couldn't shift it. It made me think about the path I'd set myself on since coming back, and it's not the one I want to be walking."

Arlo's heart clenched. Alone, and lonely even in a crowd of friends, looking in from the outside. You're not meant to be alone... Francine's words shivered down his spine.

"I've spent most of my life being scared. I don't really know why. Mum says I've got a sensitive soul." Lucian snorted. "Thin skinned, is what she means. Too thin. But what I know is that I'm sick and tired of it, because people sense it — men sense it — and it kind of makes me easy prey. They take advantage, and end up mistreating me, knowing I won't make a fuss and I'll put up with whatever scraps they throw my way. Coming here, I thought a change of location would give me the jump start I needed, but I'm still scared."

"Are you scared of me?" Arlo swept aside the warm, silky hair from Lucian's brow.

"No, no I'm not."

Arlo licked his dry lips. "Then perhaps we can try to be... not scared together?"

"Perhaps we can — try? If nothing else, it'd stop Francine trying to set you up with any more upright practitioners of the noble art of dentistry. Think of me as your armor against shit matchmaking."

Arlo laughed. It bubbled up from his belly, filled his chest, then burst out of him, filling the night sky, and Lucian joined in.

"You up for a short climb?"

Lucian nodded, and Arlo pulled a thick blanket from the pickup, along with a heavy flashlight.

"A blanket? What kind of boy do you think I am, Mr. McDonald?"

"The kind of boy who likes to lie on the ground and look up at the stars. Come on."

A short but steep climb along a clear track took them to a wide, flat ledge.

Arlo watched as Lucian spread his arms out and turned slowly.

"The stars are like diamonds scattered on a black velvet cloth." He let his arms drop to his side. "Listen to me. I sound like I'm in a cheesy romance, going on about the starry sky."

"I like cheesy romances. Come and lie down and get super cheesy."

Lucian sniggered. "That sounds — delightful."

"Just do as you're told."

"Yes, Sir!" Lucian dropped down next to him.

They sat close, but not touching, and a sudden engulfing shyness overcame him. Cuddling under the star-lit sky, kisses and maybe more. It was why he'd grabbed the blanket. They'd already crossed a threshold, so wasn't it up to him to make the next move? Any kind of move? Instead, he felt as awkward as a teenager on a first date with big ideas and no clue how to carry them out.

"It was a song, wasn't it?"

"What was?" Arlo jumped as Lucian's clear voice razored through the air.

"Putting a blanket on the ground. My dad loved country music. He played it all the time when I was little. Who sang it? Tammy Parton? Or was it Dolly Wynette? I think I've got the names right, because—"

Arlo stopped him with a kiss, pushing Lucian down and onto his back. Lucian gasped, then sighed, and Arlo's heart did the same as Lucian wrapped his arms around him.

The kiss was as dark and endless as the sky above them. Tongues twisted, fighting for dominance in the hot wetness. Lucian tasted of sweet caramel, the last thing they'd eaten as they'd sat in the park, but he tasted too of something so much better: he tasted of himself. Beneath him, Lucian whimpered and moaned, pulling Arlo closer as he pushed his hips upwards, his full, hard cock rubbing against Arlo's own arousal.

Oh, Jesus… This was everything Arlo told himself he hadn't wanted, hadn't been looking for, but here, now, with this man, it was everything his body craved and his heart cried out for.

Arlo broke the kiss. Straddling Lucian, his arms supporting himself, his hands planted either side of his head, he stared down at the man who'd crashed into his life and was shining a bright light into the corners of all his dark places.

Lucian's chest rose and fell, his breath coming in shallow, fast gasps. Moonlight fell across his face, picking out his swollen, damp lips, and his wide, dazed eyes which even the ugly glasses could do nothing to disguise.

"Why'd you stop?" Lucian panted, before he groaned. "Don't tell me you've changed—"

"No!" In the silent night, Arlo's hard denial seemed to bounce and echo off the mountains. "No way," he whispered, running his fingers through Lucian's messy hair before trailing his fingers down the side of his face, brushing over the first signs of rough, dark stubble. Lucian moaned and pushed into his touch as he closed his eyes.

"So beautiful," Arlo murmured. Lucian shook his head in denial.

"No, never been that. Too thin, too short, too—" Arlo pressed a finger to Lucian's lips, stopping the steady flow of disparaging words.

"Yes. Beautiful. Inside and out. But there's one improvement you could make."

"A face transplant?"

Arlo tutted and tweaked Lucian's nose.

"Ouch!"

"That's for talking out of your ass. Your glasses. Can you take them off? They kind of get in the way of kissing you."

He stared down at Lucian, but a worm of worry crawled through his gut as Lucian met his stare, his expression neutral and unreadable. Arlo's stomach crash landed in his boots. He'd killed the moment. Lucian would roll away and get to his feet, and suggest that maybe it was time to—

Lucian removed them, folded them in, and placed them to the side, saying nothing as he blinked up at Arlo.

Gazing at Lucian's starlit face, a lump the size of a boulder lodged in his heart. Beautiful didn't come close. Lucian's eyes were huge and, even in the moonlight, his eyelashes were thick and soot dark and way longer than they had any right to be. Without the glasses, Lucian looked younger, more innocent and untouched by the kicks and punches of life; a quiver of disquiet rippled through Arlo, and he swallowed. There were years between them, maybe too many.

As though reading his unspoken thoughts, Lucian reached up and tugged him forward.

"They're not the only things that come off." Lucian's voice, breathed into his ear, was lower, rougher, deeper than he'd heard before.

For all his sweetness, Lucian was an experienced man. All of Arlo's doubts washed away, and his flagging cock thickened.

Lucian shifted and unbuckled his belt. His hand sought his zipper, but Arlo pushed it aside and slowly eased it down over the bulge stretching the front of Lucian's jeans, feeling him shiver as the metal dragged over his swollen cock. Spreading open the denim revealed plain white boxer shorts, stretching over the solid ridge of Lucian's erection.

Arlo's mouth dried as he gazed down at the man spread out beneath him and, cupping him in his hand, he squeezed and kneaded, his heart pumping hard at the fulness pressing into his palm, at the heat, at the pulse of blood, at the tiny throbs and twitches. Pushing up into his palm, Lucian's moans sent a searing spasm of need deep into Arlo's balls, and his own needy, neglected cock demanded attention.

"Ah, shit." With trembling fingers, he wrenched his belt open, tugged his zipper down, and pushed off his jeans, taking his boxers with them.

Lucian's boxers had also gone, leaving him gloriously and beautifully naked from the waist down. Resting on his flat lower belly, Lucian's cock twitched impatiently.

"Jeez, Lucian, you're—"

"Don't say it. Please."

Arlo's heart stuttered. Don't say it? Don't say that Lucian was beautiful?

How many times had he been told he wasn't, for him

to not even stand to hear the word? Arlo ached to hold him close and tell him he was everything that word was and so much more, that those who'd said otherwise had been blind, fools, or both. Arlo drew in a deep breath. If he couldn't tell him, he could show him how beautiful he was.

He leaned down and brushed his lips over Lucian's in the softest of kisses, his heart fizzing at Lucian's shuddering sigh.

Kiss after kiss, each as soft and sheer as the lightest, airiest cotton candy. Gliding his hands down, Arlo trailed over the warm, taut skin of Lucian's belly, before finding his cock and wrapping his palm around the hot, wet shaft. He began a slow upwards stroke, guiding the foreskin of Lucian's uncut cock over the glistening head, before easing back down, all the time watching, transfixed, as Lucian moaned, and gasped, and cried, and arched his back, pushing deep into the touch.

"Oh my god, Arlo. That feels good. No, better than good, it's—"

"Shush. It feels as it feels. Just enjoy it, babe, just give yourself up to it and feel."

Above them, clouds were forming, scudding across the moon and plunging them into shadowy blackness before once more drenching them in warm, waxy light. For Arlo, the world had contracted to the beautiful man beneath him and to this moment alone. Nothing else mattered. Nothing else existed. There was only Lucian, and there was only now.

Arlo forgot all about his own pressing need as he lost himself in Lucian. Every gasped out whimper and cry, every gritted out, incomprehensible word was an arrow in his heart, piercing and bringing down his defenses piece by piece by piece.

Riding Lucian's cock with his tunneled fist, his other hand found Lucian's full, heavy balls. Rolling, rubbing, massaging, their hot weight filled his palm. Attuned to every shift in Lucian's body, his gut and nerves knew before what little remained of his rational brain, Lucian was moving towards the edge to tumble head first over the precipice.

"Arlo, I—"

"No, baby. Not yet." Arlo pressed down on the base of Lucian's cock, stemming the rising flood that threatened to break through the dam.

Lucian answered with a groaning wail as he threw an arm across his upper face. His lips stretched wide, his teeth bared in a grimace, as muttered words Arlo didn't even want to try to guess the meaning of were ground out into the night.

Arlo's own needs refused to be ignored any longer. He freed his aching cock from its cotton prison, hissing through clenched teeth as he wrapped his palm around his sensitive shaft, sweeping his thumb pad over the wet, juicy slit. In the last disintegrating corner of his brain, he questioned when he'd last been so dripping, so wet, so fucking, incredibly aroused. The answer came back, loud, clear, a sucker punch to his gut.

Never.

The word was an explosion in his heart, blasting him towards his own climax. Beneath him, Lucian had slung his arm away from his face. Gazing up at him, his eyes were a glittering, dark flame against the paleness of his face. Their gazes locked as their orgasms gained strength, their force both undeniable and unstoppable. Arlo captured both their cocks, jacking them in one hand, the drag of burning skin on burning skin slick with their combined juices was the red nuclear button that released the explosion.

Lucian cried out as he came, his hips thrusting upwards, still for the tiniest of moments, before they jerked hard as he emptied himself, spilling hot, slippery seed over Arlo's tunneled fist. Arlo's own orgasm, just seconds after, crashed through him, every part of his body twitching and jerking as he came with a force that seared the skin from his bones, evaporated the air in his lungs, and boiled the blood in his veins. His ears buzzed, white noise crackled with static in his head, the power of his climax a nuclear wind destroying what little part of him remained.

Their spent cocks, already softening, slipped from his grasp. Collapsing on top of Lucian, Arlo closed his eyes.

A light but insistent shake woke him up. For a moment he wasn't sure where he was, his brain too foggy to grasp anything.

"I hate to disturb your well-earned rest, but my arm's going numb. Plus, you're dribbling. From your mouth and elsewhere. And snoring."

Dribbling and snoring? Oh, jeez…

Lucian laughed.

"If that's an English sense of humor, it's not funny," Arlo growled, trying his best to sound pissed, but he wiped at his lips just to make sure.

"But seriously, my arm really is going numb."

Arlo rolled off Lucian, but not away. Lying next to him, he trailed his fingers over Lucian's face, before sweeping his sweat soaked hair from his brow. Lucian turned his head to him and smiled. It was soft, and dreamy, loose and relaxed, and with a jolt Arlo knew he wanted Lucian to look at him like that again, and again. You're not meant to be alone... Francine's words burrowed through the hard bone of his chest, through his rib cage, and into his heart, coming to rest in its deepest, darkest place. Maybe he wouldn't be alone. Not now.

"I really have had a wonderful day, even if the last part was a bit shit."

Arlo refused to rise to the bait. "Yeah." He affected what he hoped was a considering, thoughtful expression. "That good, huh? I'd give that a ten out of a hundred. On a good day. Which it wasn't."

Lucian's answering laugh was cool water on a hot day, and all Arlo wanted to do was to drink it in and never stop.

"I suppose we'd better..." Lucian gave a lethargic wave of his hand toward their bodies.

Arlo supposed so too, but neither of them moved, content just to lie together, their touch no longer heated but sated and content.

A harder breeze, edged with a chill, finally provoked them into moving. Pulling on jeans, they zipped and buckled up. Lucian yawned and rubbed his eyes. Arlo grabbed the chance.

"Will you come home with me tonight?" So I can take you to bed, and wake up with you in the morning...

"Oh god, I'd love to, but I promised Bibi I'd make a bouquet and displays for a wedding on Monday. It's a rush job, and I need to go in early. The groom-to-be is in the military, and he's going on a tour of duty almost straight after."

"But it's Sunday tomorrow. Can't Bibi do it? She's a florist and it's her business." Arlo tried to sound reasonable, but wasn't sure he was succeeding.

"She may own the business, but she's a truly terrible florist. God alone knows where she trained, if she even did. The happy couple deserve to remember their big day with joy, not horror. But," he said, looking down at his feet, toeing at a clump of tufty grass, "I should be free by about 1:00pm. If you are, that is. And if you'd like to meet for, erm, whatever?"

Arlo's heart flipped and flipped again. What had Francine called Lucian? Ardorkable. Lucian Arbuthnot Blaxston was adorkable in bucket and barrel loads.

"I'm free. I'll meet you at Bibi's." Even if he wasn't, he'd damn well cast aside anything to make sure he was.

They made their way to the path leading down to the pickup, Arlo's flashlight illuminating the way. Just before they descended, Lucian stopped.

"My glasses. I've left them behind."

"Wait here, I'll get them." Arlo rushed back, the flashlight picking them out on the ground. Maybe he could suggest Lucian give contact lenses a try. Picking them up, he looked through them and froze. The lenses were clear glass.

CHAPTER TWENTY-FIVE

Lucian hummed with delight as he bit down on the sweet, syrupy, crunchy baklava. He was stuffed, he couldn't eat another mouthful of the wonderful picnic Arlo had brought for their afternoon together. If he so much as thought about one more mouthful, he'd burst. He picked up another piece to test out his theory.

"Honestly, I can't eat another thing." Lucian eyed what was left of the picnic.

"You said that four pieces of baklava ago." Arlo, lying on his back, his arms crossed behind his head, smiled up at him.

"I had to make sure they were fit to eat. I mean, if they were off, we'd have had to take them back to the deli."

They were under the same tree they'd sat beneath the day before, when they'd come to the park for Jake's Day, yet it couldn't be more different. No crowds, no noise, no people almost. It was cooler, and cloud cover blotted out the sun. Lucian didn't mind, he didn't mind at all, because all that mattered was that he was here with Arlo. He swooped down and landed a sticky kiss on Arlo's lips.

"Thank you."

Arlo tilted his head. "What for?"

"For today. For yesterday. For being my gallant knight and winning me a prize. For taking me into the mountains to see the stars."

"Just to see the stars?" Arlo's lips lifted in a dark smile, and a delicious shiver tumbled down Lucian's spine.

"Can't think what else you might mean, but the stars were amazing, fabulous, awesome." *And so were you.*

Lucian pushed his glasses up on top of his head and looked out over the park. There were a few dog walkers in the distance, and some kids were playing, but they were so far away he and Arlo might as well have been alone.

"Take them off. You don't need them."

"You want me to take my clothes off?" Lucian laughed as he switched his attention back to Arlo. "What if Deputy Sheriff Ted Warren turns up? Or even Sheriff Morgan? How could I explain my immodest behavior?" His laughter died on his lips. Arlo wasn't laughing, his steady gaze serious as it met his. Lucian swallowed. "What do you mean?" He already knew, but it didn't stop him from fumbling for his glasses.

Arlo sat up and loosely wrapped his hand around his wrist, stopping him from pulling them down onto his nose.

"I know you don't need them. Last night, at Jake's Lookout, you forgot to put them back on. I know they're clear glass."

Lucian sagged, and Arlo caught him in his arms. "You must think I'm really stupid," he whispered, dropping his head forward. He couldn't meet Arlo's gaze and see the questions he didn't want to answer.

"No, I don't think that at all. But I know why you wear them. Or I think I do. Your ex, right? Miles? Come on, look at me."

Lucian hunched his shoulders, refusing to look up, because whatever Arlo said, he felt stupid because he was stupid.

Stupid for letting Miles get to him. Stupid for letting Miles make him run and hide.

A finger under his chin tilted his head up. Arlo gazed down at him, his gaze so soft and brimming with compassion and understanding, Lucian's heart stuttered in his chest.

Arlo cupped his face with his palm and gently swept his thumb across his cheekbone. The touch was warm and comforting, and Lucian nuzzled into it.

"I won't push you to tell me, but I hope you do."

Lucian closed his eyes, wanting only to feel Arlo's sure touch. He didn't want to speak, he didn't want to own up to his weakness, he didn't want to be the ground down, pathetic man Miles had molded him in to. But as Arlo's thumb brushed over his cheek, his heartbeat slowed, as regular and rhythmic as Arlo's touch. Arlo wouldn't judge him, and Lucian drew strength from the conviction; he opened his eyes and looked up, forcing himself to meet Arlo's gaze.

"I told you about him, how he always chipped away at me. I don't know why I let it happen, but I did. It wasn't as if I couldn't have walked away any time I wanted. Yet I didn't. Maybe it says something about me, that there's some defect in my character."

"No, never say that. The guy was a bully. Never blame yourself for what he did."

"I did at first, but then I felt a sense of relief, like someone had lifted a weight from my shoulders when I got that photo of the beach. Dumping me was the best thing he did. I only wish I'd had the courage to be the one to have done it."

Lucian lifted the glasses from the top of his head and looked down at them.

"They're so ugly. I chose the ugliest ones I could find, because that's how he made me feel. They were a mask, and I knew it. I knew what I was doing when I bought them." He snorted. "God alone knows what the optician thought. Mad, probably, when I said I didn't want an eye test, I just wanted some frames with clear glass. I told everybody I'd become shortsighted, so they wouldn't ask why I was suddenly wearing specs.

"When I got them, I felt better because I had a mask I could hide behind. It was easier to look at the world from behind the barrier I set up. Miles said they were the most disgusting things he'd ever seen and tried to get me to go for contact lenses. Which I didn't need, of course.

"It was the only time I openly defied him and stuck to my guns. He hated me wearing them, and I got a kind of perverse kick out of it. But of course once I began wearing them I couldn't suddenly stop, so they became a habit, like brushing my teeth or having a shower each morning."

"You can break the habit. It'll just take a little time."

Lucian turned the glasses over and over in his hands. It would be so easy to snap them in two, to chuck them into the trash, to throw away everything they represented, but…

"I should get rid of them, I know that, and I've tried. Soon after I came here, I even left them in the apartment one time before setting off for work — I hadn't been quite brave enough to throw them away — but I only got a few yards before I panicked and rushed back. I couldn't do it. I couldn't make myself face the world, even a world where I didn't know anybody, without them."

"You were alone, but you're not now." Arlo leaned forward, and Lucian sighed as Arlo kissed him, the brush of lips as soft and light as summer mist. No heat, no fire, just a simple affirmation that no, he was not alone, not anymore.

"I—I don't think I'm ready to get rid of them. Not yet. But when it's just us, in private, I could, maybe, not wear them? You know, take that bit of time to break the habit?" His fingers tightened around them.

Arlo smiled. "That sounds like a plan." He looked up at the sky. "Rain's coming. Let's go back to your apartment, where you can take your glasses off. And everything else."

Lucian grinned, extending his arm for Arlo to pull him up. Yes, that sounded like a plan.

CHAPTER TWENTY-SIX

"'Jonas Fisher... New York, Boston, Los Angeles' And now Collier's Creek. They really should include the town, don't you think?"

Lucian linked his arm through Arlo's, stopping him from walking away from the gallery's tasteful window display. He leaned in closer, peering at an ink drawing of two cowboys leaning on a wooden gate, the hands of one on the hips of the other.

"That's very Brokeback Mountain," he muttered. "I'm sure that wasn't in the window the last time I looked."

"Come on, I thought you wanted brunch." Arlo gave him an encouraging tug to get moving, but Lucian wasn't going anywhere. They'd stopped outside the gallery for a good reason, even if Arlo didn't know it was for more than idle curiosity.

"Landscapes, as well as a healthy dose of homoeroticism. Yours are way better than those." Lucian nodded to a couple of canvases. They were good, but Arlo's were miles better.

Arlo gave a non-committal hum, but his eyes narrowed as he studied them, tipping his head one way and then the other. Unlinking his arm from Lucian's, he took a step back before taking a step forward, scrutinizing the works from all angles. Lucian looked away to hide the smile he couldn't contain any longer.

Movement behind the window display caught his attention. A tall, slender man in a classic navy blue suit was studying the displayed work on the walls. He turned, caught Lucian's eye, and raised his lips in a reserved smile. Jonas Fisher himself, and he was on his own. It was now or never, and if it was going to be now, Lucian had to take matters into his own hands.

"Come on." He grabbed Arlo's arm, not leading him along the street and toward brunch, but bundling him into the gallery.

"Lucian! What the—"

But Arlo didn't get any further as Lucian plastered himself against the door.

"You need to let people other than me see your paint-ings so they, too, can tell you how good you are."

Arlo cursed under his breath.

"Gentlemen." Jonas Fisher glided toward them, an amused twinkle in his eyes. "How may I help you?"

"Sorry, but we're just leaving." Arlo glowered at Lucian, who pulled up what he hoped was his sweetest smile.

"Really, but you've only just made an entrance." Jonas smirked.

"Good morning." Lucian held out his hand. "I'm Lucian Blaxston, and this is my friend Arlo McDonald. He's an artist and extremely talented. We'd like your gallery to show his work." Crisp and clear and confident, and cutting through the faint background music of mellow jazz. At least his voice wasn't shaking, even if everything else about him was.

Jonas offered a small nod as he took Lucian's hand in a light grip. "I'm always keen to promote and showcase local talent. I work by appointment only," he said, flipping his attention to Arlo, "but I'm happy to book you in. In which medium do you work?"

"There's been a miscommunication here. I do paint, but it's just a hobby. As Mr. Blaxston knows. We're sorry for intruding—"

"Acrylics and watercolors, mostly. Some oils." Lucian shook off Arlo's restraining arm. Plunging a hand into the hip pocket of his jeans, he pulled out his cell. "I've got some photos. I promise you'll want to make an appointment when you see these."

Lucian's pulse was riding a rollercoaster. If Jonas Fisher offered them a bland smile and declared all appointments were booked until 2050... His pulse did a 180-degree turn before corkscrewing, then flipping over.

"Mr. Fisher, I apologize for my friend. His enthusiasm's—"

"Well placed and fully deserved." Jonas' brows pulled together in concentration as he studied photo after photo. "I'd very much like to see more of your work. Can you bring in some canvases?" He scrolled through his phone. "Are you free on—"

Arlo held up his hands and took a step back. "I paint as a hobby, that's all."

"Mr. McDonald, these are not the works of a hobbyist. Believe me, I've seen enough hobby to know."

"He's always free, so any time will suit." Lucian grinned, making sure not to catch Arlo's eye.

With a date and time agreed, Lucian and Arlo were soon outside on the sunny sidewalk.

"What the hell just happened there?" Arlo blinked into the bright day. He looked dazed, as though a shrill alarm clock had dragged him out of sleep way too early.

"What happened was that somebody other than me and you is going to find out how amazing, brilliant, and downright bloody talented you are. I know you're probably more than pissed off with me, but it was too good an opportunity to miss."

"You shouldn't have done it. I don't like being forced into doing things I'm not comfortable with."

Lucian's heart tumbled. Arlo had agreed to the appointment for his sake, to not embarrass him. He was going to cancel it. He was—

"But I'm glad you did." Arlo's lips lifted in a crooked smile. "Even if when he sees the canvases, it's going to be a thanks but no thanks, enjoy your hobby and goodbye."

"But he won't. He took one look at the photographs and—"

"And when did you take them? I don't remember you doing that."

Lucian's face heated. "I got up early one morning. I had to, because all the snoring and the dribbling — from you, not me — got too much to bear. I got lost on the way to the kitchen to make coffee, and ended up in your studio. With my phone. Which just happened to be open on the camera." Lucian linked his arm with Arlo's and looked up at him. "I could say I'm sorry for pulling that stunt, but I'm not. You're a talented artist, even if you don't think so.

If I love seeing your art, why not others? Come on, you owe me brunch for setting you off on the path to international artistic fame."

CHAPTER TWENTY-SEVEN

"They've agreed," Lucian burst out as soon as he was through the door.

Bibi looked up from putting together an uninspired display, and Lucian winced at the jarring clash of colors.

"Who's agreed about what?"

Lucian sighed, loud and dramatic, and he threw in an eye roll for good measure.

"Arlo's paintings, and how good they are. I made him talk to Jonas Fisher, the gallery owner, because if I hadn't taken matters into my own hands, Arlo's canvases would still be gathering dust in his studio. Bibi," he huffed, "I told you this last week. Remember? Well, the gallery has agreed on a showing. The world needs to see them and now it will. Or at least Collier's Creek."

"Arlo's paintings? Gallery?" Bibi's eyes widened as understanding flickered into life. "Oh my god, yes, of course I remember. They're going to put on a show? That's wonderful."

When? How many paintings? Would there be refreshments? Her questions came thick and fast.

"I've got a poster. I was wondering…"

"You want to put it in the window? Sure you can — just so long as you finish this for me." She nodded to the arrangement Lucian was already planning on rescuing.

"So, what are you going to wear?" she asked casually.

"What? I don't know, I haven't thought. Jeans? A… shirt?" He'd been about to say T-shirt, but that probably wasn't the best answer.

"Do you have a good suit? Or at least a smart jacket and pair of pants?" Her frown told him she thought it unlikely. Lucian shook his head before nodding and shaking it again.

"Yes, but not here." He had an entire closet full of them, back at Danebury, every one of them handmade and the best Saville Row tailoring. Perhaps he could ask his mum to courier one over. No, not a good idea. She'd want to know why, and he wasn't yet ready to tell her about Arlo.

"Then we need to go shopping, and boy, am I going to be your sartorial fairy godmother." Bibi clapped her hands. "Not here in the Creek, though. We'll go to Boomfurt, they've got some great stores. And a haircut."

"No." Arlo loved to run his fingers through his hair, but Bibi didn't need to know that little nugget.

"Just a little tidy up, that's all. We could make a day of it. Shopping, lunch, maybe a cocktail." Bibi's enthusiasm was frightening.

"You've forgotten something. One, you don't pay me enough for shopping, lunch, and cocktails and, two, who's going to mind the store?"

"Ever heard of a credit card? As for the store, leave that to me."

"I don't know... I've got a good pair of trousers — pants, I mean — which would work." But they'd work so much better if he could get rid of the inconvenient Marmite stain. "I've also got a very good hand made shirt." Ditto Marmite.

Bibi arched a newly plucked brow. "Luci, you do want to make Arlo proud, don't you?"

"Of course I do." He bristled. What kind of question was that?

"Then make sure you do." Her voice softened, along with her smile. "This is important to Arlo, isn't it? Who knows what it might lead to. So be the best you can be for him on the day."

The day wore on as they dealt with a steady stream of customers. Lucian acted on autopilot, Bibi's words on a never ending loop in his head.

Of course he wanted to make Arlo proud and if having Bibi pull him around the stores for a couple of hours was what it took, then he'd grit his teeth and bear it. After all, it was only a few new items of clothing, and a haircut that would only be the trimmest of trims. That was all. Nothing at all to be concerned about. No, nothing at all.

Lucian sprawled out on the bed, breathing hard, a sweat drenched, melted heap of goo. The bed shifted and he opened his eyes. Above him, Arlo appeared. He was grinning, his lips and chin smeared with—

"Nooo!" Lucian tried to push him away, but he was

defenseless against the onslaught as Arlo smothered his face in kisses, forcing him to taste his own salty release on Arlo's lips. "You're disgusting. You know that, don't you?"

"That's why you like me so much."

Arlo stood up, his honed body naked and his dick at half mast. Lucian's mouth watered and he narrowed his eyes, his gaze following Arlo as he moved around the bedroom. Maybe he could return the favor of an early morning blowjob. Before he could make the offer, Arlo beat him to it.

"Christ, it's going to be a circus today." Arlo sat on the edge of the bed and ran his fingers through his mussed hair. "I know it's just a few paintings, but…"

A few paintings? Jonas had taken dozens of canvases. The whole gallery was going to be devoted to Arlo's work. Lucian shuffled across the bed, sat up next to Arlo, and took his hands in his.

"You're a talented artist, and it's time you believed that. And it's not just a few paintings. The gallery is yours tonight. Yours. Your paintings, your talent. Do you really think Jonas would go to that trouble if he didn't believe in you?"

Arlo's lips tilted in a crooked smile, but his eyes remained unconvinced.

"Ouch!" Arlo tried to snatch his hands away, but Lucian held on tight, refusing to let go.

"You pinched me," Arlo complained.

"Yes, I did, so you'll always remember what I'm saying. Paintings are created to be admired. Same with floral displays. Movies are to be watched, preferably with a giant carton of popcorn, and books are written to be read.

But if they're shoved out of sight so nobody can enjoy them, then what's the point of creating them in the first place? Don't let your art literally gather dust up in your studio, because it'd be criminal not to share it with the world. Okay, Collier's Creek for now, but who knows?"

Arlo looked down at their joined hands, his nakedness exposing not just skin but his fears and doubts, too.

"What if people don't like them? What if they think I'm trying to be somebody I'm not? I've always painted just for me—"

"But that doesn't have to change, does it? You can still paint for yourself, but it doesn't stop you from showing others. You showed me, remember?"

Arlo lifted Lucian's hand to his lips, and kissed every one of his fingers. "That was different," he murmured.

"Some people won't like your work, just like not everybody can like every book they read, or song they hear. And some will come for the free booze and canapés." Lucian smiled as he coaxed a small laugh from Arlo. "But most will be there because they want to be, because they want to support one of their own. A home grown, Collier's Creek artist."

"Maybe."

"There's no maybe about it. Jonas wouldn't be putting the time and effort into this if he didn't think it was worth it, financially and for the gallery's reputation. If he didn't have faith, this evening wouldn't be happening."

"Maybe you're right, and maybe I'm overthinking it." He looked less doubtful, less terrified. Not much, but it was a start. "Jonas wants me at the gallery for much of today — something about confirming the arrangements and other stuff — and there was me thinking you just stuck 'em up on the wall." They both laughed, easing the tension. "You will be there, right, for when they open the doors? You'll be back in time?" A frown worried at Arlo's brow.

"Nah, thought I'd hang out at Randy's instead. I just luuurve their ribs 'n' steak deal." Lucian rolled his eyes when Arlo's jaw dropped. "Of course I'll be there, you dope. I wouldn't miss it for the world. And yes, I'll be back in good time from the, erm, flower fair."

A flower fair had been the first thing he could think of when he'd told Arlo he'd be out of town for much of the day with Bibi. Shopping in Boomfurt, on the day of the showing, wasn't ideal, but sudden and short notice floral emergencies had taken up valuable time, along with Bibi twisting her ankle during over enthusiastic line dancing in Randy's. It was today or nothing, because Marmite stained clothes were not an option.

"Talking of which, I'd best get ready. We've both got a long day ahead before your triumph this evening." Lucian bounded out of bed and fled for the bathroom, glancing over his shoulder to see Arlo staring at him in abject terror.

CHAPTER TWENTY-EIGHT

The shopping mall was the size of a medium-sized English city. Or that's how it felt to Lucian. He needed a sit down, a cuppa, and a toasted teacake to summon up the energy to even think about tackling the place, but Bibi was having none of it as she planned the day with military precision.

"Okay, we need to start with the suit. That's your capsule piece."

"My what?" Whatever language she was speaking, it wasn't English. Bibi tilted her head, an indulgent smile on her face Lucian refused to believe was condescending.

"Luci, do you trust me?" She locked her gaze on his.

"Yes." No…. But, for better or worse, he'd put himself in her hands, even though he shuddered at what those hands might do to him if he didn't agree. He nodded vigorously.

"Good. We decide on the cut and color, and from there we kind of branch out to the shirt and shoes."

Lucian swallowed, as Bibi added further branches to the suit tree. This was going to cost him, and he'd be dipping into the allowance his mum insisted on depositing into his bank account each month. But this was all for Arlo, so whether it cost the earth, moon, sun, and stars, it didn't matter.

Bibi led the way and, he followed, a chick trailing after his mother hen, not to one of the big department stores as he'd expected, but to a small place that would have been easy to walk past. As they opened the door, a thin, dapper man looked up from behind a counter.

"Hi. My friend's attending an important function this evening and he needs something suitable to wear."

Mr. Dapper nodded. "I'm sure we can help. How formal's the occasion? Are you thinking a suit, or smart jacket and pants?"

Bibi quirked her head, and looked from Mr. Dapper to Lucian, and back again.

"It's a showing at a gallery, but I think my friend would look good in a suit. Navy blue, lightweight wool. Slim fitting." Bibi counted out the requirements on her fingers.

"Excuse me? I prefer slate gray." He was going to be wearing and paying for it, which gave him some skin in the game. Allegedly.

The salesman and Bibi turned to look at him, both with near identical pained expressions on their faces.

"The young lady's correct." Mr. Dapper said. "We can certainly put something together that strikes the right note. And navy blue will be perfect. It would make the most of your coloring and your eyes. Or what I can see of them."

Lucian pushed his glasses back up to the bridge of his nose.

They were shown into a large backroom with rail upon rail of jackets and pants in all different colors and shades.

Mr. Dapper pursed his lips as he looked Lucian up and down, before he plucked a jacket from one rail and a pair of pants from another.

"If the young lady would take a seat, you can come with me." Mr. Dapper ushered Lucian into a changing room.

Lucian threw up a prayer of thanks he'd remembered to put on a new pair of boxers and a dark pair of socks that didn't have any holes as Mr. Dapper ordered him to discard his well-worn jeans and the T-shirt which bore the marks of his tussle with that morning's breakfast toast and peanut butter. The stiff, white stain near the hem was of a more dubious origin which, Lucian hoped, his face burning, wasn't from when Arlo had needed some last-minute tension release.

"Excellent fit," Mr. Dapper muttered, as he turned Lucian this way, then that, tugging on the pants, checking the waistband, tweaking the jacket, pulling on the sleeves.

Mr. Dapper nodded, and placed his hands on his hips, before he flung open the changing room door. Dah-da, Lucian expected him to say, as he was presented for Bibi's inspection.

"Oh my goodness," she gasped.

Mr. Dapper inclined his head. "Normally, I'd recommend trying on several combinations, but in this case…"

"No, that's it. That's absolutely perfect. Luci, you are going to be the belle of the ball!"

"It's not a ball…" But neither Bibi nor Mr. Dapper took any notice as they exclaimed over the perfect fit, so good it might have been made for him.

"You're going to need a shirt. You stock them, right?" Bibi looked at Mr. Dapper, who smiled.

This was something Lucian didn't need to buy.

"I've got a good shirt, I don't need—"

Bibi huffed. "I've seen your so-called good shirt. A gray and white pin-stripe. It makes you look like an insurance salesman." Mr. Dapper, standing next to Bibi, shuddered.

"Pale blue, or maybe pink. The palest of pale, though," Bibi said, looking Lucian up and down.

"The palest of blue, so pale it's barely a hint, would work best." Mr. Dapper beamed.

"If I'm going to be forced into buying a new shirt, a white one would be…"

Bibi's and Mr. Dapper's withering stares stole away the rest of Lucian's protest. They'd defeated him and he might as well accept his fate.

"What about a necktie? Rich magenta would be a good choice," Mr. Dapper suggested.

"If this was for a wedding, I'd agree, but I think the overall look should be a little looser and not quite so structured."

"So you want a hint of casual? No necktie, and leaving the top buttons on the shirt undone would do that."

"Yes, that's right. It'd go with the suit's contemporary, slim fit and would complete the look." Both Bibi and Mr. Dapper peered at him.

Excuse me, but I am here, you know…

Mr. Dapper raised brows as groomed and flawless as Bibi's own. "You have an expert eye, if you don't mind me saying."

"I studied fashion and textiles at college, then I worked

in the industry for a while." Bibi shrugged and Lucian's mouth dropped open. It was the first he'd heard of it. So she wasn't always a terrible florist...

The first shirt wasn't quite night, neither was the second. The third was declared a success, and a final decision was made. All without a word from Lucian. Bibi was in full on battle mode in her quest to ensure he made a statement, although what that was he didn't quite know.

"Maybe it's about time I had a look?" From the moment he'd shucked off his jeans and T-shirt, Lucian hadn't caught so much of a glimpse of himself.

Mr. Dapper inclined his head and Bibi grinned as he pulled aside a drape to reveal a full sized mirror.

"Fucking hell."

Behind him, Mr. Dapper coughed, but Lucian didn't care as he inspected the man, who couldn't be him, who looked back at him.

The look was perfect. There was no other word. The color, the cut, the duck egg blue shirt open at the collar, the whole coming together to be more than the sum of its parts... Had his legs grown another six inches? Had his waist narrowed by the same amount? Had he made gym visits in his sleep, because his shoulders had never been so broad? He stepped in closer, looking for any clue that the man who stood before him really and truly was him, and not some imposter.

"So?" Bibi moved in behind him, her smile soft and warm as her eyes met his in the mirror.

"It's..." Incredible. Amazing. "Is that really me?'" His unsteady laugh failed to disguise the choke in his voice.

"Sure is. Glad you trusted your fairy godmother?"

Lucian nodded, his throat too thick for him to speak.

Minutes later, back in his jeans and T-shirt, and bidding Mr. Dapper goodbye, they left the shop.

Lucian's stomach grumbled. "Food?"

Bibi waved his suggestion aside. What had happened to lunch and cocktails?

"Shoes next," Bibi said. "Plain black. Oxfords. Should be easy enough. You gotta have a classy look to go with the classy accent."

"Yes, mother," he muttered under his breath. Both his friend and his mum had a lot in common.

As Bibi predicted, the shoes were easy enough to find in the mall, the purchase quick and fuss free. His stomach growled long and loud. He looked at his watch; lunch was already overdue.

"If I don't have something to eat soon, I'll have to eat my arm. Or yours. And now we've got everything…" He stopped outside a coffee shop, his mouth watering from the rich and savory aromas of hot sandwiches. Glaring at Bibi, he did his best to look his most rebellious, which wasn't very rebellious at all, but it was enough for Bibi to lead the way into the coffee shop.

"How's Arlo feeling about tonight?" Bibi asked as she looked at Lucian over the rim of her coffee cup.

"Oh, you know. Shit scared. Terrified. Bricking it. He thinks either nobody will come, or if they do, they'll hate it and know him for the talentless dabbler he believes himself to be. He's wrong on all counts."

"Hmm. But you've got to remember, it takes a lot of guts to try something different. From designing factories to Collier's Creek artist in residence is a leap. I get where he's coming from, but having you by his side later, looking good enough to eat, but maybe not as good as this sandwich," she said with a grin, "will make him feel a lot better."

They concentrated on their food, but a few minutes later, and full, Lucian pushed the remains aside.

"Earlier, you said you studied fashion and textiles. You've never mentioned it before." Bibi was a talker, but she'd never talked about this, and Lucian wanted to know more.

She shrugged. "It all feels like a lifetime ago. I loved fashion, and making a career from it was everything I always wanted. I even spent six months working in Italy, for a major fashion house. My prospects were on the upswing, and I thought life couldn't get any better. I was right, because it got worse." Like him, she pushed her unfinished food away.

Shadows of sadness and regret flickered across Bibi's face. Whatever had cut short her career, it had wounded her deeply.

"I'm sorry. If you don't want to say anything more, then don't."

Bibi shook her head. "It's not a dark secret or anything, it's just something I don't talk about because there's no point. It was my aunt. She got sick." She picked up her discarded napkin and rolled it into a ball between her palms.

"Aunt Betty more or less took over raising me from when I was fourteen. My mom had died a few years before and my dad, although a lovely man, was hopeless where I was concerned — he didn't have any idea about bringing up a child, beyond making sure it was washed, clothed, and had enough to eat. He especially didn't have any idea how to handle an opinionated and pushy girl who believed the world was wrong and that she was right about everything." Her lips lifted in a wry smile.

"Dad remarried, and I didn't get on with my stepmom. Looking back, I didn't get on with anybody. She's actually a good woman. I just needed to grow up to realize it, and we get along fine now. Anyhow, dad got a big promotion, but it meant a move south. I refused to go."

"But you were a kid. They must have made you. Or put you in boarding school?"

"If they'd have tried, I'd have made their life hell. I was really horrible…" Bibi grimaced. "They arranged, whether officially or not I don't know, for Aunt Betty to finish up raising me. We had a lot in common, as she was my mom's twin. It worked for all of us." She screwed the napkin into a tighter ball and threw it on her plate.

"When she told me she was sick, I was living in San Francisco. I was achieving all my goals. I'd set up a dress-making business and I had my own label. It was small but growing, and I was getting a lot of work alongside an excellent reputation. Then I got the call. She tried to persuade me not to quit doing what I loved. But I loved her more. That's what it came down to. So, I came home. I took over running the flower store. She taught me what she could. Just before she passed, she told me to sell the place and go back to California to do what I really wanted." Bibi shifted and looked down on her knotted together hands.

Lucian leaned forward and squeezed them tight. Bibi looked up and gave him a wavering smile.

"I couldn't. Not then. It seemed disrespectful, somehow. Aunt Betty had built the business up from nothing, and I was determined to carry on. And besides…" Lucian waited, as Bibi chewed on her lower lip as though debating with herself what to say next. "Others rushed in to fill the gap I'd created, and it would have meant starting over. Aunt Betty finally passed a year after I returned to the Creek. Between coming back and then, I reconnected with old friends and made new ones. I met a few guys. And the place had changed for the better. It was a lot less rough around the edges. Not so 'cowboy'."

Their gazes met, and they both laughed.

"Truth was, I found I enjoyed being home, and the call to go back to California grew quieter."

"So you dedicated yourself to the noble profession of floristry?"

"Hmm. Not exactly. Let's just say I've always been careful to hire very able and talented assistants."

"Just as well, because you're the worst florist I've ever encountered."

"Hey!" Bibi whacked him on the arm, but there was neither force nor malice. "I can make straightforward things."

"You really can't. I have to re-do most of your attempts."

"You do not!"

"I'm sorry the truth hurts."

"I should fire you right now."

"Then everyone would discover what a terrible florist you are and recognize my creativity for the genius it is."

Bibi tried to glare, before the attempt crumbled to dust, and she laughed.

"Okay, I'm a fraud, so sue me."

"Seriously, sell up and use your inheritance to do what you really want."

Bibi shrugged. "Yeah, maybe. But we've talked

enough about me. Today is about you, and making that man of yours drool with want."

Lucian choked on the last mouthful of his coffee, now barely tepid.

"I really wouldn't put it quite like that."

"I would. Come on, we've got to finish the job."

"What do you mean, finish the job?" Lucian asked as they headed out. She smiled, but declined to answer.

All was made clear when they came to a halt outside the glass wall of a hair salon, its interior white and stark, everybody from the receptionist to the stylists to the customers, all of them tall, skinny, and coolly attractive. It was everything that made Lucian want to cower, and he stepped back. Bibi stopped him with a firm hand between the shoulder blades.

"Don't you dare try to run."

"No, no way. I'm not getting my hair cut."

Bibi answered with a hard shove, and he stumbled through the door. Hauling him to reception, she pointed to his head.

"I need somebody to sort this out, if any of your stylists are up for the challenge."

"Bibi! Honestly, I really don't need my hair cut." The smirk on the sleek receptionist's scarlet lips told him something different.

"One moment, please." She rose from her chair, and glided across the salon floor, and through a door at the back. "Alejandro will look after you," she said, returning with a tall and impossibly handsome guy who looked as though he should have been modeling underwear rather than wielding scissors and cans of hair spray — neither of which were going to come within ten feet of him.

"I don't want my hair cut," Lucian blurted.

"Yes, you do Luci." Bibi smiled up at Alejandro, bright, shiny and as lethal as a shark. "He needs it short at the back and sides, but leave it longer on top."

"Preppy?"

"Exactly. Preppy."

"No!"

Alejandro bore down on Lucian, and teased his hair, before pushing it away from his face, pursing his lips as he nodded. "Preppy hair for a preppy face. Very cute," he said, with a faint Spanish accent.

Lucian gritted his teeth. He didn't want to be cute, except for Arlo, and he tried to pull away, but Alejandro had him in a firm grip. Maybe he could thump him and make a run for it, but Alejandro and Bibi would catch him before he'd got to the salon door, dragging him to the sink for a dousing of shampoo and conditioner, and bland chat about his upcoming weekend. He was trapped, and they all knew it.

"This way." It was an order, and Lucian followed, a lamb to the slaughter.

At the sink, with a towel around his shoulders and his head tilted backwards, Bibi's face appeared above him. She was faster than lightning.

"Hey! I need—"

"You can't wear your glasses while you have your hair cut." She tucked them into her purse, giving him a wiggly finger wave as she left him to his fate.

Shampooed, conditioned, and seated in front of an enormous mirror, Alejandro, still pursing his lips, got to work. He didn't attempt conversation, and Lucian was at least thankful for that small mercy.

Closing his eyes, Lucian concentrated on not wincing with every rasping cut of the scissors. Alejandro switched on a hairdryer, set at Disfiguring Burns level, which was followed by further tiny snips, before he sprayed something lethal on his hair, leaving his lungs scrambling for breath.

"Oh, my… that looks awesome." Bibi had come back over, and her voice was little more than a breath. Lucian opened his eyes, first one, then the other. And gasped.

If he thought he'd had trouble recognizing himself in his new suit, this was another level entirely.

The man who stared back at him, with the short hair and no glasses, was… he couldn't say the word Arlo insisted he was. The last time his hair had been so short, he'd been at school. But this was no brutal short back and sides. Short, yes, but sculptured rather than butchered. He prided himself on being an artist, and he recognized the artist in Alejandro. He blinked, and looked at Bibi's reflection, then Alejandro's, then Bibi's again. Both were smiling, and he smiled back.

"That's better. Yes?" Alejandro asked. Lucian nodded. How could he even try to deny it? "It shows off your lovely bone structure, those high cheekbones. And your eyes, ahh, muy guapo."

Bibi laughed. "You're right, but I'm afraid he's already spoken for. Aren't you Luci?"

Lucian's face pulsed with heat.

"Such a shame." Alejandro sighed.

They left the salon a few minutes later, but not before Alejandro offered Lucian a quiet invitation to get in touch, along with a wink.

"Haven't you forgotten something?" Bibi asked as they made their way back to her car.

Lucian stopped. Bags. Jacket. Wallet. Cell. He had them all, so what was she...

Bibi delved into her purse and held up his glasses. He went to take them, but she snatched them out of his way.

"You don't need them. They're not prescription."

"I do." He swallowed.

"No, Luci, you don't. I've known that for a while now. Sometimes you take them off, but you're not always so careful about putting them back on as you seem to think."

"I've kind of got used to them," he whispered.

"Then it's time to get unused to them. You don't need a mask. Whatever made you hide, you don't have to do it anymore. But it's up to you whether you put them back on. I'm not going to force you either way, but it's time to break the habit. Don't you think?"

Bibi's words mirrored Arlo's. They were both right. Wearing the glasses was a habit, and habits could be broken. Yet, he chewed down on his lower lip, still unsure. But Bibi knew... Bibi, who wasn't just his employer but his good friend.

He drew in a deep breath as he shook his head; he'd glimpsed a different man today, a man he wanted to know more of, and to see again.

"Keep hold of them," he said, his voice rough, "until we get back."

"And then?"

"I don't know."

Bibi slung her arm around his shoulders and pulled him in for a kiss on the cheek. "Come on, we need to head back. Arlo's waiting for you to do him proud."

CHAPTER TWENTY-NINE

Nerves tickled Lucian's skin as he approached the gallery. A group milled around outside, and even from across the square, he could hear excited chatter. This was Arlo's big night, and he was late. As though on cue, his cell pinged as a text dropped. He read it quickly, and tapped in a response before slipping it into the inside pocket of his jacket.

"Arlo?" Bibi asked.

"Yep. Wondering where I am. Panicking. But I did promise I'd be here when it started."

Bibi squeezed his shoulder. "There was nothing we could do about it. But you're here now, and he's going to forget all about his panic as soon as he sees you."

She was right about there being nothing they could have done to get back earlier. An accident had forced them onto the back roads, adding precious time to the journey home. But as to making Arlo forget all about his fear of the evening ahead, he wasn't so sure, even with the new look and the new haircut. His hand found the back of his neck, the absence of hair unfamiliar and strange.

At the door, a tall and impeccably groomed young woman inspected their tickets before smiling and inviting them to go in.

"That dress is from…" Bibi whispered, naming a couture house Lucian had never heard of. "Genuine, and no change out of five grand. I'm meeting some friends, and we're going to stage a full on assault on the canapés. Go find your man, Luci, and watch his jaw drop."

The gallery comprised a central viewing room with a couple of smaller ones coming off it. Chattering crowds filled every corner. As he eased his way through with smiles and apologies, a few heads turned his way before doing a double take. Where was Arlo? In the crush he couldn't see him anywhere, and even pushing himself up on tiptoes to try to see over what looked like hundreds and thousands of heads proved useless.

"Lucian. Oh, my." Jonas appeared in front of him, his shrewd eyes openly appraising as he took his time to look him up and down. "Have you turned into a swan? You look incredible, a fully realized work of art."

"A swan? Thanks. I think. But it kind of implies I was an ugly duckling before." Lucian's stomach clenched; it sounded too much like the truth.

"No, absolutely not. Your plumage was a little dowdy, perhaps, but now it's resplendent." Jonas smiled, but it made Lucian think of a fox eyeing up a rabbit. Or a duckling. "Let me get you a drink."

Jonas beckoned to a passing waitress circulating with a tray of champagne flutes. Picking one up, he passed it to Lucian, who took a sip.

"Now you're refreshed, let me take you to the man of the hour." Jonas leaned in close as he guided them through the crowd, one hand resting on Lucian's lower back. "Several pieces have already been reserved. Far, far more than would normally be at this stage of a showing. Your Arlo is a very talented man, and he's going to make quite the name for himself. He's also very lucky, very lucky indeed," he added, his voice dropping.

Oh, no… First Alejandro, and now Jonas, but at least the gallery owner hadn't winked at him. Yet.

"Ah, here he is. Arlo, your very own exquisite piece of art."

Arlo, in the center of a knot of people, turned. He was clutching a glass, his smile fixed, terror blazing in his deep hazel eyes. Just as Bibi had predicted, Arlo's jaw dropped, his nerves replaced by wonder. His Red Sea of admirers parted to let him through until the two of them stood just scant inches apart, the noise and crush of the crowd fading.

"You—you look…"

Lucian brought his hand to the back of his neck, feeling once again for the heavy fall of hair that was no longer there.

"Blame Bibi. She decided I needed a makeover. It's what we were doing today. We weren't at a flower fair. I'm sorry I lied to you. I'm not sure about it, though. The hair, or lack of, and everything—"

"Shut up and come here."

Lucian gasped as Arlo pulled him in, crushing his mouth to his. Tasting the sparkle of champagne on Arlo's lips, all he wanted was to savor every drop.

Oohhs and *aahhs* from those around them broke the kiss, but Arlo kept his arm tight around Lucian as though afraid to let him go.

"You look incredible," Arlo whispered in Lucian's ear. "So damn beautiful. Your glasses—"

"I feel a bit exposed without them in front of everybody, if I'm honest, and I keep trying to push them up my nose even though they're not there. Bibi knew they were fake. She told me it was time to break the habit." He offered a nervous smile. "I guess two of you can't be wrong, so I've decided to try and be brave."

"Are you feeling brave right now?"

"Yes, because that's how you make me feel." And safe and secure, appreciated and valued. Everything he'd never felt with any other man. Arlo made him feel it all. He made him feel loved. Lucian's breath hitched and his pulse raced as the word blossomed in his heart.

Love...

He swallowed hard, and dipped his head, no longer able to meet Arlo's eyes.

"Hey." With a finger under his chin, Arlo tipped Lucian's head up. "Bravery comes from within. You just need to find it. Only you can make you feel brave."

"If you say so."

"I do. Never hide those beautiful eyes, or anything of who you are, ever again. Throw 'em in the trash, because you don't need them anymore. Come on," he said, a wicked smile lifting his lips, "let's make a run for it, because everybody's looking at you and I don't like it. You're for my eyes only."

Lucian shivered, the growl of possessiveness in Arlo's voice waking up his dick and igniting his blood. Yes please...

"But this is your big night. We can't go, not yet." God,

had that been a squeak? He coughed. "You're selling loads, Jonas said."

Arlo sighed. "Yeah, I guess you're right. Still don't want you out of my sight, though, because folks are liking what they're seeing. Like Jonas."

Lucian followed Arlo's gaze. A little way off, Jonas, a foxy smile on his lips, raised a glass before taking a sip, his focus never leaving them. Arlo's fingers dug into Lucian's waist, pulling him in tighter, but his determination to keep Lucian close was thwarted when a young woman, a near clone of the one who'd inspected Lucian's ticket, came and whisked him away to give an interview with the local newspaper.

Lucian wandered around, squeezing through the press of bodies. Jonas had been right. Many of the paintings had discreet little red stickers stuck on the frames, showing they'd been reserved, next to their just as discreet price tags. Lucian smiled. Arlo had been open-mouthed when Jonas had said how much they would sell for. By the end of the evening, even if he sold just a few, Arlo was going to find himself considerably richer.

Through a break in the crowd, he spotted Francine and Hank. Deciding to say hello, he'd only taken a step or two when Jonas reappeared.

"Lucian." His voice was a soft purr. "From the moment I met you, when you dragged a very reluctant Arlo into the gallery, I said to myself, there's a diamond in the rough if ever I saw one."

"Oh. Right. Okay." He couldn't decide if that was a compliment or a veiled insult. He was so busy trying to work it out, he didn't notice Jonas move in closer, until he felt the discreet press of the man's body against his.

Instinct made him step back, but the wall left him nowhere to go. Lucian ran his finger up his nose, pushing up his absent glasses. So much for being brave.

"Arlo has a bright future ahead of him. As I said, he's a very, very lucky man."

A flame of pride flared in Lucian's chest. "It's not down to luck, but talent." He smiled up at Jonas, happy and relieved a professional had confirmed his own amateur assessment. His smile froze on his lips.

Jonas was laughing softly, his focus laser-like.

Oh… Jonas was a bird of prey and he was a tiny mouse, and directly in his line of sight. Lucian scanned the surrounding crowd, looking for an escape, but the gallery was busier than ever. Pressed against the wall and with Jonas blocking his way, he was cornered.

"Yes, his artistic career is very bright indeed. But it's not his lucky break I'm talking about." Jonas widened his eyes, inviting Lucian to make the connection he absolutely, no way, wanted to connect to.

"Hey, babe. Sorry I left you for so long."

Thank god… But Lucian's relief vanished as soon as it appeared. His breath stilled in his lungs. Arlo was smiling, not at him but at Jonas, and Lucian prayed that smile would never be turned on him. Like an animal preparing to attack, Arlo's teeth were bared.

Jonas' own smile was bright and breezy, as if unaware of the tension crackling in the air. Clicking his fingers for one of the roving waitstaff, they appeared with a silver tray crowded with champagne flutes.

Arlo shook his head. "No, I'm—"

"Arlo, this evening is a triumph. This level of interest — marked in the number of reservations and the cold hard cash that comes with them — is unprecedented for an unknown artist. Or unknown until tonight. Mark your success, because believe me in this world you're now a part of, it's as rare as hen's teeth. I was telling Lucian, just before you arrived, that you're a very lucky man."

"I know."

Gripping the stem of his flute, Lucian's nervy gaze flittered between them. Arlo's combative stare had mellowed a little, softening the snarl into something that was more, if only a little, like a genuine smile.

Jonas inclined his head. "You are indeed. Enjoy your night, Arlo, every single moment of it. We'll speak tomorrow." Raising his glass in salute, he excused himself and disappeared into the crowd.

Lucian sagged against Arlo.

"You okay?" Arlo asked, concern coloring his words.

Lucian nodded. "Yeah. He's a bit intense."

Arlo snorted. "That's one way of putting it. I could see he was making a move from right across the room. Are you sure you're okay? Jeez, I don't know how I stopped myself from laying one on him." He rested a palm against Lucian's cheek and all Lucian wanted to do was purr as he pushed his face into Arlo's warm, sure touch.

"I'm glad you didn't. Although, aren't all great artists meant to be tempestuous and temperamental? It could be your brand. The Punching Painter."

Arlo blinked down at him, before he grinned, the last of his tension and held back anger draining away. Lucian allowed himself a silent sigh of relief.

"Do you think we could just slip away and—"

"Arlo! You're the second most famous guy the town has produced, after my illustrious ancestor, of course!"

Both Lucian and Arlo looked around at the handsome, good-natured face of Sheriff Morgan.

"I heard," Sheriff Morgan said, leaning closer and lowering his voice, "a couple of New York types talking about showing your work there. Hope you're not planning on hauling your ass back east after only being back in the Creek a few months?"

"No way. I've got everything I want and need right here."

Sheriff Morgan's friendly eyes shifted from Arlo to Lucian. "How's it going, working with Bibi?"

"Oh well, Bibi's… Bibi."

"She sure is." Sheriff Morgan nodded as he laughed.

Lucian was glad of the sheriff's easy, good natured chat, easing away any lingering tension.

"Are you sure we can't slip away?" Arlo whispered into his ear when Sheriff Morgan left them. "That suit looks great on you, but I can't wait to take it off."

Lucian's spine tingled as Arlo's eyes, dark with desire, stared into his. His heart pounded hard. "Yes—"

"Hey man, not been able to get near you all evening. You've been surrounded by all your fans paying homage. Hope fame's not gonna turn your head?" Hank laughed before he took a nervous sip of champagne, and grimaced. He looked uncomfortable and hot in his ill-fitting suit.

Lucian blinked. He'd been so caught up in slipping away, and slipping off his suit, he'd not noticed Hank's arrival.

"Just think of all those stories you can sell to the papers about what we got up to when we were young and handsome. Here, let's get rid of that." He plucked the glass from Hank's hand. "I'll get them to grab you a beer."

Calling over a waitress, he whispered to her, and she nodded with a smile. Hank looked almost pathetically grateful.

"My goodness, Arlo, this is awesome. Who would have thought it, me being a good friend of a famous artist? Oh, my, more champagne!" Francine, newly arrived and pink cheeked, plucked a glass from the waitress who arrived back with Hank's beer. Her eyes settled on Lucian, and widened to cartoonish proportions. "Luci-Ann! Oh, my gosh! I didn't recognize you! You look so, so… different. I didn't realize your eyes were so big and blue. Hank, doesn't he look good enough to eat?"

"Errr um…" Hank stuttered, and Lucian squirmed.

Arlo's arm, still around his waist, tugged him in closer, and Lucian had to use all his willpower not to snuggle into him and bury his burning face into Arlo's muscular chest.

More people joined them, bestowing their congratulations on Arlo. Lucian knew a few by sight from around town, but most of them were strangers. Arlo accepted their congratulations and adulation with good natured, if reserved, thanks. Hank and Francine, edged out by the adoring newcomers, gave him a quick wave and disappeared into the crowd.

Arlo sighed when there was a brief lull. "Do you have any idea how long we need to stay for?" he murmured. "I think my face is gonna crack if I have to keep smiling."

"It's the price of fame. You're now in the public eye."

Lucian ached to be alone with Arlo, just the two of them, but this was Arlo's first showing and he needed to embrace the opportunities it would bring, and which his talent deserved. A wave of pride flooded through him, mixed with other feelings he wasn't brave enough to examine too closely. He looked out over the crush of people.

"What's wrong?" Arlo gazed down at him. His voice was soft, yet a frown of concern creased his brow. Arlo had read him so easily.

"Nothing. Just a little overwhelmed, that's all."

"Thought that was supposed to be me. What is it that's —" but before he could challenge further, a chic middle-aged woman appeared, accompanied by a younger man carrying an expensive-looking camera.

"Mr. McDonald?" She asked with a polished and professional, but friendly, smile. "I apologize for interrupting." She looked from Arlo to Lucian, and back again. "You must be exhausted. One's first showing is always a whirlwind. I'm Melanie Coates, chief editor at Contemporary Art, and this is my colleague Paul."

"Ms. Coates." Arlo held out his hand. "I'm surprised anybody from such a well-respected journal would want to come tonight. Thank you, it's an honor."

Arlo's face flushed pink, and he looked coy; Lucian did his best to keep his face straight.

"Please, call me Mel. Jonas specifically invited me. We go back a long way. I trust his judgment and as he was singing your praises, which he doesn't do lightly, of course I was going to come. You have quite a talent. Although I'm sure you'd much rather make a run for it, would you be able to spare me some time for an interview and some shots? We're featuring a series of articles on undiscovered talent from across the country."

"Sure, but isn't it a little busy?"

Mel smiled. "I've already commandeered some space

in the yard. The light is good out there, or so Paul informs me."

Paul nodded.

"I'll see you later," Lucian said, ready to let Arlo go.

"Please don't, because I'd like to ask you a few questions, too, if possible. I always think including the artist's partner adds that essential human element."

Lucian froze, his tongue unable to form words. Partner? Was that how people saw them? Was that how Arlo saw them?

"Lucian?"

He looked up into Arlo's steady eyes.

"Is this what you want?"

Mel and Paul, and everybody else, faded. There was nobody but him and Arlo. Their gazes locked on each other. The simple question was anything but. Is this what you want? He nodded slowly, his body answering before he could think. Arlo smiled, as though something had been settled between them.

"Yes, please," Lucian said quietly.

"That's great." Mel smiled. "In which case, gentlemen, follow me."

CHAPTER THIRTY

"Thank god that's all over with." Arlo locked the door, wanting to keep the world at bay.

The evening had been a tremendous success, selling every single canvas. Jonas had gathered together some of the great and the good from the art world, unheard of for a first time showing anywhere, let alone a small Mid Rockies town.

His work, his talent, they were finally being recognized. It had been what he'd always secretly yearned for, even if it had scared the shit out of him in equal parts, when he'd picked up his paints and brushes to relieve the stresses and strains of running a business, of living in New York, and walking the tightrope of forging relationships before he fell from the wire and plummeted back to earth. Now, his brain and his blood told him he was shooting up into the stratosphere as a serious artist.

He didn't give a damn about any of it.

Something had changed this evening, some line had been crossed.

Is this what you want...

His question, and Lucian's answer, had been echoing through his head throughout the interview with Mel. Partners, she'd called them. They hadn't corrected her. The photos Paul had taken of him and Lucian... His heart had somersaulted as his mouth had turned dry. They'd looked so good together... did look good together.

Is this what you want...

In the kitchen, Peanut ambled over to Lucian, ignoring Arlo. The mutt loved Lucian as much as Lucian loved him back. As though aware he was being scrutinized, Lucian looked up and smiled. There was something shy and self-conscious about it and Arlo wondered if he, too, was thinking about the evening and everything that ultimately had nothing to do with the canvases that had hung on the walls.

"You looked amazing tonight. I was so proud of you. Proud you were with me." Proud you're mine...

"So I never looked amazing before my miraculous make over?" Lucian stood up and laughed, but it was nervous and unsure.

"I thought you were amazing from the moment I first saw you. Even with your glasses."

He said it as a joke, to take the edge off whatever it was Lucian was feeling, but hadn't that been true? As a flicker of doubt flared in Lucian's eyes, he knew he had to do something, anything, to make Lucian believe him.

Arlo took his hand and led him out onto the porch. The night was clear and bright, the stars scattered diamonds, backlit by the full moon.

A full moon, when madness ruled the world. Arlo had never felt as sane as he did in that moment.

Sitting close, he could feel the warmth of Lucian's body, and smell his cologne, heady with a soft hint of the roses Lucian loved so much; he breathed in deep, drenching his senses. All around them, the air fizzed and crackled with electricity, growing heavy as though a storm was rolling in from the mountains, gathering strength to break over their heads. But whatever sparked in the atmosphere, it came from them and them alone.

Arlo licked his lips and took a steadying breath.

"Tonight, I asked you something." He stopped, as a sudden fear fell on his shoulders. The question he'd asked... Why the sudden doubt when there had been none earlier? Whatever the answer he'd been so confident of, he had to know for sure. He had to hear Lucian tell him, to confirm or deny.

"You asked me," Lucian said slowly, carefully, as if finding his way, "if it was what I wanted. I don't think you were asking about me being interviewed with you."

"No."

Lucian said nothing. Next to Arlo, he was so still, and Arlo hardly dared to breathe. Overhead, a shooting star burst through the sky. A shooting star was an omen, and as Arlo's breath burned in his lungs, he could only hope and pray the omen was good.

"It is what I want."

Lucian's voice was so quiet, so small, Arlo could have told himself he'd imagined it, but as Lucian turned to him, the moon lighting up his face, illuminating his smile and glittering in the dark blue depths of his eyes, Arlo knew the only thing he'd imagined had been his own doubts and fears.

The kiss was the sweetest Arlo had ever tasted, as they

opened up to each other, as lips brushed lips, as tongues gently entwined. Tasting each other, feeling each other as if for the first time. But wasn't it a first time? The two of them together, being what each truly wanted.

Lucian held his hand out, and Arlo took it with no hesitation.

"Come with me." Lucian's voice, so often edged with hesitation, was clear and sure, sending a frisson dancing the length of Arlo's backbone.

In silence, he let Lucian lead him through the house and up the sweeping stairway to the bedroom. The blinds were fully open, allowing the moonlight to stream through, painting the walls, the floor, the ceiling and the bed in warm, waxy light.

Lucian released his hand, and they stood facing one another, breathing the other in. Close, yet not touching. The only sound in the room was the rapid beat of Arlo's heart.

"It feels different. To before, I mean," Lucian whispered. "Don't you feel it too?

Arlo nodded. "Do you want it to be different?" he rasped.

"No. And yes. I sound stupid, don't I?"

"You don't. Maybe we should just let everything be what it'll be." Arlo took a step closer, cupping Lucian's face and pressing a kiss to his lips.

Lucian sighed into the kiss, wrapping his arms around Arlo's neck, pushing his body close. Arlo's breath hitched as Lucian's arousal met his own thickening cock. Lust, desire, want, need, the strands weaving together, all of them held fast by something deeper and stronger.

It would be so easy to give themselves up to each

other, to gorge like starving men. But… He stepped back and drew in a deep breath.

"Arlo?" Doubt filled Lucian's voice, and Arlo pressed a finger to his lips.

"I wanna take this slow. I want us to remember tonight. Always."

Every touch. Every caress. Every gasp, every moan, every sigh. He wanted to remember every moment, and lock it deep inside his heart.

"Let me undress you. Let me take it all off, piece by piece. Let me take you apart, piece—"

"By piece," Lucian murmured against Arlo's finger, before he sucked it into the molten, wet heat of his mouth.

"Jesus." Arlo's muscles twitched and jerked as Lucian sucked in a second, then a third, slipping his lips down to the knuckles, pulling back before again sliding down. His eyelids fluttered to a close. His cock pulsed in his boxers, its push to be free from the constraints of material exquisitely painful. Lucian moaned as he pulled away with a wet pop.

Arlo forced his eyes open. Bathed in moonlight, Lucian's eyes glowed dark, his parted lips wet and puffy, aching to be claimed.

Arlo crushed their mouths together in a rough and hungry kiss. Disrobing Lucian slowly, piece by piece? It was too late for that, as greedy desperation consumed them both.

Hands and fingers fumbled, clumsy with need. Jackets, shirts, shoes and socks, pants and underwear, all of it ripped from their bodies, until they stood naked before each other.

"So, so beautiful," Arlo breathed, as he eased Lucian down onto the bed.

Lucian whimpered. Bending his legs at the knee, he let them flop open as he stroked his swollen cock.

Arlo swallowed. He could come just from watching. Heat spread through his belly as the telltale tingle teased his balls. No. Not yet, not now.

"Take your hand away. Do not touch yourself."

"Arlo," Lucian whined, but his hand fell away from his twitching cock.

So compliant. So — submissive.

He climbed on the bed, pushing Lucian's legs wider, his heavy cock bobbing against his lower stomach as he settled between Lucian's spread legs. Planting his hands on either side of Lucian's head, he stared down into eyes that were black, bottomless pools.

"When I saw you tonight, I thought my heart was going to stop. You looked incredible. I was the envy of everyone, and all I wanted was to kiss you into tomorrow."

"Then do it."

Tongues twisted and twined, wet and hot, hard yet soft, every one of Lucian's gasps and moans sending a bolt of searing heat to Arlo's hungry cock.

They'd kissed and touched, licked and sucked, so many times before, but tonight his ravenous, demanding heart craved more. To possess, to claim, to take Lucian as he gave all of himself in return.

"I want to fuck you so bad."

Beneath him, Lucian shivered.

"Will you let me?" Arlo's heart shuddered to a stop. This was Lucian's decision, his choice to say yes or no. Please say yes, please, please, please…

Arlo's scalp prickled as Lucian stroked his fingers through his hair as his lips lifted in a smile.

"Yes." The whispered word ignited in Arlo's heart.

Arlo kissed his way down Lucian's chest, flicking his tongue against the tender nubs of his nipples.

Beneath him, Lucian squirmed, laughing as Arlo kissed his way down and rimmed his belly button with the tip of his tongue. Ticklish. Arlo grinned; he'd have to remember that. He continued his journey, arriving at the dark, hot place between Lucian's legs, delighting in and savoring every gasp as he nuzzled, breathing in deep Lucian's warm musk.

"Arlo…" Lucian whimpered and Arlo groaned, his cock pulsing with need.

He sucked in another and deeper breath, closing his eyes for a second, pushing down the gnawing need to feast on Lucian as though he were his last meal. Slow, take it slow…

He licked a long stripe all the way from the base of Lucian's shaft, all the way to the top, where he lapped at the hot slit, salty with pre-cum.

"Oh, god. That's, that's so…" Whatever it was, it was lost in incoherent mutterings as Lucian writhed, pushing his hips upwards, his greedy cock demanding more.

Arlo licked again, this time to the base, burying his face deep between Lucian's legs, sucking in a breath, filling his lungs and drenching his senses in Lucian's warm aroma, a heady combination of musk and arousal, and the faint, lingering scent of the sweet strawberry body wash he liked so much. Lucian jerked, filling the air with curses as Arlo tickled his tongue across Lucian's perineum.

"Christ, Arlo. You said you were going to—"

"Shush, baby. Doesn't the entrée always taste better after the appetizer?"

"No. Not when I'm starving hungry."

Arlo chuckled, his heart glad when Lucian joined in. He eased his way down, raising Lucian's legs, exposing his entrance. Slowly, slowly, slowly, he massaged his tongue around the rim of the muscle, feeling every pulse and flicker. Closing his eyes, he sucked and licked, adding more pressure with every sweep of his tongue, pushing and gaining entrance.

Above him, Lucian stiffened. Arlo stopped and looked up.

"Lucian?" Arlo's heart hammered, fearful he'd hurt him.

"I'm okay," Lucian whispered. "It's just been some time since…"

Arlo's jaw clenched. Some time since another man had… The heat of possessiveness burned through him. He took a breath, steadying himself before speaking.

"If you're not ready, we don't have to do this."

"I know, but it's what I want. With you."

Lucian's words were so soft, so simple. With you… A fist punched its way through Arlo's chest and squeezed his heart.

"Are you sure? Really sure?" Arlo whispered.

"I don't think I've ever been so sure of anything."

Arlo nodded as he began to kiss and lick once more, opening Lucian up, his own desire burning through his veins as he tasted Lucian's dark heat.

He slipped from the bed, accompanied by words of complaint, which fell silent as he produced a condom and lube from the nightstand. He hesitated for a moment before he switched on the lamp, flooding the room in a soft golden glow.

"I need to see you. I need to look into your eyes." What they were about to do was too precious, too important, to be hidden in the darkness and shadows.

"Yes," Lucian whispered.

Slicking up his fingers, Arlo massaged at Lucian's entrance. He'd tightened up a little, but they had time, and with gentle insistence, Lucian relaxed. One finger, then two, pushing in and steadily stretching. Their gazes locked, and Lucian gave a tiny nod.

Arlo kneeled on the bed and tore the foil from the condom. His hands were shaking. Jesus, his whole body was shaking. With nerves, with lust, with desire. But most of all, he was shaking because this, here and now, with this man, was everything he'd never felt before. It was overwhelming and his cock flagged.

"You know, you can get medication for that."

"What?"

"Disappearing Dick Syndrome. DDS, for short."

Lucian's eyes were wide and guileless, but the edges of his lips twitched.

The little fucker... "Yeah, it's gonna disappear for sure. Right up your ass."

Lucian barked out a laugh as Arlo grinned, coaxing his cock back to fullness. Rolling on the condom, he slicked himself down. Heavy, irregular breathing replaced Lucian's laughter.

Positioning himself against Lucian, he looked up. Their gazes caught and held. Lucian's pupils had devoured the irises. Dark with desire, yet there was more there, something deeper.

With a hard flip of his heart, Arlo knew what it was. Trust and belief. Trust and belief he'd not hurt him, that he'd not use him, that he'd keep him safe.

"I'd never hurt you. I promise. You know that, right?"

"I know."

Arlo paused before he pushed forward, breaching Lucian's muscle. Lucian cried out, but he lifted his legs higher, wrapping them around Arlo's waist.

"Now," Lucian rasped. "Fuck me."

It was the green light Arlo's brain and body needed. He drove in deep, every thrust met with one of Lucian's own. Every gasp and cried out curse, every plea for more urged him on.

Arlo's eyes had closed, but he wrenched them open, forcing them to focus on the man beneath him. Lucian's eyes, too, were open. Wider, darker, hungrier than Arlo had seen before, his lips red and swollen, as his teeth clamped down hard on them. The need to possess rose in him once more, forcing him forward, each thrust more urgent than the last.

"Is this what you wanted? Me inside you, fucking you hard, nailing your sweet ass?"

Lucian laughed, breathless, edged with hysteria. "You call this hard? You call this being nailed?"

"Fuck you."

"Oh, yes please."

Arlo yanked Lucian's legs up onto his shoulders, all but bending him in two. He pumped his hips, his cock pounding like a well-oiled piston. Faster, deeper, changing his angle, dragging the scream from Lucian as he pummeled, over and over, at his sweet spot.

Lucian's fingers dug into his hair, clutching and

pulling, sending nervy spasms of pain across his scalp. Their bodies, slick with sweat, slid and rubbed against each other. Lucian bit down hard on his lips as his eyelids fluttered closed.

"Open your eyes," Arlo demanded. "I wanna look into them when you come."

Arlo's own orgasm was rising, gathering strength, ready to thunder through him. But so was Lucian's. Arlo could hear it in his rising breath, in the racing beat of his heart pressed against his, and in the swelling of his cock, wrapped in his palm.

Lucian's eyes drifted closed again.

"I told you not to fucking close your eyes."

Lucian's eyes widened as he gasped, as his body stilled for the briefest moment before he spasmed and jerked, as he cried out his climax.

Oh, Jesus, so beautiful, so fucking beautiful. And mine, so mine...

With a final hard thrust, Arlo's back arched, his eyes locked on Lucian's. His orgasm spewed from him as he bellowed, loud, feral, animalistic, as he emptied himself into the condom buried deep inside Lucian.

CHAPTER THIRTY-ONE

"Luci! Your man's here," Bibi hollered.

In the back, where he was checking inventory for a delivery, Lucian's heart fizzed. Your man... The fizz spread through him, making him tingle from the top of his head to the tips of his toes. He threw the inventory down and dashed through to the front.

Leaning on the counter, Arlo smiled as he chatted with Bibi, but as he turned his attention to Lucian, his smile grew bigger and brighter until it filled the whole store.

"Hey," Arlo said.

"Hey." Lucian's smile was the perfect match for Arlo's.

"Okay, you guys, I've had it. All this doe eyed, sweet as candy gawkiness is just too much to take. You're putting me off my dinner tonight. Luci, you can go now. I'll finish up here." She looked at her watch and grinned. "Thirty minutes before your official finish time. You can make it up tomorrow."

"You're all heart, Bibi. A heart with clogged and furred up arteries."

Bibi snorted, and with a wave, Lucian grabbed Arlo's hand and fled before she could change her mind.

"Let's grab dinner, and then—"

Lucian shook his head. "You're always feeding me. Let me return the compliment. Come back to the apartment and I'll cook." He had the ingredients, he had it all planned, but Arlo tilted his head and stared down at him with suspicious eyes.

"You're going to... cook? Your culinary skills are a little limited. If I don't feed you, all you eat is Marmite on toast. Is that what you're offering me? Because, let me tell you, mister, that ain't good enough."

Lucian snorted. "I do have skills — and no, I'm not talking about, you know." Lucian lowered his voice when two elderly ladies walked past. "Come on. Let me surprise you."

Cheese risotto. Easy peasy, lemon squeezy. Even he couldn't screw that one up.

"Stop looking at me. It's putting me off."

"Just watching a master chef in action. I might learn something." Arlo laughed, but he retreated to the couch, leaving Lucian to wade through the recipe he'd pulled up on his cell.

He'd read through it, and it sounded so easy. Finely chop onions. Fry them in olive oil until golden. So far, so good, he could do that. Then add arborio rice. Except the grocery store hadn't had any, and he'd been faced with the only option of quick cook long grain. Rice was rice, and he'd thrown it into the cart.

"'Add the wine to the partially cooked rice, stirring until it's absorbed,'" he read. "'Then add the stock, ladle by ladle, as the rice mixture absorbs the liquid. Keep stirring. Add the cheese once the rice is cooked and the liquid absorbed. Your risotto will be beautifully oozy.'" Hmm...

A pile of grated cheese sat next to the chopped onions. The grocery store hadn't had Parmesan, either, so he'd bought something that looked a bit like cheddar, even if it was an alarming shade of yellow. It'd tone down as it cooked. Along with the onions there was a jug of stock, and a bottle of white wine. Or rather a third of a bottle of wine, as he'd had to taste it the night before, just to make sure it was the right kind of wine.

"Okay. Time to cook. Onions first, then the rest."

The onions hit the hot oil, spitting and sizzling, quickly turning not golden but black. Shit. The oil was too hot. He turned the heat down and scraped at the pan, but most of the onions were sticking like glue.

"Think you might have had the heat too high," Arlo called from the safety of the couch.

Talk about stating the bleeding obvious... "Everything's in hand."

Time to add the rice. Lucian ripped the bag open with his teeth, half the contents spilling out over the floor. He poured what remained into the pan and stirred, mixing the rice with the blackened pieces of onion. He peered down into the pan; it didn't exactly resemble the photo on his cell.

The rice started to burn and stick to the bottom of the pan, joining forces with the onion. Fucking hell... this was supposed to be a throw in the ingredients and stir recipe, and hey presto! Instant domestic god. Lucian poured in the wine, turning the rice and onion mix into a bubbling thin soup.

"The knack to risotto is to make sure you add the liquid slowly and to keep on stirring." Arlo abandoned the couch and wandered over. "Like this."

From behind, Arlo coiled his arms around Lucian's waist. Covering the hand holding the spoon, Arlo moved it in small circles.

"Add the stock when it dries out a little." Arlo poured a small amount of stock as he continued to guide Lucian's hand with the spoon. "Hmmm, I think you should cook for me more often."

Lucian's knees began to buckle as Arlo nuzzled into his neck, sucking on the tender, sensitive skin just below his ear. Leaning back into Arlo, he groaned. Maybe dinner could wait.

"Pour and stir, pour and stir," Arlo whispered against his neck.

Pour and stir... He could get used to cooking if it came with having Arlo wrapped around him, kissing and nuzzling into his neck.

"I think it's on the edge, don't you?" Arlo's voice was a husky, deep growl, reverberating across his warm skin.

Oh, yes. He was certainly on the edge. Lucian pushed back against him, rubbing his ass against the growing bulge in Arlo's pants. Yep, dinner could definitely wait. "Why don't we—"

"Add the cheese?"

"What?"

Arlo chuckled, sending a ripple of hunger through

Lucian, hunger that absolutely, definitely had nothing to do with risotto.

"Can't have a cheese risotto without the cheese, babe."

Arlo scattered in the cheese, added a pat of butter, stirred — and stepped back. "Now we need to let it rest for a short while. To kind of settle down."

"But I want it now," Lucian said, spinning around, glaring at Arlo who stared back at him with a shit-eating grin. Bastard...

"It's best when you've waited. I promise, it'll taste so much better."

Lucian huffed and looked down at his crotch, the tenting in his jeans already subsiding.

Arlo laughed. "Okay, let's eat. I might let you have some dessert later."

Lucian's dick twitched. Dessert, that was certainly worth waiting for.

CHAPTER THIRTY-TWO

Sitting across the table from one another, they dug into the risotto.

"What rice did you use?" Arlo asked, chewing slowly.

"The only kind the store had."

"The texture is a little…"

"Unusual?"

"Hmm. What was the cheese?"

"Erm… just cheese. I was too late for the delicatessen, and the grocery store's choice was a little limited. All they had was yellow hard cheese and spreadable cheese triangles." Lucian peered down at the neon yellow sludge on his plate. The spreadable cheese might have been the better option.

"I appreciate the thought, babe, but it might be a good idea to leave me to do the cooking in future."

Lucian sucked in his breath. Arlo had just given him the opening he needed, but now the time had come nerves consumed him. What if he'd miscalculated? What if he was making a huge mistake? What if he'd got this so wrong? What if—

"What's the matter? You look like you're about to throw up. The food's not that bad. Or not really."

"It's not the food, it's... well, I've got something I want to say, but I'm not sure how to start."

"What's wrong? You're worrying me." Arlo's hazel eyes clouded with anxiety. "Lucian, just tell me."

Lucian swallowed. This was harder than making risotto.

"I've—I've been thinking. About going home."

Arlo's face stiffened, but he stayed silent.

"Point is, I don't think I'm ready. To go home. Not yet." Maybe never... But they weren't words he could say, not at the moment, not when Arlo was staring at him, his expression unreadable, giving nothing away about what he thought, what he felt.

Lucian let his head drop forward. Oh, god. He'd got it wrong, so bloody wrong. Arlo was saying nothing because he was thinking of something to say, something nice, to let him down gently, to tell him he should book that flight home, to tell him—

"And I'm not ready to let you go home. Not now, not next week, next month, or even next year."

"What?" Lucian peeked up at Arlo, hardly daring to believe what he'd heard.

"I don't want you to go. That's the simple truth. I guess I've kind of gotten used to you hanging around."

"You—you don't? And I guess I've kind of got used to hanging around you, too."

"Come here."

Lucian jumped up and fell into Arlo's open arms, snuggling into his lap. He closed his eyes as Arlo wrapped his strong arms around him, sighing as he held him close. So warm, so safe...

"Are you sure about this? You've got a life back in England. A home. A family. You live in a castle."

Lucian chuckled. "It's not a castle, it's a manor. And yes, I have a life there, but it's not been too good for a long time. I love my home and my family, but I—I love being here with you more."

"And I love... you being here. With me. Maybe we can see how—"

"Maybe we can give it a shot?" Lucian looked up at Arlo.

"I think we could. I know you're going to have to go back at some point, to sort things and speak to your folks, and I get that. But maybe I could go with you?"

Lucian's heart leaped as he met Arlo's sure and steady gaze. He nodded.

"I'd like that. So, I don't need to give Bibi my notice just yet?"

Arlo's lips lifted in a slow, dark smile. "No baby, not just yet. Come on."

Lucian gasped as Arlo swept him into his arms and carried him toward the bedroom. Catching his breath, he buried his head into Arlo's chest, hearing the steady beat of his man's heart. No, he wouldn't be resigning, nor booking a flight home.

No, not just yet...

CHAPTER THIRTY-THREE

"Hey, Arlo. And Peanut, too! Come in. Glad you could make it. How's fame treating you?" Francine laughed, and Arlo groaned.

Since the showing at the gallery, so many more people had come up to say hi, or had waved to him from across the street. His payment for coffee in CC's had been refused, as instead the barista had asked him to autograph a napkin. It was excruciating.

"I'm not famous," he said, defensiveness in every word.

"I wouldn't say that."

He would, but Jonas was already talking about a major showing at his Boston gallery, much to Lucian's excitement.

"Everybody's talking about you and when I was in the library earlier today, they had a copy of that magazine you gave an interview to, on a stand, right there on the desk where you check out your books. I was very proud when I told the librarian I was one of your oldest friends."

Arlo followed her through to the kitchen. Lucian had squealed in delight when he'd read the piece in Contemporary Art. Sure, it'd talked about him being an artist to watch out for, and with a bright future. It had been insightful about his work. But it hadn't been the words that had got to him, but the photographs of him and Lucian together. Lucian had looked incredible, gorgeous and unbelievably sexy as he'd gazed into the lens. He'd also looked so young, the difference in their ages as emphatic as though somebody had run a neon yellow hi-lighter across them both.

"Take a seat and make yourself comfortable." Francine put her hands on his shoulders, almost pushing him down at the table. "It's been so long since we all sat down to lunch together, but as Lucian's with Bibi at a flower fair, Hank and I thought it'd be good to grab the opportunity. We didn't want you sitting down on your lonesome with nothing but a sandwich."

Lucian, not Luci-Ann. At least she now pronounced his name correctly. But...

"How do you know he's at a flower fair?" Bibi must have told her, because he sure hadn't, and he doubted Lucian had.

"Oh, Bibi mentioned it. Lunch is cooked, but it just needs heating." She bustled over to the stove and concentrated on stirring the contents of a large pan.

Hank was already in the kitchen, telling their dog Gomer he was the most handsome boy. Arlo grinned. The dog was even quirkier looking than Peanut and had about half as many teeth. Gomer abandoned Hank and limped across to a tail wagging Peanut; Hank ushered them into the yard.

"It's getting colder." Hank shivered as he shut the door. "There'll be snow on the mountain tops soon."

The temperature had dropped over the last couple of days, and high winds had stripped the trees of much of their red and gold. Summer had receded to little more than a memory, and fall would soon be claimed by winter, already waiting in the wings. Arlo's thoughts were turning to the winterscapes he was already painting in his head.

Scratching at the door was followed by some half-hearted barking.

"Go on, let them in." Peanut hated being cold, and even though he was wearing his coat, Arlo didn't like the idea of his little mutt shivering in the yard. Hank opened the door, and the dogs slunk inside and retreated to the corner, and Gomer's basket.

"Just a simple lunch." Francine ladled out a rich meat stew before placing a plate piled with homemade bread in the middle of the table. Not a vegetable in sight... Maybe it was just as well Lucian wasn't with them.

They talked about the showing, but also about the neighbors, and Hank and Francine's kids, who were no longer kids, but young men and women in their late teens and early twenties.

"Lucian should get to know Kyle and Jed," Francine said. "The twins are only a couple of years younger than him, but that's still the same age group. Right?"

"Er, yeah, I guess so." The twins were good enough kids, but other than being close in age, Arlo couldn't think what Lucian could have in common with them. He glanced across at Hank, who was inspecting something at the bottom of his bowl of stew.

They carried on eating, the sounds of spoons on bowls

accompanied by little yelps and snuffles from the dog basket in the corner.

"We used to do this a couple times a week, at least," Francine said, breaking the silence that had descended over the table. "When you first came back to town and were finding your feet. In fact, we used to see a lot of you. Not so much, now."

Lunches. Dinners. Coffee. Invites to family parties and BBQs. To movie nights, where the food and drinks usually came with a gay friend, a gay cousin, or a gay cousin of a friend, every one of them guaranteed to make Arlo want to run for the hills and never look back. At least she'd stopped doing that since he'd got together with Lucian. He peered around the kitchen, half expecting a random guy to jump out of a cupboard.

"Life's been busy in the past few weeks. The show, and... other things." Lucian, Lucian, and more Lucian. But a worm of guilt wriggled in his stomach that his best and truest friends might think he no longer had time for them. "Why don't you come on over to our place? The weekend, maybe? I'll cook."

"Our place?" Francine's eyes widened, the spoon she held frozen part way between her bowl and her mouth. "Has he moved in with you?"

Arlo stilled, his shoulders tensing. *He*...There was something he couldn't name, in her tone, in the way she'd avoided using Lucian's name, in the way she was looking at him. Whatever it was, it felt accusatory. Our place... It had been a slip of the tongue, but that was how he thought of his house now, as being theirs, his and Lucian's. He put down his spoon, his taste for the meal fading.

"No, but he spends most of the time there with me.

He's still got his apartment at Mr. DuPont's because it's convenient for work…" Even though he's hardly there and I'm going to ask him to move in… The words should have been easy to say, but they withered on his tongue.

"Francie." Hank glared at Francine, who pressed her lips together in a straight line.

Arlo looked between the two of them, all their attention on each other. They'd forgotten him. Something was going on, and whatever it was, he wasn't going to like it.

"I'm sorry, Arlo. I didn't mean to question you, but I was taken aback. By you saying your home belonged to both of you. Because he's going home soon, right? I remember him saying he was only going to be here for a few months. Did he mention up to Thanksgiving? Or was it Christmas? The holidays are coming fast. He's such a nice boy, even if he is a little quirky, but hey, he's been good for you. He's taken you out of yourself, and that's got to be a good thing."

The food in Arlo's stomach curdled.

"Plans have changed. He's not leaving. He's going to stay on in the Creek. We haven't talked too much yet about the longer term—"

"Excuse me?" Francine stared at him, mouth agape.

"He's not leaving."

"I heard you, Arlo. But what do you mean, he's not leaving? I thought he lived in some big old castle back in England."

"It's a manor, not a castle. He does. Or did. But now he lives here." And soon he'll be living with me.

"But—"

"Francie."

The hard note of caution in Hank's voice cut across

them, plunging the kitchen into a prickly, awkward silence.

Arlo put down his spoon and pushed the unwanted food away. Whatever was going on here, it needed to stop. Now. It was time to collect Peanut and leave. But he had one more thing to say before he did.

"Francine, Lucian's not a boy. He's twenty-four. And he's not been some kind of temporary diversion."

"That's not what I said. I agree he's been good for you. Didn't I just say that? But I'm sorry, if I called him a boy it's because he feels like little more than that to me. He's about the same age as the twins, so how else am I to think of him?"

The twins… Jesus Christ. Kyle, still plagued with acne and hardly more than monosyllabic, obsessed with gaming on his computer, and hardly ever leaving his bedroom. Jed, jock extraordinaire, his brain as muscle bound as his body. They were as different from Lucian as it was possible to get, and Francine was comparing Lucian to them? He bit his tongue, tasting the metallic tang of blood, anything to stop himself from launching a full on attack. Francine was his friend, even if at the moment it didn't much feel like it.

"Arlo," she said with a heavy sigh, as though scolding a child who should know better. He gritted his teeth. "We worry about you. Don't we, Hank?"

"Francie, leave it. It's not our business."

It sure wasn't, but whatever warning Hank thought he was giving, she refused to heed it as she turned back to Arlo.

"We do worry. I'm not going to deny it. We've worried about you since the day you came back to the Creek. You were so down and defeated after Tony. And I'm not saying Lucian's the same—"

"Then what are you saying?" Arlo gritted out.

Francine flinched at the steel in his voice, but she was determined. "Tony was a nice boy, too, or so I thought. And what did he do? He crushed your heart and threw it away. He was too young to be settled down—"

"The difference in our age had nothing to do with why we parted." His stomach clenched, what he'd eaten of the rich stew laying heavy and fatty, making him feel sick.

The age difference, which had never been a factor early in the relationship, had later become one, as Tony had grown to want something different from the life they'd shared. But Tony and Lucian were not the same, as different from each other as the ocean and the desert.

"Oh, Arlo, can't you see you're going down the same path? I know it's flattering when somebody who's so much younger shows you attention. Why, that nice boy who works in the bakery, he's always flirting with me—"

"What's that?" Hank lifted his head out of his hands.

"And I've got to say I rather enjoy it," Francine said, taking no notice. "Because it's validation that I'm still worth flirting with. At my age, too. But it doesn't mean anything. It's just a little playfulness. And that's how you have to see this thing you have with Lucian."

She lurched forward and covered Arlo's hands with her own, holding on tight.

"We don't want to see you repeating the same mistakes. Another much younger man? Really? Arlo, I know you think a lot of him, I can see that, but the plain truth is he's not for you. So this boy's extending his time here, but he will leave. He'll go back to his own home, to his own friends, to his own country, and to his real life. Arlo, he's not for you. Don't you see that?"

Arlo pulled his hands out of her grip. Francine's words were a hurricane, flattening everything in their wake. Everything except for him.

"What gives you the right to talk to me like this? Who are you to say who is and who isn't good for me?"

"Arlo, I'm only—"

"I tell you what you're doing, Francine. You're putting our friendship on the line. Yes, I was a mess after Tony. I won't deny it. But do you think you know everything that happened? You don't. You only know what I've chosen to share with you, and nothing else."

"Arlo, please. I just don't want you getting hurt again."

Arlo snorted. "Yeah, well, you've sure got a strange way of showing it. Maybe he will go back home, but maybe he won't. But that's for us to discuss, and for us to decide. What we don't need is any of your help," he said, spitting out the word, "which is only the interference of a controlling busybody who can't keep herself out of anybody else's business. Isn't whipping Hank's ass enough for you without trying to do the same to mine? Let me tell you this, lady, you're not doing that to me. Keep your nose out of my and Lucian's business."

Francine reared back, gasping, as Arlo pushed himself to standing.

"Hey, that's enough, Arlo!" Hank jumped to his feet, his chair toppling to the floor.

"Yeah, buddy, you're right. It is enough. What I do with my life, and whomever I do it with, isn't any of her business." He jammed his forefinger at Francine. "I reckon Gomer's not the only one around here you need to keep on a leash."

CHAPTER THIRTY-FOUR

Lucian settled himself in front of his laptop and clicked the link. A moment later, his mum appeared on screen, thousands of miles away.

"Hey, honey!" Her bright smile and warm voice tugged at the homesickness he'd all but forgotten about. Behind her, he could see an orange and yellow flame crackling in the enormous stone fireplace, its mantle crammed with the many family photographs she liked to surround herself with. "Look who's come to say hi." She ducked out of sight of the camera for a second, reappearing to hold up a small, grizzled mutt of a dog.

"Wally!" Lucian cried. He put out his hand, as though he could reach through the screen to ruffle the dog's rough fur. Wally yapped and lurched forward. Lucian could swear his daft little dog was smiling. The tug of homesickness became a hard yank.

"So, honey, how are things working out in cowboy country?"

"They're working out good." More than good."

Out of sight of the camera, Lucian wrung his hands together. It was time to tell her about Arlo, but it was also time to tell her he wouldn't be booking his flight home anytime soon. The knots in his gut pulled and tightened.

"That's great, honey, it really is. Although, I still don't understand why you chose to—okay, okay," she said, holding up one hand in surrender as with the other she hugged Wally to stop him from trying to crawl through the computer screen. "But you'll be coming home soon, and oh my goodness, I for one will be so happy to see you again.

"I've missed my baby boy sooo much. Lucian, honey, Danebury has not been the same without you, not at all. Eddie and Bella feel the same. We were saying, just a couple days back, that maybe it's time for you to come home, now you've had some time out. It's too late for you to work on dressing the house for our Christmas events because those arrangements have already been agreed, but we have the New Year's Eve ball where you can work your floral magic. We've already amended Danebury's website to announce your impending return from your sabbatical."

Sabbatical? Was that what they were calling leaving home to go halfway around the world to take time out from the shit storm his life had become?

"You'll be thrilled with what we've got arranged for when you get home…"

He had to stop her, but she was a huge truck heading straight for him, freezing him in its headlights.

"Mum…"

"Honey, the perfect premises have become available in the middle of the high street in the village. We've already spoken to the landlord…" She laughed. "Which was all fine and dandy, of course, as we are the landlord."

The offer to set him up in business, his own florists… He'd forgotten all about it, and here was his mum, laying it all out in front of him as a done deal. She was talking, but he couldn't hear a word of it. He had to say it now, to stop it all in its tracks.

"You probably need a couple weeks to wrap everything up, but maybe we can agree on a date so we can book you a flight home. Oh, here's Eddie."

Lucian's brother appeared, pulling up a chair next to their mum. His wide grin split his face in two.

"Hello, Lu. Has Mum been filling you in on what we've got planned for you?"

What we've got planned for you… Lucian's stomach hollowed; he opened his mouth to speak, but nothing came out.

"This is a great outcome," Eddie went on, their mum smiling and nodding in agreement. "You'll have the independence of having your own enterprise, but still be working alongside the core Danebury business — but just at a bit of a distance, as we don't want any more bee and bride incidents." A slap on his arm and a deadly glare cut off Eddie's guffaw. "Sorry. It was just a joke. Clearly not a very funny one."

Lucian jumped into the microsecond of silence.

"A great outcome for whom? Thanks for planning my life without consulting me."

His mum and brother gave him identical stares. Guilt spasmed in his gut. They had talked about this before he left, but he'd been too ground down in the dirt to do anything other than nod and agree with a disinterested murmur.

"Lucian, we've only got your best interests at heart. Just like we always have." Thousands of miles away, his mum's lips curved downwards, her whole being dripping with hurt.

Oh, shit...

"Before I left," he said, trying to keep his voice from shaking, "I wasn't in the right state of mind to talk about my plans. I just needed to get away for a while, to reset. We all agreed. And—and I have done. Reset, that is."

"And we're all so glad of that, honey, we really are. Happy that you seem happier, because you do. Happy that you've got a more positive—"

"What is it you're not telling us, Lucian?" His brother's sharp blue eyes burned into his across the miles and through the screen.

Fuck... This wasn't how he wanted to tell them, but what he'd wanted and what was happening were two different things.

"Oh!" His mum's eyes widened, and her mouth formed a perfect, lipsticked *O*. "Have you met somebody? A handsome young cowboy? Because, goodness knows, that's what every Wyoming man is. A brief fling can do wonders for boosting self esteem and—"

A cowboy? A fling?

"Yes. No, and no. What I mean is, yes, I have met somebody. No, he's not a cowboy. And no—" Lucian swallowed hard. "He's not a fling."

The only sound to be heard was the crackle of flames in the fireplace, and Wally, who'd long since jumped down and was barking and growling out of sight.

"I've decided to hang on here. We've talked about it —
me and Arlo, that is, because that's his name. Arlo. Arlo
McDonald, not Arlo That-Is."

He was babbling as two pairs of blue eyes stared out of
the screen, out of blank faces. Lucian raised his hand to
push up the non-existent glasses. Neither his mum nor his
brother had noticed he wasn't wearing them, nor had they
noticed his hair had been all but cropped.

"How long are you planning on staying in…" Eddie
gave a dismissive wave of his hand, the gesture unfreezing
the nerves that had turned Lucian into a rambling mess.
Anger rose in him. How dare his brother dismiss the Creek
and everything it had given him?

"Collier's Creek. It's a fine town. There's a lot more
here than cowboys." He shot a glance at his mum.
Although, it had to be said, there were rather a lot of them.

Lucian drew in a deep breath. He wouldn't stumble
over his words. He'd be clear and calm and explain who
and what Arlo was, as he made them understand.

"I was an emotional, mental mess when I left to come
here. We all know it, and we know why." Neither said
anything. Out of sight of the camera, Lucian's hands
shook, but he had to be clear about what he wanted, and
who he wanted; he wouldn't let them steamroller him.
"When I decided to come to Collier's Creek—"

"I really don't think sticking a pin in a map constitutes
the basis for a well thought out decision." Eddie huffed as
he shook his head.

Lucian squeezed together his sweat slick hands.

"How I chose this place isn't relevant, but my being
here is and that's because of Arlo."

Off camera, indistinct words caught Eddie's attention,

and he scowled. "Bloody hell. I need to sort something out. I'll leave Mum to talk some sense into you. We'll be seeing you soon, Lu." Eddie stared pointedly into the camera before he disappeared.

"Don't mind your brother, honey, he's just protective of you. We all are, but I guess we all show it in different ways. Eddie's gruff, you know that. He's a lot like your late granddaddy."

Lucian shrugged. When did protective cross over into being domineering? Guilt rippled through him, but they all had to stop trying to plan his life, and he had to stop letting them.

"So, tell me about your Arlo," his mum said gently.

Your Arlo… The words wound themselves around his heart and warmed every little piece of him. Because Arlo was his.

As concisely as he could, he told her all about Arlo McDonald. About his art, and about coming back to Collier's Creek. About his beautiful house on the edge of town with the incredible mountain views. He even told her about Peanut. But there was so much he hadn't told her, and he braced himself for the questions he knew would come.

"He sounds like an interesting man who's achieved a lot in life. Way more than most twenty-four-year-olds would do."

Twenty-four. His age, but not Arlo's.

"That's because he's not twenty-four. He's forty-four." Lucian battled to keep the tremor out of his voice. Why should Arlo's age matter? It was the essence of the man that was important. But he knew his mum's concerns, and he braced himself for the questions she would ask next.

"Oh, honey. Why? After everything that happened before… Why are you treading this path again?"

Lucian closed his eyes, just for a moment, not bearing to see the anguish on her face, but he need to answer her questions and look her in the eyes as he did so.

"I'm treading this path precisely because it's not the same as before. Arlo's older, sure, and I'm not dumb enough to not realize that, yes, maybe that was part of the initial attraction, but—"

"So what is this? You like this Arlo because he's twenty years your senior?"

Lucian could hear the irritation and impatience rising in his mum's normally level voice, and he bit down on his tongue so hard he winced. He couldn't allow this to veer off into displays of temper on either side.

"First of all, he's not *this Arlo*. Don't refer to him like that, Mum, otherwise I'm going to log out and end this conversation." He waited a second before his mum nodded her agreement. He tried to slow his breathing to relieve the tension holding him in its iron grip; it didn't work.

"His age is just one facet of who he is, but it's essentially irrelevant. I tried hard to keep my distance, to not get involved, because I was determined to not get involved with anybody." Had he tried to keep his distance? He wasn't sure he believed himself, so how could his mum?

"But who he is, that's what broke through my defenses. Arlo's kind and thoughtful, and he makes me feel good about myself. He listens to me and he's interested in who I am and what I think. He doesn't try to mold me into what he believes I should be. We make each other laugh and we're so much on the same wavelength. We just fit together, and I—I feel safe with him. These are all the things Arlo is, and they're the things that really matter."

"They do matter, honey. But so does age." His mum held up a hand to quell the protest fizzing in Lucian's chest. "Hear me out, okay? Maybe Arlo is all the things you say he is, but a twenty-year age gap is a lot, and with it comes differences in life experience. The stage a person is in their life influences what they want out of it. The priorities of a forty-four-year-old are not those of somebody of twenty-four, they just aren't. You said he sold a successful business in New York, but now he's returned to his hometown, in the middle of nowhere. Why did he do that?"

Lucian met his mum's clear, level gaze. Out of sight of the camera, he rubbed his sweaty palms over his thighs.

"Because his last relationship fell apart. It's what made him decide to change his life and come back here." Arlo's life with a younger man...

"Does he know about you and Miles?"

"Yes. I told him everything. I almost had to stop him from getting on a plane to London so as he could come and punch his lights out."

His mum smiled. "That's certainly a big plus in his favor, then."

Lucian laughed, the moment providing some much needed relief, but his mum's face quickly grew serious once more. She leaned forward, filling more of the computer screen.

"Honey, I love you. You know that, right?"

"Mum..." Please, don't play the 'I love you and want to protect you' card...

"But it's because I do that I'm pushing you on this. Everything you just said, all those good things about Arlo?

259

You said the same things about Miles in the beginning, and you said the same things about the guy before. They were older — older than I'd have wished, but I said nothing because we all have to learn about life — but they hurt you, and they hurt you badly. You were a wreck after Miles." She shook her head. "That guy was a piece of work. I was so worried about you, and so were your brother and sister—"

"Were they? I must have blinked because I didn't notice."

"Honey, come on. That's not fair. They've always been there for you. They just do it quietly, and without fuss. Remember when Daddy passed and how distraught you were? The way they insisted on taking turns in sleeping with you in your room while you processed what had happened? Lord knows, no way in this world could I have coped without them, because I was almost comatose with grief."

Lucian closed his eyes and ran his hands down his face. He remembered, just as he remembered Rex Burley-Tait, the nastiest of the school bullies who'd made his life hell — until Eddie had approached him for a 'quiet word'. Perhaps it had been a coincidence Rex had been off school for the rest of the term, because of a broken arm and a dislocated jaw. When Rex returned to school, the dethroned bully made a point of ignoring him.

"They want the best for you, just as much as I do."

"I know that, Mum. I know you all love me, just as I love you all back. But I know what — who's — best for me better than anybody else. You've got to stop worrying and trust me on this. You all have. Please?"

"Oh, Lucian," she sighed. Lucian's heart clenched. Not

honey, not this time. "I'll never stop worrying about you, because that's what moms do, and you're my baby boy, remember? It doesn't matter how old you are, it's what you'll always be to me. You ask me to trust you not to make the same mistakes again. But I don't know if I can."

"You can trust me, because I trust Arlo. He's nothing like Miles. I feel good about myself, more than I've ever felt before." He ran his hands through his hair. What he had to say next couldn't come as a surprise, but he had to say it. He had to make it clear. "I'm not ready to come home yet." Maybe I never will... but if he said those words now, they'd be a punch to the stomach of the woman he loved so much.

She nodded. The only clue his words had pained her was the tiny inward pull of her brows.

"You're not a kid, and your life is your own, and I need to remember that even though it's hard sometimes. But promise me this. Don't let your emotions blind you. This isn't the first time we've been here. If you have any doubts, any inkling that something isn't working, promise me you'll be out of there and on the first flight home. Because if you don't do that, my promise to you is that if I think things aren't right, I'll be hightailing it out to haul your sorry ass back home. I won't stand aside and see you down in the dirt ever again."

Lucian blinked as tears burned behind his eyes.

"I promise. You won't need to channel your mama bear." He gave her a quivering, wonky smile.

"Where you're concerned, I'll always be your mama bear, and I won't be afraid to use my claws. Oh, and honey? I love the new look. You're my beautiful baby boy again."

CHAPTER THIRTY-FIVE

"What's up? You've been quiet and kind of distracted all evening. Most times I can't shut you up — except with one thing." Arlo grinned and waggled his eyebrows to make Lucian smile. It didn't work.

All around them, the lively buzz of chatter and laughter from the restaurant's Friday night crowd only highlighted how low key and subdued Lucian was.

Lucian pushed aside his barely touched pizza and attempted a smile, but it was as thin, gray and washed out as an old rag.

"Babe, you're starting to worry me."

Lucian snorted. "Seems like I'm a worry to everybody. Oh, I'm sorry." He slumped back into his chair. "It's just that I spoke to Mum earlier. I told her about us."

"You did? That's great. Or it should be."

Lucian shook his head as one hand found his fork and turned it over and over. Arlo leaned forward and rested his hand on his, stilling Lucian's agitated movements. Nerves crept through his stomach. Whatever Lucian had told her, she hadn't liked it, and he had the creeping feeling he knew why.

"I'd planned what I was going to say, and how. But, you know, best laid plans and everything." He shrugged. "My brother was there too, for some of it. They expect me to pack up and leave, to go home and just… just fall into line and do what I'm told. It's like I don't have any say over my own life. I said, no, I wasn't ready to go home because of what I have here. And then I told Mum you were older. She put two and two together and came up with five."

Arlo said nothing, biting down hard on anger, frustration, and a kind of inevitability. Of course Lucian's mom was worried about him, worried about the age difference, worried history might repeat itself. He got it, he got it all. He wasn't anything like that fucker Miles, but they didn't know, because they didn't know him.

"Lu—"

"My family, they're protective." The words rushed from Lucian. His eyes were wide, as though beseeching him to understand. Arlo ground his teeth together. Lucian needed to talk, and he needed to let him.

"They always have been. When the shit hit the fan with Miles, I was glad of it, I suppose, until it got too claustrophobic." Lucian thrust his fingers through his hair. "I told Mum you're nothing like—"

"I would never treat you like he did," Arlo ground out. How could anybody could ever harm a hair on Lucian's head? It made him feel sick, and so angry he could get blood on his hands. His heart hammered hard. A light touch, resting on the backs of his hands, cleared away the red mist that had overtaken him.

"I know you wouldn't. All that matters is us, when it comes down to it. What I think, what you think, what we think."

Arlo nodded and wished it were that simple.

They continued with their meal, but it was half-hearted, and when they pushed their plates aside, they left more than they'd eaten.

Guilt swirled through Arlo's stomach. He'd caused a rift between Lucian and his family. They were close and Lucian was the youngest; it didn't matter that he was a grown man, it was who he'd always be to them. He cast a glance at Lucian, who looked fed up and so downcast it was a physical pain in Arlo's chest. *And he looks so damn young…*

The thought crashed into him, a baseball bat to the head, making him dizzy and breathless. Young. Too young… those words again. From Hank and Francine. Friends, good friends, friends he'd always been able to trust and depend upon, despite the bitter, angry words of their last meeting. He'd stormed away, refusing to listen to anything they'd had to say. They'd been wrong, and he'd been right… because he and Lucian were right. They were right for each other.

A bug burrowed under his skin. Were they? Were they really?

What the fuck… Why the hell was he thinking like this? Why were they letting others' views get in the way of who they were? Arlo grabbed for his beer, but his hand was clumsy and he knocked it; catching it quickly, he only just stopped it from spilling all over the table.

"Now who's distracted?"

"Yeah, let's get out of here."

Minutes later, they were outside on the sidewalk, their table taken by the next in a long line. They made their way past all the busy bars and restaurants, and the park where a few people still lingered. An empty bench beckoned, and they sat down.

"What did you tell your mom about me, other than being an old man?" He'd meant it as a joke, but his words fell flat and heavy.

"That you're kind and thoughtful. That you make me feel good about myself. That you're great at sex. That you let me be me. That your blow jobs make me weak at the knees—"

"That I'm—what?" Arlo's bolt of terror deflected when Lucian laughed, the first light-hearted sound he'd heard from him all evening.

"Okay, I didn't mention the sex stuff, but I did say the rest of it because all that and a load more is true."

Arlo placed his arm around Lucian's shoulders and pulled him in, warmth filling his chest as Lucian nuzzled close.

"Your mom focused on the age difference because there is a big gap between us, so I understand her concern even if I don't share it."

The words burned Arlo's throat. He hated what he was saying, but their ages were a fact. They could ignore it, but others didn't seem able to. But maybe other people's problem made it their problem, too. Too young... too old... don't let history repeat itself...

"You think I don't understand?" Lucian wriggled out from under Arlo's arm and turned and stared at him.

Dusk was falling fast, and although the shadows were

stealing over Lucian's face, his eyes had never looked larger or more intense.

"Most of my boyfriends in the past have been older, and most of them have been crappy for one reason and another. But not all of them, and not because of their age.

"Miles was in a league of his own, older and crappier than all the others put together, and he was a huge mistake, but he wasn't a mistake because he was older. He was a mistake because he was vicious and a control freak, who got a kick out of whittling away at me and making me doubt myself all the time, always telling me I was stupid.

"Sub par was the term he used, and he said it with a great big smile on his face, and if you're told something for long enough, you end up believing it. I didn't know then why he treated me like shit. I don't know now, and I don't think I ever will. But it's what he did, because that was him, not because he was older than me. My mum can't see beyond the age difference between us and so she's lumping you into the same category. It's not right, and it's not fair."

Lucian's voice wobbled, and Arlo tugged him back into his arms, holding him tight as the strain loosened a hard flood of tears. Hugging him close, he gently rocked him, not telling him it was okay, not telling him it was alright, not telling him it would all come out fine. The words would mean nothing as he said them, just as they'd mean nothing as Lucian heard them. He let him cry until there were no more tears left.

"Sorry," Lucian muttered, sniffing into his chest. "You must think I'm such a wuss, letting it get to me. I'm supposed to be a big boy now. I can even tie my own shoe laces."

"Don't exaggerate. You forget I've watched you get dressed."

Lucian laughed as he hiccuped.

"Come on, let's dry those tears." Slowly, gently, Arlo brushed his fingertips along the tracks of tears wetting Lucian's cheeks. He was doing a better job of spreading rather than drying them, but it didn't matter because all that did was caring for Lucian, giving him the comfort he so sorely needed.

"Better?"

"Yeah, a bit. Thank you. Sorry," he said again, "for making your shirt wet and snotty." Lucian offered a watery smile.

"Hey, never say sorry to me for showing how you feel."

Lucian nodded and mumbled an okay. Arlo hated seeing him upset. If his mom was afraid he was anything like Miles, he had to show her otherwise.

"What if they were to meet me? Remotely, I mean."

"It's the obvious answer, isn't it? But not yet."

Arlo jolted. "Why not?" It didn't make sense. He could do it with or without Lucian present, allay all their fears, make them understand how much he thought of Lucian... how much he... liked him.

"I know them. Obviously. But they know me, too. My mum, and my sister, and my brother in particular, they'd think I was begging for their approval and I can't let them think like that. It sounds crazy, but I have to make them believe I can make my own choices and that I don't have to seek validation. If I arranged a video call, that's what it'd look like.

"I want you to meet them, I truly and honestly do, but I

won't push you in front of them and beg them to like you. They need to see I can make my own choices without falling on my face. I know it doesn't make sense, it doesn't to me either, but I just know that for now it's the right action to take. Or not take. If you see what I mean."

Arlo ran his fingers through Lucian's hair. "Whatever you want, baby."

Lucian took his hand and pressed a kiss to his palm, and a muted, muttered 'thank you'.

"Come back to the house with me tonight?" He'd work out all the knots and tension holding Lucian tight, leaving him relaxed and boneless and sated.

"I—I think I'd like to go back to the apartment. I've a lot to think about, plus I have to be up super early to get some wreaths and tributes ready. I really don't want Bibi adding to the poor family's distress."

They both smiled. Bibi, the world's worst florist. But Arlo couldn't help the twist of disappointment in his heart.

"Hey, I really need to get an early night, you know."

"You can get an early night in bed with me."

In the growing gloom, Lucian's smile turned wicked.

"Sure, I'd get an early night, but I wouldn't get any sleep. Come on, walk me back. Make Mr. DuPont's night as you kiss me under the streetlamp."

CHAPTER THIRTY-SIX

Arlo watched the door close, and waited for Lucian to give him a wave from his window before he headed off. He was restless and driving home to an empty house held no appeal. Just a few weeks before, he'd been used to it — had made himself get used to it — but now the thought of walking into the silence dragged his spirits down. With no conscious decision, he headed back into town. He'd get a beer some place, find a corner table for one, and think about Lucian's revelation to his family and the implications for them both.

He walked in a daze, jumping and spinning around as a hand fell on his shoulder. Hank stood before him, with Francine a step or two behind.

"Hank. Francine." Tension rippled through his muscles. He was in no mood to take any lectures, no matter how 'well meaning'.

"Arlo." Francine stepped forward and rested a hand on his forearm; he resisted the urge to shrug it off. "I was going to come find you tomorrow, but as we're here... I want to say sorry. For what I said, and how I said it. For meddling, when it wasn't my place to do so. You called me a busybody, and I guess you were right." Her features pinched, as though she were in physical pain. She had no right to seek his forgiveness, and he had no cause to grant it, but—

"When you said I was putting our friendship on the line, it crushed me. Here." She pressed her free hand to her chest. "I was awake all night, thinking about it all. I never want to risk that. You're too precious to us both." She glanced at Hank, her husband's expression as impassive as ever. "Whatever you do and whatever decisions you make, whether it's about Luci-Ann, or anything else, I want you to know you'll always have our support.

"I — we — love you dearly, Arlo, and we couldn't bear for anything to come between us." She stepped back. "That's... that's all I wanted to say. I have to get back. I'm hosting my bookclub this evening and all my ladies are expecting drinks and snacks, and goodness knows I haven't got a thing prepared, and—"

"Come here." He pulled her into his arms and placed a kiss on top of her head. She and Hank were his oldest, staunchest friends and though he had every right to wave her apology aside, he wouldn't and couldn't. "Thank you," he said, giving her a hard hug before he let her go.

Francine nodded as she wiped away a tear. "So, we're good again?" she asked in an unsteady voice, a watery, hopeful smile lifting her lips.

"We're good."

"Why don't you boys grab a beer or something? With

all my book club ladies arriving soon, you'd both be doing me a favor."

"Arlo?" Hank raised his brows in question.

"Sure, that'd be good."

With a kiss for Hank and a relieved smile for Arlo, Francine made her way home, leaving the two old friends on the sidewalk.

They stared at each other, like two dogs sizing the other up. Hank rolled over first.

"Thanks for that just now. Francie's been worried sick. She knows she stepped out of line, and we had a long and frank talk after you left."

So you tore her a new one... "It's not easy owning up to being wrong, and apologizing. But let's forget it. Like I said, we're good."

"Then let's get that beer."

They made their way through the throng of those who were getting their weekend started. Outside Randy's, where a sign announced the Collier's Creek Cowboy Combo were the evening's main act, an excited crowd gathered, each and everyone dressed in denim and checked shirts, their cowboy hats balancing on their heads.

A couple blocks down, Hank turned off into a side street and Arlo followed him into a small bar. No music, no gigantic screen blaring out sports, it was instead a place for talk. Most people sat at the bar, but plenty more gathered around wooden tables, chatting in the soft, low light.

Settling down with their drinks, Arlo shifted in his seat as Hank studied him over the rim of his glass.

"What?"

"You look kind of ill at ease and distracted."

Distracted. Arlo sipped his beer. It seemed to be the word of the evening.

Hank leaned forward. "You've gotta believe Francie, about how sorry she—"

"I know she was, but what she said over lunch, it kinda pressed a nerve even if I didn't want to admit it." He sighed and took a gulp from his bottled beer. Hank's gaze was locked on him. He put the bottle down and slumped back into the chair. "What she said, I understood even though I didn't want to. I know Lucian's a lot younger—"

"Yes, he is," Hank said bluntly. "No point trying to overlook it, either. What Francie was trying to say, even though she screwed up bad, was that ain't always going to be easy to navigate. You found that out with Tony. There were maybe fourteen, fifteen years between you. With Lucian, it's twenty—"

Arlo ran his fingers through his hair. "Jeez, I'm old enough to be his father. It's what you're saying, because it's the truth. Are people looking and thinking—"

"Some folks will disapprove just because they can, but they'd disapprove if you chose mashed potato over French fries. Disapproval happens, so get over it. You're both adults and you're doing nothing illegal. Reckon most would think you were lucky."

Arlo looked across at his friend. Hank's gaze was direct and steady, but his lips twisted in a smile.

"But you and Francine do disapprove, don't you?"

Apologies had been sincerely offered and accepted wholeheartedly, a years' long friendship pulled back from the brink of destruction. Yet, Francine's words over lunch hadn't only cut him to the bone, they'd quietly burrowed beneath his skin whether he'd wanted to recognize it or not. And now, with Lucian's family…

"It's not, and never was, about approval. We just don't want you to be disappointed and left alone again. I guess we didn't handle it too well. But you said you understood what Francine was saying. What d'ya mean by that?"

Arlo sucked in his lower lip as he tried to order his thoughts.

"When I came back, it was to reset my life. I wasn't interested in meeting anybody because I didn't want to put myself through any more shit. It crashed and burned with Tony, and you and Francie know that more than anybody because you helped pick up the pieces. But he wasn't the first guy it all went wrong with, was he? If my track record at holding onto anybody long term was my resumé, I'd never get another job. Tony and Lucian are different men in all kinds of ways, yet parallels exist, even if I tell myself I don't want to see them."

"If you mean young and cute, then sure."

"Hank, you're not supposed to notice when young guys are cute."

Hank laughed. "Why can't I notice? It's allowed, nowadays. But it's as far as I go." His laughter died, and he grew serious. "The age difference is the only thing Tony and Lucian have in common, as far as I can see. You just said it yourself. Arlo, whatever you may think, our concern's not about that, not at its heart. But what does concern us is that you're getting too attached. For a man who said he wasn't interested in getting settled with somebody again, you're doing a fine job of doing just that."

"Francine was always keen to set me up, yet you're concerned about me getting attached to someone. That

273

doesn't make any sense, Hank." He remembered Wilbur, just the last in a long line of Francine's handpicked men who'd made him shudder.

Hank grimaced. "Yeah. I told her to ease off, but she just didn't want you sitting alone in that big ol' house of yours. Even she realized you needed more company in your life than us. She thought they were suitable. Professional guys. Guys like you."

"Jesus." He met Hank's eye, and they both laughed, the moment providing a release of tension.

It didn't last, as Hank leaned forward.

"We'll support you, just as Francie said. Whatever happens with you and Lucian. We've been friends since we were kids, and I want to carry on being your friend. I've been with you through the good times and the bad, and I think that's earned me the right to speak to you honestly. I know you don't want to hear this, but you need to ask yourself some hard questions about what kind of future you think you might have with him."

"How do you mean?" Arlo's stomach knotted; he knew what those hard questions were that he didn't want to answer.

"Whatever reasons he had for coming here, he's only passing through, Arlo. He's said as much himself. We couldn't stand aside and say nothing, not when we saw you getting so attached. It was meant to be a word of caution, that's all, but you know how it went. But what kind of friends would we be if we hadn't said anything? Not very good ones, that's for sure.

"We'll support you, man, we made that promise and me and Francie, we'll keep it. All we're asking is that you be clear-sighted about what's going on — and about whether he'll swap his life back home and everything he knows for one in a small Wyoming town. Maybe he'll stay, who really knows, but if he doesn't, that's gonna hurt bad. And you've had enough of being hurt. We don't want to see it happen, Arlo. We don't want to pick you up off the floor again if he's only in the Creek to mark time."

"Mark time?" Temporary, and just something to do before Lucian left and never looked back.

Hank rubbed hard at his forehead. "That sounded—"

"Like what it is."

"No. I'm not saying it'll happen for sure, just that it's something you have to consider before you get in any deeper. You gotta look at the situation from all sides. Ah, shit, I'm screwing this up… We just don't want to see you heartbroken again, but that's what's gonna happen if he decides in a few months' time that he's gonna go home to his castle."

"It's a manor, not a castle," Arlo said dully, but what-ever it was, it was thousands of miles away.

A different country, a different way of life, a life Lucian was born to. A life so different from the one he'd come back to the Creek for. Everybody else seemed to understand that, so why couldn't he?

Tiredness overwhelmed him, sudden and crushingly heavy. Everything Hank had said made agonising, painful sense. Too attached… Maybe it was time to loosen that attachment and ultimately let it float free. You need to ask yourself some hard questions… His heart broke with the painful, gut wrenching truth of it. The bar was suddenly too hot, too stuffy, the walls pushing in on him. He scraped the chair back and stumbled to his feet, wanting only to get out.

"I'll call."

Hank's anxious voice chased after him, but disappeared into the night as Arlo pushed his way outside, the backs of his eyes burning, his breath searing his lungs, as he fled into the cool night.

CHAPTER THIRTY-SEVEN

Arlo stared up into the night sky, the stars chips of ice and just as cold. He shivered as a hard gust of wind swept through the yard, and he pulled the blanket tighter. Next to him, Peanut whimpered and pawed at his leg.

"Come on, boy, up you come." Arlo picked up his dog and settled him onto his lap. Peanut nuzzled hard, as if trying to climb inside Arlo, still whimpering, whimpering that sounded too much like tears. "Shush." Arlo stroked, slow and rhythmic, and Peanut began to settle and quieten. It was a shame Arlo's heart couldn't do the same.

Arlo picked up the brandy he'd poured but had yet to touch, turning the glass around and around in his hands as he turned both Francine's and Hank's words over in his head.

In his fury, he'd dismissed Francine's words as those of a busybody who wanted to mind everybody's business. But Hank? Like the man himself, his words had been low key, measured and steady, not steamrolling but inviting him to stand back and think. A man who more often than not thought before he spoke.

He stared, unseeing, into the night sky. What was it Francine had said... His chest tightened as her words came back to him...*can't you see you're going down the same path*.

Was he? Was that what he was doing? He shook his head. No, he couldn't believe that, because everything could and would be different with Lucian. Because Lucian was different. Because Lucian made him feel different.

A gust of wind, harder and colder than earlier, sent an icy shiver through him.

Yet... weren't there parallels? Tony had put aside his dreams and plans for his future, ready instead to invest in a life with him, until he'd wanted to withdraw his investment, until he'd decided he wanted those dreams and plans and a different future more than he'd wanted him.

Wasn't that what Lucian was doing? Changing his plans. Not going home. Investing his future in him. Allowing a wedge to form between himself and his family. And all of it because of him?

The wind picked up again, bringing with it a faint but unmistakable feral cry, as somewhere deep in the mountains a life came to a sudden, brutal end. Arlo shivered. Carrying Peanut inside, he locked the glass doors, gladder than he'd ever been to shut out the night.

Too restless to go to bed, he switched on the TV and stared at the flickering images, his fevered brain unable to understand what he was seeing and hearing. Switching it off, he threw aside the remote.

Wandering into the kitchen, he stood by the counter, not knowing why he was in there. The refrigerator hummed, and he pulled open the door before slamming it closed. He wasn't hungry, he wasn't thirsty. Maybe he could paint. It'd always soothed and calmed, but he shuddered at what his febrile brain might cause to appear on the canvas. Thrusting his hands through his hair, he walked up and down the kitchen, as antsy as a caged animal.

His gaze fell on his laptop, on the coffee table in front of his couch. Danebury Manor. He'd never looked it up after his first abortive attempt.

It didn't take a moment to power up, and a few taps on the keys made his jaw drop.

Danebury Manor. The perfect setting for stylish weddings, balls, charity functions, corporate events for blue chip companies... He flicked through them. Danebury was incredible. It was older than the United States by a hundred years or more. Brick and stone mellowed by time, it blended perfectly into the green landscape. How the hell could Lucian bear to leave it?

About Us... Arlo clicked the tab. A photograph filled the screen. The Blaxston family. Mother, brother, sister, seated in a bright and sunny room lined with paintings. A Labrador sat at the feet of Lucian's brother. Next to Lucian was a small wire haired mutt. Arlo smiled. Wally, Lucian's pet dog.

His smile faded. Lucian looked happy. He was with the family he loved, with the family who loved him back and who wanted only the very best for him.

Arlo scrolled down, past the potted bios of each family member until he got to Lucian's. Floral artist... recognized as one of the leading in the country despite his youth... winner of prestigious industry awards... innovative... flair... work featured in movies, TV, and in magazines...

trained at one of Europe's most renowned schools for floral design…

Arlo slumped back into the cushions. Lucian had so much waiting for him back home. If he stayed, how long would it be before he realized his wings had been clipped and that he wanted to fly once more, just as Tony had done?

"Oh, god." Arlo rubbed his brow, at the dull headache taking root. He hadn't wanted to get involved, he'd told himself that so many times. But with Lucian, it had been impossible not to get involved, to not fall—

No, he couldn't say it, because saying it would only make things harder, more painful, more heartbreaking, when he told Lucian it was time he returned home.

CHAPTER THIRTY-EIGHT

"Here you go. I think my tea has more depth and intrigue than the movie." Lucian laughed as he set down the mugs on the coffee table in front of his battered couch.

Arlo answered with a vague smile, and Lucian peered at him.

"Are you okay? You were very quiet at dinner."

"Just tired. Jonas has been taking up a lot of time, getting ready for the Boston showing. He seems to want me involved in everything, all the way down to the size and shape of the canapés." Arlo shrugged.

"Better than keeping you too much at arm's length, though. Maybe he fancies you." Lucian snorted. "He'll have me to contend with if he makes a move on my man!"

Arlo didn't answer, and Lucian tucked himself into the corner of the couch and sipped his tea, studying Arlo through his lashes. Yes, tired, that was all. Which was why he'd been so quiet and preoccupied over dinner, just as he'd been quiet and preoccupied over the last couple or so weeks. Why he'd bailed on them getting together once, twice, maybe three times. Yes, he was tired, that was all.

"How are things with your folks?"

Lucian jolted, Arlo's question taking him by surprise. It was the only cloud on his sunny horizon, and his shoulders slumped.

"Awkward. Mum still thinks I'm making another wrong decision. Which I absolutely am not," he added quickly.

Arlo shrugged again, the gesture sending a ripple of irritation through Lucian. No comment, no denial, no backing of Lucian's assertion, just a non-committal, unreadable shrug.

"But at least she seems to have accepted my decision not to go home, even if it is grudging. It's Eddie and Bella who've fired the big guns, because they've made their views very clear. Eddie's even threatened to cut off my allowance if I'm not home by the 5th of November. Which I won't be. They'll just have to pin a photo of me on the guy when they throw it on the bonfire."

"What are you talking about?"

"Guy Fawkes Night, on the 5th November. Or Firework Night, as it's also called. It's an old tradition in the UK, and we always have a firework display at Danebury, followed by a bonfire where we sacrifice the guy, as in an effigy of Mr. Guy Fawkes himself. He tried to blow up the Houses of Parliament, back in whenever. Just a shame he didn't succeed. It's quite a night, and next year you can come home with me and we'll celebrate it together. My family'll be cool with my decision by then, because I'd have worn them down, and you'll have won them over."

"So they're still not happy?"

"No." Lucian sighed. That was one way of putting it. "Still the baby, remember? But they have to understand it's not what I am. And there's one very good way of doing that."

Nerves fluttered deep inside his belly. He was staying in Collier's Creek, he was going to make a life here, with this man who was his first thought of the day, his last thought at night, and every thought in between. They'd decided together, so the next step was inevitable, yet his stomach knotted when it should be leaping and dancing with excitement. Nerves, yes, that was all it was, because what he had to say was a big step for them both. He took a deep breath.

"I've been thinking. It doesn't make sense for me to carry on living here." He glanced around his tiny apartment, and at the few homely touches he'd added. "Perhaps it's time for me to... what I mean is..." The words stumbled on his tongue. Arlo stared at him, his green-gold eyes unreadable, his expression set in neutral. "Perhaps it's time I moved in with you," he finished lamely.

Arlo said nothing, looking away and running his fingers through his hair.

"Arlo?" Lucian whispered, "don't you like the idea? Don't you think it's the next step? As we've decided, I'm staying here. It—it would kind of make us official. Of course, I'll contribute to the bills. But I think it'll be safer if you do the cooking, because I think you'd soon get fed up of Marmite on toast, or really horrible risotto." Lucian laughed, his attempt to lighten the suddenly dense, choking atmosphere falling flat as Arlo remained silent. "You're worrying me, Arlo, you're really fucking worrying me."

Arlo hung his head, his shoulders rising and falling

with each breath. He looked up, his face a picture of pain. Lucian's stomach burned as the tea he'd drunk turned to acid.

Oh no. No, no, *no*…

"Over the last couple weeks, I've been thinking hard. About us."

"Look, if me moving in is a bit much, for now, I'll stay here. I know us getting together wasn't in either of our plans, so I get it if I'm being too full on and—"

"You're not being full on." Arlo took his hands in his. Their warmth and strength should have been a comfort, so why did it feel like they were holding him up and stopping him from drowning? "What you just said, about us getting together not being in our plans, it's right. Neither of us were looking for—"

"I know that. I kept questioning myself, over and over, about whether it was even wise for us to be friends, let alone anything else. But the heart wants what the heart wants, right? And—and my heart wants you."

"Oh, Lucian," Arlo sighed.

Lucian pulled his hands out from Arlo's. "What do you mean by *oh, Lucian*?" Understanding was knocking at the door of his heart, along with fear and a rising anger. "What is it you're finding so hard to say to me?"

"I…" Arlo's voice trailed off, and he licked his lips.

"You what, exactly? I never reckoned on you being mealy mouthed. Why can't you tell me what's on your mind?"

Arlo winced, and a thrill pulsed through Lucian that Arlo, so often sure and steady, was none of those things now. The thrill faded as fast as it had come, because there was damn all to be thrilled about as they stared at each other, inches yet universes apart.

"I don't think you staying here, in the Creek and—and with me—is a good idea. For either of us."

Understanding, fear, and anger burst through, reducing the door to a pile of splintered, broken pieces.

"You don't think it's a good idea? You don't think me staying here is good for me? What gives you the right to decide what's good for me, and what isn't?" Nausea rose in Lucian's throat. "Miles thought he knew what was best for me. Every other man who's crashed into my life has thought they knew what was best for me. My mum, my brother, my sister, they all think they know what's best for me."

Lucian jumped up, his knee knocking the little table and toppling over his mug, flooding the surface with the remains of his tea.

"I'm not trying to dictate to you—"

"Don't tell me that." Lucian pulled his hands aside as Arlo got to his feet and tried to catch them, stumbling out of arm's reach. "Don't lie to me, because that's exactly what you're doing. Everybody seems to think they know what's best for me, but I never, ever thought you'd join the list. Poor Lucian, too stupid, too immature, to know what to think about anything. We'll just have to do the thinking for him. Why doesn't anybody have enough faith that I'm capable of making the decisions that are best for me? Why don't you, Arlo? Why don't you have faith in me?" His voice had dropped to little more than a shaky whisper, his burst of searing anger already going cold.

"Baby, I do have faith in you."

"Doesn't sound like it. Just like it doesn't sound like I'm your baby anymore."

"You'll always be that."

"That already sounds like a goodbye."

"Lucian, please. Let me explain."

"What's to fucking explain, Arlo?" Lucian snapped, his anger heating once again. "Yeah, why don't you explain in simple language a fool like me can understand? Because it's what you've made me feel like. Well, go on. Explain why you've broken my heart. Explain why my world has crumbled at my feet. Explain, as you kill me, why I should still want you."

"Sit down. Please?" Arlo sank back onto the couch; Lucian hesitated before he perched at the opposite end. He waited. Arlo wanted to explain, so he could damn well start.

"When I came back here, it was to change my life. You know what happened with Tony."

"You had a bad breakup. You were battered and bruised. I get it, because I've got the T-shirt, seen the TV show, and read the book, remember?"

"I know. But Tony wasn't the first guy I committed myself to. Every serious relationship I've had has failed, and every time it was heartbreaking, but with him it was crucifying."

Arlo looked down and sucked in a breath, his hair falling forward. Lucian itched to run his fingers through it, but he clenched his hands into fists.

"Each time, I've thrown myself in. Wholeheartedly. Believing this will be it, this is the one that's going to last a lifetime. None of them have."

"That doesn't mean we can't work. You're

condemning us to fail before we've properly started. I'm not Tony, I'm not those others. You're scared. Do you think I don't get it? Because I am too. I came here to get over what happened with Miles.

"That bastard ripped me apart, almost from day one. Fucking hell, I even grew my hair longer than it'd ever been and started wearing non-prescription glasses, all so that I could hide behind them. I was a basket case. He made me believe I was unworthy, that I was sub fucking par. That I was unloveable.

"But then you happened, Arlo. You made me believe in myself again, when everybody else in my life had long stopped. He took my self respect away, along with my dignity and pride, but he never took away the belief that love was worth fighting for, worth putting myself on the line for. If after everything I've been through, I can still believe in that, why can't you?"

"Love?"

"Yes. Love. I love you, Arlo."

The heavy, rapid thump of Lucian's heart drowned out every sound. He'd said the word he'd been wary of. It was out in the open and waiting for Arlo to pick up and hug to his chest.

"Love. Oh, baby, you've got so much love inside of you. Don't waste it on me."

"Why would it be wasted? I don't understand."

"Because I'm not a good bet. If I know anything about myself, I know that much."

"I don't believe that. You're a very good bet for me."

"No, I'm not. I just don't believe I have it in me to make a relationship go the distance. Something's missing. In me. There's some kind of defect, and I wish to god I knew what it was. I won't subject you to that — I don't want you to end up being a casualty of my failure."

Arlo reached for Lucian's hands and Lucian let him take them, too tired, too weak, too defeated to not let him. He watched Arlo's thumb sweep over his knuckles.

"You came here to take a breath and create some space between you and what happened with Miles. It was a kind of sabbatical, I guess, from your life."

"Sabbatical. It's what my family has put on the website. Some fucking sabbatical."

"But the thing about them is that they're temporary. And that's what you being here is. You've got your whole life in front of you, with an amazing talent with a whole stage to show it on.

"Your family loves you and has your best interests at heart, even if it doesn't always feel like it. You have so much waiting for you. And then you met me, and what's happened? I've driven a wedge between you and your folks, and you're ready to give everything up for me. I'm not worth the risk. Don't bet your heart on me, because it'll end up broken. Both our hearts will."

"Talk about fucking brutal." Lucian pulled his hands away and hugged himself around the middle, holding himself together as the blood from the wounds of Arlo's words bled out. He shivered, frozen to the bone.

"My family's angry and upset, but they would've come round. I was prepared to leave everything behind me, that big bright future you talk about. I could have that big bright future here, with you. But you don't want it, do you? You don't want me."

"I do want you. I want you too much, and that's why

we need to stop, because I'll end up hurting you more than you can ever know. I'm not prepared to let that happen."

Lucian laughed, hysteria breaking through as he held himself tighter, as he fought to stop himself from falling apart.

"You'll end up hurting me? What's with the future tense? You're hurting me now, Arlo. Now. You're hurting me more than you could ever fucking know."

"Lu—"

"No." Lucian pushed his arm out. "Everything you've said, about saving me from a broken heart, it's bullshit. But do you know what's worse? It's that you've shown yourself to be a liar and a coward."

"What?" Arlo jerked back, his eyes wide.

Lucian leaned forward. "Yes, you heard me. You're a liar. A liar by omission. You're running scared, Arlo, not for how you'll end up crushing poor little Lucian, you're scared for yourself. You're scared to take a chance on a new beginning, you're scared to put your heart on the line, you're scared of what could be. You've been hurt before, but you never wrote the book on heartbreak. But the book you did write? It's called cowardice. Everything you've said has been a smoke screen to hide your craven heart. I never took you for being a coward, Arlo, but it's what you are."

"Lucian, please. I—"

"Just go, Arlo. Take your excuses and your lies and your cowardly heart with you."

CHAPTER THIRTY-NINE

"Fuck it." Lucian sucked his thumb pad. Made to bleed by a thorn on a rose stem. A red rose, the flower of love. Ha bloody ha.

"I'll take over wrapping them for you, ma'am." Bibi nudged him away from the counter.

"I don't expect a whole heap of cussin' when I spend my hard-earned dollars in the town's stores."

Piss off, you dried up old bag. Lucian glared at the woman, who answered with pursed lips.

"No, of course not. I apologize for my assistant. Lucian, there's something in the back I need you to take care of."

"Like what?" Bibi was giving him her shark smile, and he couldn't have cared less.

"Find something."

Lucian slouched through the door and into the back, and collapsed against the table.

Three days since he'd told Arlo to go, three days of checking his cell, three days of picking it up and putting it back down again, indecision throwing him one way, then another. Should he call? Should he go out to the house? Should he plead, beg, grovel for Arlo to change his mind? But Arlo had made it clear he neither wanted nor loved him enough. His stomach rolled over and over. He'd crawled to enough men, and he refused to do it again.

Lucian pulled up a chair and sank down into it. Flopping forward over the table, he rested his head on his crossed arms and closed his eyes.

The door opened with a bang, but he couldn't be bothered to look up.

"What the hell is wrong with you? You've been like a bear with a sore head for the past couple of days. You can curse as much as you want, here in the back, and with me, but not in front of customers."

He buried his head deeper into his arms.

"Lucian, I'm talking to you." Bibi prodded his shoulder.

He buried some more.

"Lucian?" Bibi's voice lost its angry edge. A gentle hand on his shoulder replaced the prod. "What the hell happened? This isn't like you. Should I go get Arlo?"

"Arlo?" He didn't know whether to laugh or cry. He turned his head to look up at Bibi. "No. I don't want you to get Arlo. Not now, not ever."

Bibi's eyes widened as understanding dawned.

"You've got to be joking. I mean, you are, right?"

"Wrong. As of three days ago…" Three days, fourteen hours and fifty-seven minutes, twenty seconds and counting, "Arlo and I have slipped from present and future tense into the past."

"Oh, no. Luci, I'm so sorry. You were so cute together.

At first, you seemed like such a wrong match, but once you looked a little closer, anybody could see you were so right for each other."

Lucian sat up. "Just a shame he doesn't see it that way."

"Then you just have to convince him otherwise. Wait a moment." She rushed out of the door into the store and was back a few moments later. "I just made sure we won't be disturbed. We've closed for lunch."

He looked up at the wall clock. "At ten o'clock in the morning?"

"My store, my rules. Do you want to tell me what happened? If it were later in the day, I'd say come over to my place, drink too much wine, and blubber."

"I've already drunk too much wine and blubbered until there was nothing left to blub. I feel like such a damn fool," he whispered.

"Then join the millions of us all around the world. Talking — or not to anybody other than Arlo — won't solve your problem, but it might just make you feel a little less alone." She rubbed his arm, and the tears rose in him. He sniffed and nodded, but it took only a second before the flood gates cracked and burst as he told her everything.

"It's turned out he's the worst of the lot. At least my old boyfriend Miles — the one I came out here to get over — didn't bother to pretend. I always knew he didn't much like me, except for one thing. There at least some kind of warped honesty in our relationship, but Arlo, he—he made me believe we had something good, something that would take us into the future." A discarded leaf lay on the table, and Lucian rolled a fingertip over it, rolling and rolling until he'd reduced it to nothing more than flattened mush. You and me both, leaf.

"I don't believe he did it on purpose. I've always trusted in my gut, and it's never let me down. And do you want to know what my gut's saying about Arlo?"

"That he's giving you an acute case of wind?"

Bibi rolled her eyes. "No. That was you, when you turned up here, you jerk. What it's telling me is that he's scared."

"That's what I said to him. I just told you."

"Yes, I know. But think about it for a moment. Try to take the heat out of it, even though it's difficult.

"Arlo got seriously hurt by a younger guy, bad enough to make him abandon his career and the business he built up and move across the country to come back home. He's returned to lick his wounds, which was what you came here to do, too. He's told himself he won't let himself fall in love again, because number one," Bibi said, counting on her fingers, "he equates love with heartache and heart-break. Love means failure, and who wants to fail? Number two, that long-term relationship he poured himself into, that ended up crashing and burning and leaving him like a piece of wreckage? It was with a guy who was a lot younger than him."

"How do you know all this?"

Bibi's lips tilted into a small smile. "This is Collier's Creek. Everybody knows everybody's business even if they think they don't."

Lucian cringed at the idea anybody could know about his sorry business. "But what's that got to do with me? I'm not Tony, and he's not me. I told him that, but he wouldn't listen."

"I know, but deep down he'll be scared of getting caught in that whole shit storm again. Sure, it's not logical, but when has emotional fear ever made any sense?"

"Emotional fear?" His world had come crashing down, but Lucian couldn't help the smile pulling at his lips. Bibi sounded just like his mum.

Bibi shrugged. "It's why, ever since he came back to town, he's been keeping his distance. He's smiled and been nice as pie as he's thrown back all those eager advances that have come his way. It's because he's afraid. Look at all those guys Francine's lined up for him? My goodness, that woman has the most terrible eye for men — excluding Hank, of course — so it's no surprise there was never anything more than a handshake and a how d'ya do. And then you come along, throw a pitcher of beer all over him, and his world's turned upside down again."

"What do you mean?"

"Oh, Luci. Do I have to spell it out for you? You're everything he's told himself doesn't work for him. You're a walking, talking, breathing, living failure."

"You think I'm a failure? Thanks, Bibi, thanks a fucking lot." Arlo had kicked his legs out from under him, and now the woman who was supposed to be his friend was stamping on him in her six-inch heels. "I think it's time to re-open the shop." He got up, only to be pushed back into his seat.

"No, you're not a failure. You weren't listening to me. Failure is what you represent to Arlo. You're everything he's told himself not to get involved with, but he forgot all that the moment he saw you — until something or someone reminded him, and fed that fear which for a while he forgot all about.

"Do you remember what I said to you, weeks and weeks ago, when you told me he wanted to keep what was happening between the two of you to friendship?"

Lucian shook his head. He could hardly remember his own name.

"I said you'd be here for when the snow came, but you'd be gone by the time it'd melted. Make him believe that won't happen. Because that's what he's fearing. Arlo wouldn't have woken up one morning and decided that was it for the two of you. I've seen you together, Luci, and I can tell you that man was head over heels. And he still is, even if he's telling himself and you something different. He loves you, I just know it."

"Then he's got a funny way of showing it."

"Something stopped him in his tracks. Maybe more than one thing, and he's put them all together and come up with some dumbass number that's all kinds of wrong. If you want to shoot for any kind of future with him, find out what's spooked him and then kill it dead."

"Loves me? You think?" Lucian shook his head, blinking back the fresh tears stinging his eyes as he pushed himself to standing.

He couldn't talk about this anymore, but there was one last thing he had to say, which would knock down everything Bibi had said, like a bowling ball smashing into the pins.

"He's never once said he loved me, and I didn't push him to. But I—I told him I loved him, thinking it had to make a difference. It didn't, because he never said it back to me. And that said it all. It told me everything I needed to know."

CHAPTER FORTY

Arlo stared at the canvas, the mountainscape flat, gloomy, and uninspired. He'd been working on the painting for the past week, plunging himself into his art the way he'd always done to keep his dark thoughts at bay. It'd always worked before; picking up a brush and mixing colors had never failed him in the past, but they were failing him now.

I love you, Arlo...

Why couldn't he say it back? Why couldn't he admit what was in his heart? His scared and cowardly heart...

"Fuck, fuck, fuck." He hurled his brush at the picture. The jar of water followed, smashing to the floor and shattering into a million vicious little shards. It dripped down the canvas, making the watercolor paints run and bleed, like so many tears and so many wounds. Tears and wounds he'd caused, that had been nobody's fault but his. He ripped the canvas from the easel and kicked it away.

A small, frightened whimper from the corner at the back of the studio made him spin around. Peanut, curled up and shivering on an old blanket by the wall, next to some heaped up boxes, stared at him with fear and sadness in his dark brown eyes.

"Hey, boy, I forgot you were there. I'm sorry. Come here and let's go down and get a treat."

Peanut whimpered again and pressed himself into the wall. Guilt rippled through Arlo as he gazed at his pet, every part of Peanut's little body quivering.

Lowering himself onto all fours, so he was nearer to Peanut's size, Arlo inched along until he was in front of his dog. Tentatively, he put his hand out. Peanut sniffed, then licked, before he edged forward. Taking Peanut into his arms, Arlo rocked him, stroking and nuzzling him as he told him over and over that he was a good boy and how sorry, how so, so sorry he was for scaring him, as he begged the little mutt for forgiveness.

The tears he'd not let flow streamed hard and fast, soaking into Peanut's warm fur.

"What the hell have I done, boy?"

Peanut licked his face in response, lapping away the salty tears.

"I did it for him, you know that, right? Doesn't matter what I feel, doesn't matter how much it hurts me. It's him that matters, not me. He'll realize it soon, he'll realize what I've done is the best thing for him. He'll realize it, and then he'll thank the lord he didn't make the biggest mistake of his life. Because staying here with me would have been just that. A mistake. He's young, but he's been hurt too much already. And I'd have hurt him, Peanut, I would've. I couldn't let that happen because I—because I feel for him too much. Way, way too much. He deserves better than me—"

The deep chime of the doorbell reverberated through the house. Peanut yelped and jumped out of Arlo's arms. Arlo's heart hammered and the pulse in his neck pounded as he fumbled for his phone, as the hope rose in him, the hope he absolutely shouldn't have, pressed against his chest. His body sagged as he opened the app to show him who his evening visitor was.

The doorbell rang again, their finger stuck to the button. He could ignore it, pretend he wasn't in, but with both his vehicles in the drive and the studio light on, he wasn't going to be fooling anybody. He tapped the mic icon to speak.

"Bibi."

Bibi glowered into the camera. "Open up, Arlo. I need to speak to you."

"It's getting late."

"It's seven-thirty. Let me in, it's important."

"Look, you obviously know we've split—"

"Bullshit," Bibi spat. "He laid himself on the line for you, and all you did was trample all over him. Okay, this isn't my business, but I'm making it mine. I need to speak to you, and I'm not doing it through a fucking intercom. Let me in *right now*."

Jesus… Just let the woman in, let her spit and snarl at him and call him every name under the sun, the moon, and the stars, because god knew he deserved it. Clicking the icon to unlock the front door, he gathered Peanut up in his arms and rushed downstairs.

Bibi stood just inside, her face thunderous as she stalked towards him.

"I was in a restaurant waiting for somebody, and just about to order a drink when I got a call." With her hands on her hips, her eyes filled with fire, she glared at him. "I was waiting for my date, but I don't suppose he'll be that now because I had to call and bail."

"What are you talking about?" Arlo held onto Peanut, still in his arms, armor against this woman with fire in her eyes.

"Just put the dog down." She advanced a step.

"Bibi, are you sure you didn't already have that drink?"

"Just put him down, okay?"

And get this — whatever it was — over with. He placed Peanut on the floor and the little dog scampered away.

The hard slap came out of nowhere, the force of it making him stagger backwards, his ears ringing, the sting burning into his cheek as he went hot and cold.

"Jesus Christ, woman—"

"That's what Lucian should have done, but he didn't, so I'm doing it for him."

"What we do, what decision we make, it's not your business, and as for this," he pointed to his throbbing cheek, "you're lucky if I don't file for assault."

Bibi smirked and tossed her head, her glossy bob swinging. "So sue me, mister."

Her words echoed in his head, overriding the burn of the slap. He'd said the same thing to Lucian, about the damage to his ugly glasses when they'd attempted to kiss, his heart swelling as Lucian had laughed... Arlo's knees shook; he staggered over and collapsed into one of the couches.

Bibi stood over him, eyes bright with anger. She shook her head and huffed as she sat down heavily next to him.

"I'm not sorry I did that, because I reckon you deserve it."

Arlo didn't answer because he reckoned he did, too.

"You said you got a call? Is—is Lucian okay? What's happened?" Fear flooded through him, burning his blood. Was Lucian ill? Had there been an accident? His heart jumped, the beat erratic and out of control.

"No, of course he's not okay," she snapped, "he's not been okay since you did a number on him. He's even started to wear those ugly glasses of his again."

"What?" Arlo's heart twisted. Lucian had pulled the mask back on when it'd taken so much courage to put it aside. And it's all because of you, a little voice sneered into his ear.

"Yeah, those fucking glasses, you heard me right. Jesus, Arlo, you've made the biggest mistake of your life. You thought you should part? Then let me tell you, you've got your wish because that was what the call was about. He's booked a flight back to London. He's paid Mr. DuPont his notice period, and he's asked me to take him to the airport. Tomorrow, Arlo, he's leaving tomorrow."

The fire was burning up in her again, and she jumped up, stabbing her finger at him.

"I've lost the best florist I've ever had, who's also become a damn good friend, and you've lost the best man who ever came along and lit up your dismal life. Or you have if you let it happen. Is that what you're gonna do? Are you going to let the best thing that ever happened to you board a flight and leave your life forever?"

Bibi stood over him, shaking with fury.

Leaving… Arlo's blood froze in his veins. Sickness rose from his gut, threatening to spew out. He swallowed hard. Leaving. But that's what he wanted Lucian to do, because it was what was best for him. What he'd said, what he'd done, it had all been for Lucian's sake.

"It's for the best if he leaves," he croaked. "I'm not good for him, I'm protecting him from the inevitable pain—"

"Bullshit, bullshit, and more bullshit. How many more times are you going to make me say that? Inevitable pain? You know how pompous that sounds? And nothing's inevitable, or not unless you believe it is.

"You're not protecting him," she said, her voice softening as she once again sat down. "It's yourself you're protecting, Arlo, and you know what? I get it, I really do. You've been hurt bad in the past and you don't want history to repeat itself. And don't look at me like that — do you think you can keep anything secret here? Nobody's been gossiping about you. Or not so much. The thing about the past is just that — it's in the past. Lucian had nothing to do with what went before, but he could be a big part of your present and your future." Sadness and disappointment glittered in her eyes, dousing her fiery rage.

"If you don't take a chance on Lucian, you'll regret it for the rest of your life, and you know what'll happen? You'll end up as a lonely, bitter old guy living on the edge of town with nothing in his life except a funny looking little dog, fading memories, and dreams of what might have been. It doesn't have to be that way, but the only way to make sure is to pull your head out of your ass and not be scared." She got up and gazed down at him.

"I'm picking him up from his apartment tomorrow at ten o'clock. Stop me from giving him a ride, Arlo. Stop him from catching that flight."

CHAPTER FORTY-ONE

Lucian put the second of his two suitcases in the trunk of Bibi's car. He had arrived with little, so he wasn't leaving with much, and the battered cases seemed like a testament to his life in Collier's Creek.

Stupid...

So a brief love affair had ended. They hadn't been much more than a holiday fling, really. Yes, that was the way to look at it, because this town wasn't for him. He'd only ever been passing through and now he was going back home to the life he knew, and that really, absolutely was for the best. His hand tightened on the edge of the trunk. He'd been telling himself that for the last week, each word a heavy strap, holding him together; without the words he couldn't believe in, he'd spill out over the floor into a million pieces he'd never be able to put back together again.

He slammed the trunk lid down hard and picked up his small backpack, checking again he had his passport along with all his travel documents.

"I'm ready." He looked at Bibi, who leaned against the car's hood. She looked at her watch and said something under her breath, but it was too quiet for him to hear.

"You okay, Bibi? You keep looking at your watch. Not keeping you, I hope." He tried to inject some life into his voice, but it fell as flat as under baked bread. "I suppose we may as well go now. No point in hanging around." No, no point at all.

"Just need to check something. The traffic." She walked off, hunkered over her cell.

They'd already checked on the traffic status, and everything was clear; it would be a straightforward ride into Denver. Maybe she was jittery because he was leaving. Guilt gnawed at him, as he'd only told her yesterday he couldn't stay in the Creek. He'd heard the disappointment in her voice when she accepted his decision, and he'd closed his eyes to stop the tears, knowing it was the disappointment of a good friend rather than his employer.

"Traffic still good?" Lucian asked, as Bibi returned, shoving her cell into her purse.

"What?"

"The traffic? You were just checking on it."

"Oh, yeah. Just wanted to make sure. No sudden change. I guess we might as well go."

"Bibi?"

"Yeah?"

"Just this." Lucian dropped his backpack at his feet and enveloped her in his arms.

"I'm so, so sorry for dumping on you like this. These last few days, I—I wondered if things might change, but they haven't and they won't." He buried his face into her soft hair. "I just can't stay here any longer, I just can't. I know I'm dropping you in it, and that there are orders to fulfill in the store, and I'm not sure how you're going to do it because you're such a crappy florist… Sorry, I shouldn't say that because you're not really that bad. I suppose."

In his arms, Bibi was shaking. Oh god, he'd upset her and made her cry, and if she cried, he'd cry too. The shaking got worse, her shoulders heaving, then dropping, and heaving again. Her tiny sobs grew louder, sobs that were…

"Oh, Luci," she said, laughing. "I suck at being a florist, and yes, I really am that bad. Which is why I've got somebody coming in to help, starting tomorrow. She's good, but nowhere near as good as you. Nobody could be."

"I really am sorry. About how it's all turned out. But maybe it's for the best and next week or next month or next whenever, I'll look back and think, yeah, it was."

Bibi swept his hair, the hair he'd had cut especially for Arlo, away from his brow.

"Do you believe that?"

A lump jammed tight in his throat, and he shook his head.

"I'll miss you. I've never had an assistant quite like you. When you're settled back home, I'll come visit. Maybe I'll meet an English lord and live in a castle just like your one."

"It's a manor, not a castle. And you really wouldn't want to marry an aristo," he said, smiling, "because if they're not gay, they prefer their horses and dogs to the women in their lives."

They both laughed and Bibi checked her watch once more, her lips curving downwards in resignation. "Looks like it really is time to go. You ready?"

"Yes."

Moments later, they were in the car. Lucian's little apartment receded, and as Bibi turned the corner, it vanished. Lucian closed his eyes and leaned his head against the window, not bearing to see the small town where he'd been happier than he'd ever been fading into the distance.

CHAPTER FORTY-TWO

Arlo screeched to a halt, scattering dust. No Bibi, no Lucian. He checked his watch again. Ten-twenty. Would twenty minutes define the rest of his life? His stomach lurched, and he fought against the rising nausea. About to swing the wheel around to take the road out of town toward the interstate and Denver airport, he slammed on the brake, jumped out, and ran to the house.

Mr. DuPont had to have Lucian's number... Arlo jammed his finger on the bell, cursing himself for the millionth time for letting the battery on his cell go flat and flinging it aside as he rushed from the house, not thinking to bring it with him so he could charge it in the car... No answer. He rang the bell again. He hammered on the door. Not a sound, not a twitch of the drapes. Nothing, nothing, nothing.

In his rear-view mirror, the house, the street, the town receded from view. On the highway, he put his foot down.

The traffic, thank god, was light, and wherever the traffic cops were today, they weren't any place near him and as the open road took him closer to the interstate and the airport, his hammering heart slowed. He was going to do it. He was only twenty minutes behind them, he was going to catch them up, he was going to get to Lucian before he got on that flight that would take away the best thing that had ever happened to him.

As the ramp for the interstate came into view, the traffic increased. Arlo swore under his breath. He checked the time, his heart lurching. He could do it, he could make it, he could get to Lucian in time to stop him making the biggest mistake of both their lives... he just needed the traffic not to—

"No. No, no, no, no, *no!*" He stamped on the brake, shuddering to a stop.

Up ahead for as far as he could see, the interstate was a sea of red brake lights. Arlo slammed the heel of his hand against his horn, joining the cacophony. Vehicle doors were opening as drivers and passengers shielded their eyes and peered into the distance. No, this couldn't be happening, it just couldn't... Arlo squeezed his eyes tight to stop the hot tears of frustration, rage and his own damn foolishness from pouring down his face.

In the lane next to him, a trucker, high in his cab, had an eagle eye view.

"Can you see what the problem is?" Arlo called out.

The trucker shook his head. "No, but it's got to be an accident. Haven't heard any sirens yet, so maybe it's just happened. Probably some jerk late for his flight. Happens all the time on this stretch."

Arlo's stomach hollowed out. His hands around the wheel gripped tight, his knuckles whitening. An accident... late for a flight... oh, dear god, no, not that.

Sirens ripped through the air. Cop cars and an ambulance, somehow, against all the odds, getting through as drivers maneuvered , creating just enough space.

"Hey, can I borrow your cell? I've got a—a friend who's somewhere up ahead... I have to check..." Arlo waved toward the emergency vehicles, his voice shaking, refusing to believe the unbelievable.

The trucker looked from Arlo to the ribbon of metal that seemed to stretch into forever. With a curt nod, he leaned down and handed it across. Arlo's fingers trembled as he tried to punch out Lucian's number, but, clumsy with fear, it took him three attempts.

"Hello, this is Lucian Blaxston..."

Arlo squeezed his eyes shut. "Pick up Lucian, for the love of god, pick up..."

"... leave me a message after the bleep..."

"It's me." Arlo glanced up at the trucker, who picked his nose as he gazed into the distance. "I—I'm wrong. I've made the worst mistake of my life. Everything I believed, or tried to convince myself I believed, about us, it's wrong. Baby, don't get on that flight, don't—"

"Thank you for your message. Goodbye."

Arlo stared at the cell, his hand tightening around it.

"Hey, buddy!"

Arlo jolted and looked up. The trucker stared down at him, his arm outstretched. "Gotta call the depot, because this ain't going anywhere fast." He jerked his head to the stationary traffic.

In the far distance, Arlo could see the flashing blue lights, and his stomach flipped over. He had to know. He had to know if...

He got out, and threaded his way between the cars and

trucks, the pickups, and the motorcycles, between all the folks who leaned against hoods and trunks, who stood in small knots complaining about missed appointments, about being late, about missed flights…

Arlo pushed through, not caring who he bumped into, not caring about the jerk and asshole thrown his way, as he peered into one car then the next, looking, looking, looking, meeting the eyes of their scared, bored, ill-tempered, or worried occupants. Way, way ahead, the blue lights still strobed, but the sirens had fallen silent.

"Where is he? Where the fuck is he?"

His head jerked this way and that, the sweat of fear and agitation soaking the old shirt he'd pulled on, still buttoning it as he'd run for his car, to stop the biggest mistake in his and Lucian's lives from happening.

Cupping his hands on either side of his mouth, Arlo sucked a deep breath before he hollered.

"Lucian!"

CHAPTER FORTY-THREE

"Can you see what's happening?"

Lucian looked from Bibi, standing on the roof of her car, to his watch, and back to Bibi. They'd been stuck for almost forty minutes and it didn't look like they'd be moving for another forty. Or more. Way, way more.

Bibi clambered down and shook her head. "No. The emergency services are still there, and the cops aren't letting anything through. I think it's a couple of station wagons. At least there's no truck involved, thank the lord."

Lucian shivered. They were huge and nothing and nobody would survive if a car got entangled up with one.

"Then there's nothing we can do." They both climbed back into the car. "If I miss my flight, they'll put me on the next one out."

It'd mean hours spent hanging around the airport, lots and lots of extra time to think about everything he didn't want to think about ever again.

He delved into his backpack and pulled out the little bag of goodies he'd packed to nibble on as he waited for departure. Glancing through the windshield, he sighed. Might as well have them now…

"Ta—dar!" He held up the Tunnocks Teacakes. "One each. I love you dearly, Bibi, but not enough to let you have both." He met her smile as he handed one across.

"You will send me some once you get home, right? I'm gonna be expecting a regular care package. And some of those crunchy chocolate bars. What d'ya call them?"

"Erm, Crunchies."

Bibi licked her fingers clean as she finished her Tunnocks. "I don't think this jam's going away anytime soon. You might end up coming back to the Creek with me."

Lucian shook his head. "I'll stay at the airport and get the next available flight. Not really a lot of point in going back to Collier's Creek." No point at all.

"Are you sure about that? I mean, really sure?"

"Yeah." Lucian stared down at the red and silver foil wrapper that had covered the teacake, which he'd rolled into a tight ball. "If there had been any point…" Any hope… "I'd have known that already, wouldn't I?"

Bibi shrugged her shoulders. "I guess." Her gaze flickered from Lucian to the stuck traffic and back again. "There's something I should tell you. You promise you won't be angry with me?"

Lucian frowned. "Why should I be angry with you? What have you done?"

"I went to see Arlo. Last night. After I got your call. I told him you were leaving today, and he needed to get his head out of his ass."

Lucian swallowed, the sweetness of chocolate now

cloying and fatty on his tongue. "But he hasn't, has he? Did you tell him what time we were leaving?"

Bibi nodded. "It was why I kept checking on the time. I thought he'd come, Luci, I really thought he would."

Lucian looked down. How could he be angry with her? She was a good friend, and he was going to miss her more than he could say. He collapsed into her as she enveloped him in her arms. Across the central panel, it was awkward and uncomfortable, but to Lucian, it was everything he needed right now.

"He never called me, not after that last time. Maybe I should have swallowed my pride and fought harder… got on my knees and begged. But I couldn't. I've done that too many times in the past and all it's got me is another kicking and a gutfull of shame and self loathing. I have to accept that he doesn't love me, not the way I love him."

Why pretend his love was in the past, something over and done with, something finished. He loved Arlo, right here and now, and he'd carry on loving him tomorrow and the day after, and the day after that no matter what he told himself. He'd go home with his tail between his legs, slap a sticking plaster across all the hurt, and pray it left nothing more than a tiny scar that faded with time.

Yeah, some fucking hope.

"Hey, look at me Luci." Bibi pulled out of their clumsy embrace. "The person you have to live with most in this life is yourself. And that means you have to feel good about you. Everybody else, no matter how much you love them, comes second, because the only one who can truly look after you is you." Her lips dipped in a wry smile. "I know that from personal experience, which I'll share with you when I come visit you in your castle—"

"It's not a castle, it's a manor," they said in unison, before chuckling.

"But seriously, sometimes you have to swallow your pride, but sometimes you have to wear it like it's your best coat and only you can know which of those choices to make."

"Maybe."

Closing his eyes, he rested his head against the window. He'd made his choice, just as Arlo had. The only problem was, the coat he'd pulled on didn't feel as if it fit.

"Lucian! Lucian Blaxston!"

Arlo swung around looking for any sign that Lucian was nearby. Everybody stopped what they were doing, everybody stared. Everybody except the one person he wanted.

Arlo pushed on, bumping, jostling, knocking his way through the knots of people surmising about the holdup. He called out again, and again, and again. Nothing, except more worried stares as people moved out of his way, as though his craziness was contagious.

He stopped, his heart pounding in his chest as he caught his breath. A few yards ahead, a guy with dark floppy hair got out of the front of a car. Lean, dressed in tight dark jeans... He'd found him. He was going to tell him how wrong he'd been, how stupid, how—

The guy looked up, the guy who wasn't Lucian, before he opened the back passenger door, and reached in to help a small kid out. Arlo sagged, his legs shaking, feeling sick as the adrenaline high plummeted and crashed. He ran a hand over his face, sweat dampening his palm as he collapsed against the nearest car.

"Young man? Young man?" The voice was frail, but insistent. "Are you alright? You look like you've had a shock. Here, have a sip of hot tea."

A wrinkled face stared up at him from the open window. The old man was stick thin and looked older than time, but his eyes were sharp as they met his own.

"Go on, it'll do you good." He held out a flask with a gnarled but steady hand.

"Thank you, but I've got to find my friend. He's here somewhere, and if I don't get to him and tell him—" That I love him, and that I've made the worst mistake of my life… Arlo turned away from the old man's faded light brown eyes, eyes that seemed to see way too much.

"He?" The old man hesitated, just a beat, before he smiled, his creased faced softening.

"You'll find him, if you're determined enough. You just need to carry on looking and not give up. He'll be here, and waiting for you. He's not caught up in the accident, if that's what you're thinking, because that's some ladies. Mom and daughter in one car, a nun in the other. If that's supposed to be some kind of message, I don't know what it is." The old man chuckled.

"Cars are wrecks, but the ladies aren't much more than shaken up, with a few cuts and bruises. Or that's what we've heard coming down the line. So nothing to worry about, least ways not concerning your friend. Was that you I heard hollering? For Lucian? Is that right?"

Arlo nodded, too relieved to speak, too relieved it wasn't Lucian the blue lights flashed for, too relieved

Lucian was waiting for him. Now all he had to do was find him and make him believe he was worth waiting for.

The old man smiled, holding Arlo's gaze. "Then go find him," he said quietly, "and tell him what it is you need him to know before it's too late."

CHAPTER FORTY-FOUR

Lucian jerked, his eyes straining wide. His heart pounding, his breathing fast and shallow as he swung his head from one side to the other.

Arlo had been calling for him, had been racing to find him, to tell him... The dream faded, taking its desperation with it. Lucian wiped a hand across his sweaty brow and took one deep breath, then another, and another, trying and failing to use all the little tricks his mum had taught him.

A dream, nothing more than a bundle of all the stresses and strains of the last few days. He looked at his watch. It'd take a miracle for him to catch his flight. He snorted. He didn't much feel like believing in miracles anymore.

He peered through the windshield. A couple of cars ahead, Bibi was talking to a guy in a plaid shirt. They were smiling at each other, and Bibi's giggle drifted across. Since when did Bibi giggle?

Lucian settled back into his seat. He could check his cell for social media. That was all, because he wouldn't be checking it for anything else. Maybe he text his mum, tell her what had happened, tell her not to come and pick him up from Heathrow. He could... he couldn't be bothered. Everything, even the tiniest thing, was too heavy and too much.

He closed his eyes and drifted. That voice... known and beloved, a voice he'd never forget no matter how much he wanted... that voice, calling and frantic, accompanied by a banging on the roof of the car, by the door being wrenched open, by Bibi shouting, Bibi shaking him—

"Oh, my god. Luci, wake up. Wake up!"

"Errggh... What? What's happened?" Panic seized him. Had there been some kind of atrocity, some kind of emergency, some kind of—

"Lucian Blaxston, where are you?"

Lucian froze. The voice that wasn't a dream was growing louder, was coming closer.

"Over here, over here, over here." Bibi was waving and screaming, jumping up and down. "What the hell..."

Lucian peeked out of the window. Bibi had covered her mouth with her hands as she stared back down the interstate, but she wasn't alone as dozens, scores, of people all looked in the same direction, jaws dropping, fingers pointing, knuckles pressing against lips.

"Lucian, I need you to get out of the car. Please."

A thud accompanied by gasps from the crowd, a thud that sounded close by.

No. He wouldn't open the door and get out. He was on his way to the airport, back to his proper life, a life that had no place in it for Arlo McDonald.

He opened the door and slipped out.

"Lucian?"

He looked up. "What…?"

Arlo stood on the roof of a large, heavy SUV.

"I've been looking for you, calling your name over and over again."

"I was dreaming."

Arlo shook his head. "No. This isn't a dream. This is the here and now, and you and I are very much awake."

Lucian shielded his eyes from the sun, which had grown hotter and brighter, making Arlo little more than a silhouette, but a silhouette whose green-gold hazel eyes bore into his.

"Why are you here, Arlo? You said we were over. You told me to go home. You didn't want me. You didn't love me. Even after I told you what I feel—felt—about you, you never said it back. So, why the hell are you here?"

"Because I had to find you. I had to tell you I was wrong. I had to tell you I'd made the biggest and worst mistake in my entire life. And I made it because I was scared.

"You were right. I was scared, and I was the coward you accused me of being. I was scared history was going to repeat itself, scared to take a chance. Scared that I was taking you away from everybody you love and the incredible life you could have back home. Scared that one day you'd wake up and know you'd made the wrong decision, and that you'd hate me for it."

"But wasn't that my decision to make? Whether to stay or leave? Whether to take a chance? To believe that this time it could — it would — be different? You had no right to make that decision for me, yet you did."

Arlo nodded, the pain in his face breaking the fragile little nugget that was all that remained of Lucian's heart.

"I tried to convince myself what I was doing was the best for both of us but I knew, in here," Arlo said, pressing a hand to his chest, "that I was lying not only to you, but to me too. Hurt now, or have a whole world of hurt later. Those were the only choices we had. Or that's what I told myself."

"Why were you so convinced it — us, you and me — would crumble to dust? We wanted the same thing, or so I thought. I was prepared to lay it all on the line and give love another shot because despite all the shit that's been thrown at me, I believe in love. But you didn't. You showed me that by retreating, by telling me to leave because you weren't good enough for me, and that I should go home and live out the incredible life that was waiting for me. You gave up on us without a fight. And maybe I did too, because, maybe, we're not worth fighting for."

A collective gasp rose around them, accompanied by mutters and groans. Cell phone cameras flashed. Lucian didn't care. He didn't care that his and Arlo's sad little drama was being played out in front of strangers who'd have a story to tell over a beer and a bowl of chips, or to laugh over as they showed friends the video they'd taken.

"You accused me of being a coward. You were right to, because that's what I was.

"I let myself listen to others' doubts about us and what we could be together. Words, I know now, that were meant in good faith, even though they were wrong and felt like knives in my back. But they fed my fear that I wasn't capable of a love that would last a lifetime because look at the mess I'd already made. I couldn't let myself fail again, baby," Arlo said, his voice cracking, "but most of all, I couldn't fail you."

Arlo's head dropped forward and Lucian's heart clenched so hard it took his breath away.

"Am I too late?" Arlo's whispered words cut through the silence of the crowd as he looked up, his gaze finding Lucian's. "Am I too late to put this right? I was wrong, so damn wrong, and I want to spend the rest of my life making it up to you. I love you, Lucian, I've loved you from the moment you crashed into my life."

Lucian's lips lifted in a small, quivering smile. "You've loved me from the moment I drenched you in cheap beer?"

Arlo nodded, his smile matching Lucian's. "Yeah, I reckon so. And you still owe me for the dry cleaning bill." He jumped down from the SUV, landing in front of Lucian to the gasps and excited chatter of the watching crowd. "Please stay. Maybe we could have that incredible life here, together, in Collier's Creek?"

Hope and love, so much love, glittered in Arlo's eyes. Lucian nodded. An incredible life... it could only be incredible if Arlo was in it.

"Yes," he whispered. "I'll stay."

Arlo pulled him close, and Lucian sank into the warmth and strength that had made him feel safe from the very start.

"I love you, baby, I love you so much, and I was such a fool for almost letting you—"

Lucian stopped his words with a kiss.

"Oh, my god. He said yes, everybody, he said yes," Bibi cried out.

The crowd whooped. Car horns blasted. Cheers erupted. Claps gathered strength, rising like a wave rushing to the shore.

"Oh, my, this is like a movie," somebody shouted, as more cell phone cameras flashed.

"I, erm, think we've made a spectacle of ourselves," Lucian muttered as they broke the kiss, before burying his face against Arlo's chest to hide the pulsing heat in his cheeks.

Arlo's chuckle rumbled through him as his arms tightened around him. "They'll be telling their grandkids all about the happy ever after they witnessed. They won't believe 'em, but all that's important is that you believe. Do you?"

Lucian nodded, his throat too thick to talk.

"Okay, folks, we're going to be getting you going any minute now." A burly traffic cop pushed through the crowd. "Please get back into your vehicles. Everything's back to normal, nothing more to see. Apologies, folks, for the inconvenience, but you're now free to carry on with your day."

"Do you want to carry on your day with me?" Arlo smiled down at him.

"I've not got anything better to do, so might as well."

Arlo huffed. "The car's — somewhere."

"Bibi?" Lucian said, turning to find his friend.

"Go. I'll drop your stuff off later at Arlo's." Blowing him a kiss, she hopped into her car.

"Ready to go home?"

Lucian smiled. Yes, he was more than ready.

EPILOGUE

SIX MONTHS LATER

"Hey, what are you doing here? I thought Jonas was keeping you tied up all morning. In a manner of speaking." Lucian couldn't keep the smile from his face or voice as Arlo sauntered into the flower store.

"He did keep me tied up, and very satisfying it was too."

"Not sure I like the sound of that."

Arlo barked out a short laugh. "Want to get lunch?"

Lunch? How could it be lunchtime? Lucian looked at his watch, and his jaw dropped. When did one o'clock happen? His stomach growled, a reminder breakfast had been a long, long time ago.

"You're on. Jed!"

A head appeared around the door that led into the back of the store, with a face that bore a startling resemblance to Hank.

"Need you out here. I'm off for lunch, so I'll see you later."

Seconds later, they were outside. Lucian looked up at

the flower store and grinned, the way he did every day, as the thrill that would never get old tingled through him. He caught Arlo's eye, and his face heated.

"Okay, okay, I know I should be used to it by now."

"Why would you want to be? You've done wonders to the place. Best thing that's happened to you here in the Creek was buying the business from Bibi. Or the second best thing." Arlo smirked.

"She jumped at the chance. It was the lifeline we both needed to do the jobs we love."

Lucian glanced across the square to where his friend had set up as a dressmaker. Like his own business, Bibi's Buttons and Beaus was going from strength to strength.

"I'm so proud of you, baby." Arlo wrapped his arm around Lucian's shoulders, pulled him in, and planted a kiss on his head. "Come on, let's eat."

As they walked away, Lucian couldn't help but look back at the sign above the door — no longer Bibi's Blossoms, Blooms, and Bouquets, but Floristry by Lucian Blaxston.

"That was good." Lucian threw down his napkin onto his empty plate. "But I really should get back to the store. It's not fair to leave Jed on his own."

"I thought your new apprentice was doing okay?"

"More than okay. He's a fast and eager learner — even if sometimes he tries to run before he can walk. I thought he was going to kiss me when I told him I'd fund his place on the floristry course."

Arlo raised a brow in mock outrage. "Kiss you? Not

sure I like the sound of that. I wonder what his jock friends think of him training to be a florist? I bet they're giving him hell."

"I'd like to see them try. Jed's huge and his hands are the size of prize hams, but some of the displays I've had him make are incredible because they're so delicate. Taking him on was a good move."

"It was. Hank and Francine were worried about his lack of direction, so you've made lifelong fans of those two. Jed'll be fine on his own for a while longer. What's the point of being the boss if you can't take advantage of the perks that come with the position? You work hard all the time. Taking a longer lunch break once in a while won't hurt you or the business."

Arlo was right, but Floristry by Lucian Blaxston was so much more than a flower store. It was an investment in the life he was making in Collier's Creek and with Arlo. He had to nurture it so its roots went deep, allowing it to grow tall and strong.

"I guess so. Jed's smart and he'll call me if there's a problem, but I still don't want to leave him for too long. Thank goodness I've got a fully qualified florist joining us at the end of the month. It might only be part time for now, but it'll make things easier and give me the breathing space I need. Once they're settled in, we'll finally be able to make the trip to Danebury."

His heart lurched. He missed Danebury and his family so much, but home was now the little Wyoming town he'd found with the aid of a pin and a paper map. But home was more than a place. Home was the gorgeous, kind, caring man who just got him and whom he loved so much it could steal his breath away. Home was Arlo McDonald.

"It can't come soon enough. It's time I saw where you grew up, and met your folks properly."

"You don't know how much I want that," Lucian said. "Video calls are all well and good, but it's just not the same. I know they're dying to meet you, too. Mum was devastated when she had to cancel her trip out here."

His mum's favorite horse had, at the last moment, refused a jump. It had sent her flying and resulted in a broken leg and a fractured hip and pelvis, rendering all travel impossible.

"I know, baby, but she's all mended now, and that's the main thing. She looks more glamorous every time I talk to her."

Lucian smiled; she never seemed to age. "I think she has a portrait of herself hidden away in the attic." Or maybe good genes, or bone structure, or all that time she'd spent centering herself, or getting in touch with her inner goddess...

The calls home Arlo joined him on were full of warmth and laughter, but the memory of the first call he'd made home after Arlo had chased him down and persuaded him to stay and make a life together was never too far away.

His family had, in turns, been upset, angry, and worried. He'd understood, he really had, but no amount of pleading for him to see sense had made any difference because he loved Arlo more. It was that simple.

After the call, and seeing him shaken, Arlo had demanded to speak to them — in private. They made the arrangements and Arlo took his laptop into his studio, closing the door behind him. He'd emerged two hours later and hadn't divulged a word of what had been said, but when Lucian had got in touch with his family a few days later, the stormy skies had cleared.

Lucian checked his watch and sighed. "I'd best get back."

"We've got a call arranged with your folks later today, haven't we?"

"What? Erm, yes, we have."

Arlo nodded. "Good."

Lucian tilted his head to the side. All of Arlo's focus was on his coffee cup, which he held in a death grip.

"Why? What is it you're not telling me?"

Arlo's hands stilled, and he looked up. His lips lifted in a self-conscious smile.

"I was going to tell you later, before the call—"

"Arlo!"

"Okay, okay. The reason I was with Jonas for so long today wasn't just to discuss the showing in New York—"

"That's still going ahead, isn't it?" A sudden panic seized Lucian. Arlo's works had been displayed in Boston, Seattle and L.A., where they'd been met with critical acclaim and high sales. New York would be taking it up another level, placing Arlo squarely on the artistic map.

"That's all fine, so don't worry."

"Then what…?"

Arlo leaned forward, his smile so bright it was blinding.

"London. Jonas has a lot of contacts there and he's been busy pulling in favors. Everything's arranged. There's going to be a showing at the beginning of June, which means we can combine it with visiting your family."

"Wh—what? That's brilliant news, but why didn't you tell me before?"

"Because I didn't know for sure that it'd happen. I only found out today."

"Oh, Arlo, that's… that's…

Lucian launched himself across the little table, knocking the remains of his coffee into his lap, but he didn't care because all that mattered was pulling Arlo in close and kissing his talented, wonderful, amazing man into tomorrow and beyond.

"That's incredible, and the best news ever. Didn't I tell you from the start what a talented artist you are? If I hadn't shoved you into the gallery—"

"You wouldn't be sitting here with cold coffee soaking your crotch."

"Yeah, well…" Lucian unwound himself from Arlo and grabbed a handful of napkins and dabbed at the spreading wetness, which was seeping through to his underwear. "But if it wasn't for me making you…" He frowned at the wet patch, which seemed to grow larger by the second. "Awww, people aren't going to think I'm incontinent, are they?"

He dumped the sodden ball and pulled out another handful from the dispenser. How could half a cup of coffee turn into a gallon?

"You think my critical and commercial success is down to you? What are you looking for, some kind of kickback? Don't even think it, mister, you ain't gonna get anything from me."

Lucian stopped dabbing and peered up at Arlo. "You think? You owe me big time, and you're about to pay." He grinned as he pulled out his cell. "Jed, it's me. I won't be back for the rest of the day." He paused as he listened; his gaze met Arlo's, and he grinned. "Yep, something's come up that needs careful handling. I'll see you tomorrow."

Their breathing leveled out. The sheet lay crumpled on the floor, leaving their sweat soaked bodies naked. Mid-afternoon sun flooded through the window, warming their bare skin. Arlo turned on his side. He ran a finger along the valley of Lucian's backbone and was answered by a shuddering groan.

"I think you've broken me," Lucian muttered as he shifted and gazed at Arlo.

"Oh, I don't think so. You're very… flexible." Arlo's heart stuttered, as it always did, when Lucian's lips lifted in a soft smile, his eyes brimming with love.

It'd been six months since he'd made the frantic, panic-filled journey to stop Lucian from leaving, yet fear would creep up on him, and whisper in his ear, reminding him of how close he'd come to losing the best thing that had ever happened to him. But, it was happening less and less and, pray god, the whispering would soon fall silent for good.

"Arlo, stop thinking."

"How do you know what I'm thinking?" He cleared the grit from his throat.

Lucian offered a lazy shrug. "Because I know you. I'm here. You, me, us. We're here, together. It's all that matters."

Arlo pulled Lucian to him. Holding him tight, he never, ever, wanted to let him go. Nuzzling into Lucian's soft hair, he closed his eyes. He could stay like this forever, the two of them bound to each other, their skin sticky with sweat and cum, the tangible, visceral evidence of their lovemaking. He kissed the top of Lucian's head; Lucian didn't stir, his even breath and the gentle up and down of his chest plastered to Arlo's own, telling him he was asleep.

Arlo let his mind drift. His life had changed beyond recognition in just a handful of months.

The night Bibi had confronted him, he'd been in turmoil as he'd told himself lies, that everything he was doing was for Lucian's sake. As the sky had turned from black to the blue-pink of first light, exhaustion had finally pushed him into a fitful sleep full of broken dreams. When he'd jerked awake, there had been tears on his face and his heart had pounded so fast he'd been scared it would burst. But it'd been nothing to what had really terrified him. With a clarity so razor sharp it cut him to his core, he'd known that giving up Lucian would be catastrophic, for both of them. Scrambling for his watch, fear had filled his heart as the minute hand had ticked over to ten o'clock.

In his arms, Lucian stirred and pushed closer, as though trying to climb inside Arlo's skin.

"I'm here," he mumbled, so quietly Arlo could almost believe he'd misheard. But he hadn't.

Calm settled over him like the warmest, softest blanket. His breathing and his heartbeat slowed, one synchronizing with the other, as he drifted into a calm, dreamless sleep.

"Lucian, honey. I thought you'd forgotten about our call."

"Of course not. I had, erm, a floral emergency." Out of sight of the camera, Lucian crossed his fingers.

"Hey. Sorry we're late," Arlo said as he took a seat on the couch next to Lucian. "Things came up at the last minute that needed taking caring of."

Like me riding your cock… How could Arlo be so calm? Lucian shifted; he was sure his mum could read his mind.

The three of them chatted and laughed, the conversation light and easy. Lucian jumped in, no longer able to keep quiet about their news.

"Mum, we've got something to tell you." He looked at Arlo and smiled. Over to you… They'd agreed Arlo would tell his family about the trip they'd be making to England.

"Hello Lu, Arlo." Eddie beamed at them as he joined the call. "Christ, what a day. We've just finished hosting a corporate event for a firm of accountants. They all got pissed, two of them fell into the ornamental pond, and another one attempted to run around the folly stark bollock naked. Fortunately, two of the gardeners were able to dissuade him before—"

"Eddie!" Lucian and Eddie's mum batted his arm. "Lucian and Arlo have something to tell us. Tales of inebriated bookkeepers can wait."

Lucian bit down on his grin as his brother's face fell.

"Go on, honey."

Arlo leaned forward. "We're coming over, at the beginning of June—"

"Oh my goodness, that's wonderful news." Lucian's mum clapped her hands together before she burst into tears.

"Mum—"

"Don't mind me, honey. I'm crying because I'm happy." She dabbed her eyes with a paper tissue as Eddie gave her a light cuddle. "I just want to give you the biggest hug ever. And you too, Arlo honey, for making my baby boy so—so—h—appy."

Eddie handed her another tissue to mop up a fresh flood of tears.

"That's great news," Eddie said. "We've all missed you so much Lu. And Arlo? It's about time we welcomed you into the family properly…"

They carried on talking. Arlo told them about the London showing, which prompted more tears along with enthusiastic congratulations. Bella appeared for the last couple of minutes, as excited as her mum and brother about the impending visit. At last, with waves and kisses blown across the miles, and with promises to let the family know as soon as they confirmed the date, Lucian ended the call.

"We're going to Danebury. You're going to meet them properly. I still can't believe it."

Arlo grinned. "I can't believe it's happening, either. They were ecstatic."

"Yeah, they were. But they're not the only ones." Lucian jumped up from the couch, snatched up Arlo's hand and pulled him to his feet. "Come on, let me show you how ecstatic I can be, too."

Arlo's grin grew dark. "Sounds like a plan, mister."

Bacon, eggs — and burned toast.

Arlo smirked as he leaned on the doorjamb and

watched as Lucian scraped the toast over the sink. Lucian was getting better in the kitchen. After six months of living together, now only one thing out of three was some charcoal edged offering.

"Should have waited for me, babe."

Lucian scowled. "It's only a bit... singed." He looked down at the lump of coal in his hand before sighing and chucking it in the food waste bin. "Who needs carbs? And anyway," he said, dishing up the rest of their breakfasts, "I've got to get to the store early. We've got a busy day today — and I'm going to be playing catch up since you lured me away for the afternoon."

Arlo huffed. "You lured me in the end, I seem to remember." He dug into his food; he was hungry, and no wonder, when he and Lucian had spent all afternoon, half the night, and again this morning... his dick twitched. His eyes narrowed. It was still early, they could—

"Oh, bollocks."

Across the table, Lucian mopped up runny egg yolk from his chin. A golden blob also sat on his bottle green polo shirt, next to the discreetly embroidered Floristry by Lucian Blaxston. He rubbed at the mess, making it worse.

"Don't you dare say anything," Lucian growled, not looking up as he continued to spread rather than clean off the stain.

"It honestly never even crossed my mind." Or not if he wanted to keep his balls attached. "But you have a whole pile of them upstairs in the closet, so maybe throw that one in the laundry?"

Lucian glared across the table.

Arlo met his gaze and fought to tamp down the grin

that was scratching at his lips. Lucian's attempt to look fierce was so damn… adorkable.

Lucian was the first to crack as a smile broke out across his face. "I told you before that I was feral," he said, as he dashed out of the kitchen.

Arlo put on some more coffee, his thoughts settling on the day ahead.

Spring had come to the town and the surrounding mountains, decorating them in the bright colors that made the world fresh and new and full of hope. He had a landscape that needed some final touches, but later, when the working day ended for them both, he'd suggest they take a ride up to Jake's Lookout to gaze up into the night sky and count the countless stars. Maybe they could get the blanket out and—

His cell, in the hip pocket of his jeans, pinged as a message dropped in. Abandoning the coffee, he pulled it out, his lips pressing into a tight line as he stared at the number that was part of his past. After a moment's hesitation, he opened up the message, bracing himself for what it might contain. He read it, re-read it, and re-read it again, before letting go of a long, deep breath. This was the final dotted *i*, the last crossed *t*, the turning of the last page in the book that was his life before Lucian.

"I suppose I better get off," Lucian said, rushing into the kitchen as he tucked his clean polo into the waistband of his jeans. "I've got a delivery of…" Lucian's hands stilled. "Arlo? What's the matter?"

Arlo held out the cell. Lucian took it, worry creasing his brow.

Arlo said nothing, only watched as Lucian, just as he'd

done, read the message before re-reading. The creases in Lucian's brow melted away.

"He's... Tony's agreed to sell the beach house? It's the best news!"

Arlo took the cell back, glancing at it before he closed the message, relief flooding him as he thrust it back into his pocket.

"Yep." He couldn't keep the smile from his lips or his voice. "It's taken him long enough to come around. Guess his lawyer finally drummed some sense into his head."

"I'm so glad." Lucian wrapped his arms around Arlo and brushed a soft kiss over his lips.

"Me too, baby, me too."

A shaft of golden sunlight lit up the kitchen, bathing them in its soft warmth as the final clouds of his old life were, at last, chased away.

"This is an incredible day, and one we should celebrate," Lucian murmured into his chest. "You can take me up to Jake's Lookout tonight and make me see stars."

"The weather report says there'll be clear skies, so— Ouch! Why did you pinch me?"

Lucian glared up at him. "Because the stars in the sky are not the ones I'm talking about."

Arlo grinned as laughter bubbled up inside of him. Lucian glared some more, still trying, and still failing, to look fierce before a wide, sunny smile shone from his face.

"Okay, I guess I deserved that. Come on, I'll give you a ride into work."

Together, they left the house, walking into the warm, bright morning.

Yes, it was going to be an incredible day.

I hope you enjoyed reading Meeting Mr. Adorkable, it was certainly a pleasure sharing Lucian and Arlo's story with you. If you have a moment to spare, a short, honest review would be much appreciated. Thank you.

Did you enjoy meeting Cameron in CC's coffee shop? The great news is, Cameron has his very own sweet and sexy romance. Check out Collier's Creek book six, Nic Starr's Blue Skies.

There are six wonderful romances in the Collier's Creek series, HEAs guaranteed. Keep reading to find out more!

While we're talking, if you've enjoyed the small town vibe of Collier's Creek you might like to visit Love's Harbour, my little coastal community deep in the heart of England's West Country. Animal Instincts is an age gap grumpy/sunshine story, and Hearts Colliding is enemies to lovers — listen carefully, and you can hear the sexual tension crackling in the air!

The next book in the Love's Harbour series will be published early in 2024.

COLLIER'S CREEK SERIES

BECCA SEYMOUR
BEST KIND OF AWKWARD

ELLE KEATON
MANDATORY REPAIRS

SUE BROWN
SHERIFF OF THE CREEK

KATHERINE McINTYRE
ALL THE WRONG PAGES

ALI RYECART
MEETING MR. ADORKABLE

NIC STARR
BLUE SKIES

A FEW WORDS FROM ALI

To find out more about me, my books, and to sign up to my newsletter (irreverent, chatty, packed with news and heads up on sales I'm running), check out my website at:

www.ryecart.com

As a thank you for subscribing, I'll send you a juicy sweet with heat story.

I also have a readers group on Facebook, which is mainly where I hang out on social media. Come and join me!

Ryecart's Rebel Readers

Printed in Great Britain
by Amazon

35049175R00195